To the monsters we all have hiding inside us

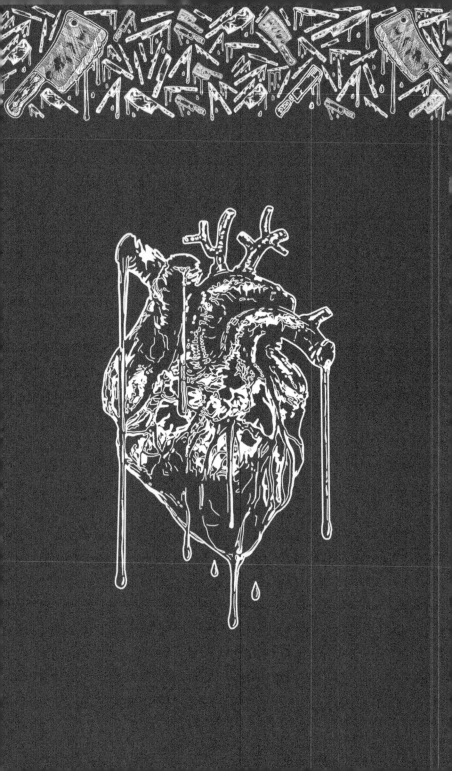

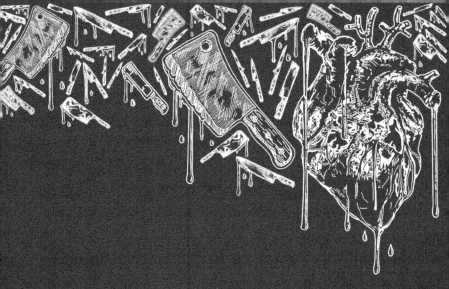

PROLOGUE

ILLI

There are many places I'd rather be at two in the morning on a Saturday than the shitty forest at the edge of Mounts Bay.

There's more skeletons in this place than all the fucking cemeteries in the state combined, easily. There isn't a cop in the Bay that would set foot in this place without a gun pressed against the back of their skull. That should make it my kind of place but the posturing bullshit that comes with the Twelve means I fucking loathe it.

There's a crunching noise, the kind where there's no coming back from, and my attention drifts back to the clearing as the jeering and shouts die down.

Well *fuck*.

I was kinda hoping the kid would have a little less backbone but there she is. Her hands are still dripping in blood and the rock she used to bash the other guy's head in is laying at her feet, glistening with his blood and brain matter.

The shift in their minds is like a tangible thing as an uneasy sort of respect ripples through the crowd. She isn't one of them anymore. Nah, she's something else entirely now.

I watch as D'Ardo speaks to the little girl, all formal and shit as if he isn't some little street urchin who grew up and stole a black crown of his own. When she tips her head back and claims herself to be the Wolf a savage grin spreads across my face. She sure has some fucking fire in her, how the hell her skinny little bones can contain it, is beyond me and shit, I hope that backbone is enough to get her through this life. If D'Ardo has anything to do with it, she'll be bound and broken in his bed in the next five years.

I try not to think about my best friend's perversions and apparent enjoyment of young girls, reasoning with myself that he hasn't touched her and claims he won't until she's ready. But what the fuck does *ready* even mean? What girl in her right mind would be *ready* to deal with that man?

Then again, I can't judge. I *am* the Butcher of the Bay.

The crowd starts to move away and I wait in the shadows for D'Ardo. He slings an arm over the girl and leads her towards me, whispering in her ear and completely ignoring how fucking uncomfortable she looks. Once he's out of the company of the rest of the Twelve, four of his loyal supporters flank him. The big blond idiot grins and makes a joke at the little girl. She gives him a half-hearted smile but she's staring around with keen eyes. I've never seen a kid so miserable in my life, which is fucking saying something considering where I came from. D'Ardo doesn't notice, of course. He only notices what he wants to about her, which is that she survives fucking *anything*.

"We should go and get a drink to celebrate," says D'Ardo, and I scoff at him holding my hand up to wave at the little girl.

"Planning on getting her drunk and vulnerable already?" I ask, and he shoots me a warning look. That shit doesn't work on me, I could pound that boy into the ground and we both know it. I don't know why I'm trying to warn her, or maybe I just want to get a rise out of her, whatever it is, she doesn't acknowledge I've spoken at all. Just looks out over the forest like she's waiting for the ghosts to walk out and find her.

D'Ardo keeps a hand clamped firmly on her shoulder as he rolls his own back. We head through the forest towards the cars and there is a hushed sort of reverence that follows. Infamy is a weird thing but I can't say I hate it. I like being known as the Butcher, I like everyone knowing who the fuck I am when I walk into a room because there's nothing better than the fear in people's eyes. I glance down at the little girl and wonder if she knows what she's in for.

"Doesn't she have a family or some shit to go home to?" I ask once again trying to get her the fuck out of this. I know exactly where she came from, our paths had crossed in the group home for all of a fucking month, but I'll never forget the look on D'Ardo's face when she showed up. I knew she was going to be around for the long haul.

He smirks at me and turns his attention to the little girl. "The group home won't even notice she's gone, why not have a celebratory drink?"

The girl cuts us both a look and says, "If the two of you are going to talk like I'm not standing right here with you I'm going to go back and you can drink by yourselves. I'm not interested in playing this dick-jerking game."

A surprise laugh bubbles out of my throat and although D'Ardo laughs with me the look he gives her is a challenge. I wonder again if she sees it, if she knows his plans for her.

If I were a better man, I'd warn her.

I keep my mouth shut.

When we get to the car park, D'Ardo leads the kid to his car and stashes her carefully in the back. His organization is big enough now that he has a driver, the grinning blond idiot that slides into the driver's seat. Another of the thugs climbs into the front passenger seat, carrying enough weapons that he looks dangerous enough but I know for sure he's a shit shot. I quirk an eyebrow at D'Ardo and he waves me off casually.

"Just meet me at the bar, idiot."

I've gotta say, I'm not a fan of being called an idiot. I narrow my eyes at him but D'Ardo just puffs out his chest as if that will make him look more dangerous. I'm not impressed.

THE BUTCHER OF THE BAY

PART ONE

BY

J BREE

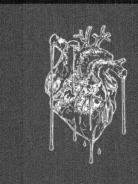

"I'll buy you a bottle of whiskey, you grumpy fuck," he says, and then he slides into the car.

The kid looks over her shoulder at me through the window and I start to feel something close to guilt. It's stupid, it's none of my business, but it doesn't matter what I say to myself, the guilt still curls in my gut.

Fuck it, I slide into my own Mustang, vintage and the one true love of my life, and I wait a minute before flooring it after them. Nothing better than an open road, a gas pedal to the floor, and the smooth changing of gears. I pass them easily, the cheap thrill enough to burn away the bad feeling in my gut, if only for a minute.

The bar D'Ardo picks is owned by one of his little friends amongst the Twelve. I'm not a fan of the guy, but he pays me well enough when he needs someone to disappear in a blood-soaked way and I enjoy the work.

I don't really give a fuck why he wants them to disappear, Mounts Bay is not the place to live if you have a conscience.

We find a booth in the back empty and waiting for us, and I smirk at the way the crowd parts. I can see Matteo's hackles begin to rise as he notices that the stench of terror is coming from those staring at me. He's not a fan of being the lesser evil in the room.

He ushers the kid into the booth before sliding in after her. I take a seat on the other side and when the smiling blond idiot attempts to sit next to me I pin him with a look and snap, "Not fucking likely, dickhead."

He stands by the table instead.

As soon as a bottle of whiskey and three glasses are delivered to the table, Matteo pours out shots and hands out the glasses until we're each holding one.

"A toast; to power."

The kid snorts at him and downs the shot like a pro. "To whiskey, for being the only good in the world."

My eyebrows shoot up at her. There might be a bit more fire in this kid than I thought.

"To bashing some dickhead's skull in with a fucking rock," I say, just to see how she will react but there's not a grimace or a flinch in sight. She's smart. Too fucking smart to be getting herself involved in D'Ardo's personal brand of fucked up. I don't fucking trust her, not one fucking bit.

And to think, someday, a few years from now, I would wake up every damn day thanking a God I didn't believe in for putting that little girl through some of the worst depths of hell and sending her to me.

I'm kind of a son-of-a-bitch like that.

Butcher of the Bay - Part One

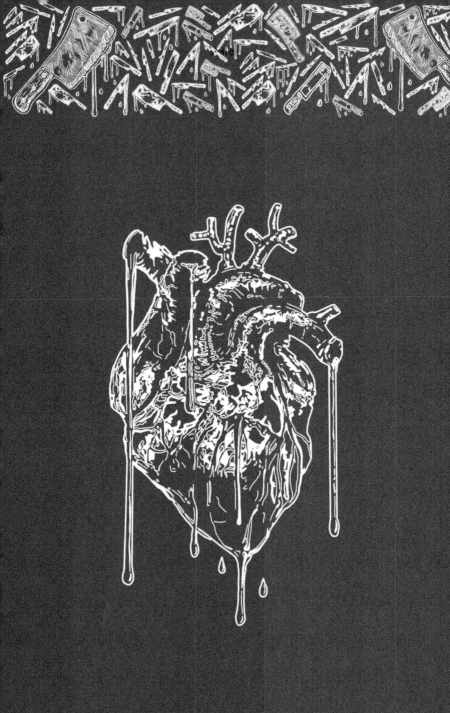

CHAPTER ONE

ODIE

My father is a drug addict.

I think it started as a secret, something he didn't want me or my mother to know about, just like he'd kept his business a secret. You see, my father broke the number one, most important rule of being a high-profile drug dealer; never sample your product.

I grew up in small towns all across France, never staying in one place for more than two years. It made for a miserable, lonely sort of childhood because every time I started to make friends my father would pack us up and move us in the dark depths of the night.

We always moved at night.

We have been living in Villefranche-sur-Mer for almost two years and my feet have begun to itch. I know it's coming. Maybe it's just my body having gotten used to the idea of always being on the move so now I crave it. I love the town, I love being so close to the ocean and all of the scenery I can sketch and paint when my father is out of town, but I know our time here is coming to an end.

I don't realize it is only my time that is up.

I round the corner at the beach to find Martin, one of father's men and someone I always considered an uncle figure, waiting for me with an armful of flowers. My birthday is still a week away but he always remembers. A grin bursts over my face.

"What are you doing here at this time of the day? Do you not have more important things to do than a beach romp?"

He laughs as I bat my eyelashes at him, and hands over the flowers. "I have some news for you today, sweet Odette. Your father has arrived and is looking for you."

My stomach drops. I hate the man, loathe him really, and this time away from him with only my mother has been like a dream.

"And what is he here for today, hm? Does he need something from my mother? I don't think she has any jewels left to sell for him."

Martin gives me a stern look, like he still sees the small child I once was and not the nineteen year old woman I really am. "Your father is a good man, respected in his business. You need to learn to hold your tongue before it gets you into trouble, sweet girl."

I grit my teeth so I don't roll my eyes. Martin is not such a ruffian that he would strike me in public but once we get back to the cottage I share with my mother his slap will certainly sting. I tuck my sketch pad more firmly under my arm and nod, casting my eyes back to the ground in an act of obedience. It doesn't sit well with me but better to play the part to get through this little visit quickly. Once I arrive wherever my father intends on abandoning us this time I will find my voice again.

Martin takes my free arm and walks me along the narrow streets, bustling with tourists and beachgoers and life. It's easier to pretend to be happy and fulfilled this way, the aching emptiness in my gut much quieter around all of this noise.

"How has your mother been? She looks tired." Martin murmurs, a smile on his face at those around us but his arm is tense in mine.

Drunk. Distant. Broken by my father. "She's been better but I think the sea air has been good for her, and the sunshine. The summer has been a warm one and I think it's made a difference."

The dutiful daughter, lying through her teeth to save her mother's reputation. I love her and I know, deep down, she loves me too. She just loves my father more.

"I think I'm going to take her home for some time. She needs to be back with her real friends. I will ask if your father will allow you to come too."

Allow me, I'm an adult! I wait until I know the bite will be out of my tone before I speak. "I can choose to go, Martin. I can make that decision by myself. I would like to go to one of the universities there. I will get a job if my father does not want to pay for it."

Martin's arm tenses even more in my arm and I hide my grimace. I will definitely pay for these words back at the house. He huffs before he says, "This is the way of our world, Odette. If your father does not want you to return to Paris then you will obey him. That is what good girls do."

I do not want to be a good girl. I want to be a free girl, a girl who owns her own life, a girl who belongs to no one. I don't ever want to be good but I'm also a trapped girl, chained to the life I was born into, so I shut my mouth, carve it into a pretty smile, and nod as if it isn't killing me to agree.

The streets grow quieter as we get closer to the cottage, the atmosphere darker as if the stones and bricks in the buildings around us know just how deeply I dread facing my parents together again.

"Why are you slowing down? Your father is excited to see you again! He has missed being around his most beautiful jewel," Martin says, and I start to think maybe this is all a trap. Maybe my father sent his favorite friend after me to try to gain my trust and complacency. Mercy, am I about to be murdered for taking up painting? For going on a walk?

Dread pools deep in my gut, replacing the emptiness with that acidic bubbling. Maybe he found out about Louis and I'm going to be murdered for daring to take a lover.

"Calm down, sweet girl. Your father is excited to see you. Some of our friends are here today too," Martin murmurs, and it doesn't help one bit.

When we take the corner down the alley I see my father's car and it takes every ounce of strength I have not to frown or show some other sign of hating the fact that he's here. Martin smiles at me again, opening the door like a gentleman and I take a deep breath before walking in, ignoring the pile of summery jackets hanging by the door, all of them expensive designers that must belong to the wives of my father's business friends. He would never allow my mother or I to own such things, not unless we were in the city with him and he wanted to show us off for the night. No, all of the beautiful and expensive things my mother once owed have long since been sold off to fund the steady decline my parents are spiralling in.

I take a deep breath as I move to the small kitchen area, my shoes silent on the old and worn rug I'd found at the local markets to warm the place up a bit last winter.

The cottage was definitely not the type of place my father would ever lower himself to live in but he didn't care about abandoning my mother and I here. The look of disdain on his face as his eyes trace the cracked tiles on the floor and the thin film of grime on the kitchen cupboards, that no amount of scrubbing had been able to remove, makes it clear that despite his addiction he sets himself to a *very* different standard.

I, however, love this house with a deep sense of kinship.

I see myself in all of the cracks in the walls and the worn kitchen floor. It doesn't matter that the outside of me is considered beautiful. I know how much the men my father spends his time with lust after me and have done long before I was a decent age. All that matters is that inside, I am broken.

My mother pours cups of coffee and tea for each of the men and their wives who have joined us today, as if these dirty businessmen would ever sit around with hot drinks. Really, she's just trying to hide her own addictions. Her hands have a fine tremble, but she is not nervous, the tremble is there from withdrawals.

I swallow my sigh and give her a sweet smile as I take over, gesturing at her to sit. I look like an obedient daughter, and the approving look my father shoots me tells me he has taken it that way, when really I'm too nervous to stay still. There is nothing my father hates more than fidgeting so I taught myself to find productive and useful ways to not sit still during these little meetings to try to stop him from finding a reason to beat me. He never really needed an excuse but if I did find some way to displease him he tended to make them more severe.

He always avoided my precious face.

No one else acknowledges that I've arrived, the mood in the room somber and tense, and the conversation resumes once Martin takes a seat. When I was younger I didn't understand that my father's business was not legitimate, no child ever thinks their father is really a monster, but now I can listen to them talk about taking care of the rival drug lords without flinching at the body count.

I move around the room silently, unaffected, handing out drinks to those who will take them. No one will meet my eye.

"All that matters here is that *Signor Mecedo* is happy with the offer," my father says, waving away the teacup and gesturing at the bottle of whiskey my mother has left out.

When none of the men take the hot drinks I offer, I move over to the cabinet that my mother keeps all of her good glassware in, what little of it has survived the constant moving, and start handing out glasses of wine and spirits instead.

Martin nods approvingly at me as I hand him a glass and I hope this act of obedient daughter is enough to stop him from helping my father punish me later.

"And you don't think it is too high a price to pay? This is your legacy we are talking of here," he says as I move away, and his words slowly filter into my head. Legacy? My father has nothing, his addiction has bled our family dry.

My father huffs under his breath and downs the whiskey in his glass in a single mouthful. "Girls are not legacies. If I had a son, that would be my legacy. This is an exchange of property."

It takes a moment for his words to sink in. And then I realize, the price my father has paid is *me*.

Betrayal is a cruel first love.

I thought I had known true love but the butterflies in my stomach and the lust in my veins was nothing but an infatuation, a veiled deceit, *a lie*.

I had decided to wait until my father's friends had left the cottage before confronting him but before I had the chance, my long-time, very secret, boyfriend had arrived and asked to escort me to the airport... a nine hour drive through the countryside of France. For a fleeting second I thought he was whisking me away, saving me from this *transaction*.

I was wrong.

I look over at the man who has broken every part of my trust as though my eyes could flay him alive; Louis Caron. He is the son of one of my father's associates, a refined gentleman and everything I have ever wanted in a man. He looks perfect in his suit, even with the grimace stretched over his face.

I could slap it off, just smack him until all of the rage is slated but I don't think it will ever burn out.

"Odette, do not look at me like that. I have already told you there is nothing I can do to stop this and the tears in your eyes are killing me," he mutters, and looks out the window at the passing colors of Paris. I hate the big city. I only ever come here in passing and it's as though the freedom and bustle of life is just too out of reach for me. I refuse to look out at the city. I refuse to be mocked by it all.

"If you were a real man you would find a way," I reply with

a sniff, refusing to cry the angry tears because I feel so helpless.

Not one person had tried to stand up for me. Not my drunk of a mother, not the men and women I had thought of as aunts and uncles, not even my boyfriend. No one. And while there may not be a gun pressed against my temple right now I know there is still one aimed at my head somewhere. I know Louis would shoot me if my father asked him to, he's made that very clear to me.

I fix my eyes on him and wish there was some way for my gaze to hurt him. I am so furious at this gutless man that if I had a gun, I think I'd shoot him and feel nothing but a bone-deep satisfaction.

Yesterday, I was so content sketching children playing in the ocean and now I'm plotting futile attempts at murder.

"I must do as your father says. He has promised you to another man, my hands are tied. I spoke to him and he assured me that you will be taken care of. A girl like you should not be hidden away in little backwards towns. You should be draped in jewels and on the arm of a rich man. I wish very much that man could be me, but it is not."

He says this as though it is nothing but an arranged marriage, as if money has not exchanged hands over me. I flick my wrist at him dismissively, a way I know sets him off in a rage but I'd rather he hit me than sit through this without fighting back. "I don't think you wish that at all. I think you got what you wanted out of me and now you're glad to see me go. Pathetic."

He shrugs at me, completely unrepentant, and it only makes my anger burn brighter. Fear of what is happening hasn't set in yet, the anger still thrumming through my blood and I snap, "Maybe I should tell my father, hm? Maybe I should tell him you deflowered his precious daughter and the marriage he's arranged for me is built on a lie? I assume I went for a higher price for my supposed *untouched* status?"

Louis's head snaps back around and his eyes are like saucers. "Odette, you cannot tell them! You would get us both killed if you do. Your father is not a good man, he won't think twice before killing you."

I snort at him, completely unlike the refined lady I'm supposed to be, the one my father insists on me being without ever training me to be. Maybe that's why the fear hasn't set in yet. Maybe I'm so used to my father's ridiculous expectations that this is just the next avenue for his crazy to rear its head.

I do know that there is no point in fighting them all now. As a child, I would often come home from school to find him washing blood from his hands. Good men do not often find themselves covered in blood. I have more chances of reaching my new husband and hoping he is a better man than my despicable father.

The car slows and Louis turns in his seat to speak to the driver. I finally take notice of where we are once again and sigh. The airport. Another hellish flight. My father had said the deal was with a Señor. Was I heading to a Spanish speaking country?

My English is barely passable but my Spanish is non-existent.

If my new husband doesn't speak at least a little French I am going to have a hell of a time.

"How am I supposed to talk to this man? Or am I just supposed to spread my legs and open my womb to him without a word spoken between us?" I mumble, not really expecting Louis to answer but he heaves a sigh at me.

"He is a very rich man, Odette. If you give him a male heir he might just leave you alone. You would be able to travel the world and do whatever you like without worrying about the trivial things in life. It's not a life you could have if you stayed here and you would finally be free of your father. Think of this as a new start."

A dry laugh bursts out of me. I long to worry about the trivial things in life. I want to get a job and pay my own bills and have a real family. He's speaking to me again as if I am a pretty bird stuck in a cage to be admired and played with but never respected.

His eyes finally look back at me and I see the lustful longing there. Ah. Of course. He's not at all remorseful about letting me go, except for the beauty of my face and the pleasures of my body. It is disgusting and I strongly consider spitting in his face.

Before I make my decision the door on my side opens and I look up to see my father standing with his hand extended to help me out. How he got here before us is a mystery until I spot the private jet. Of course, he stuck me in the car for hours and hours to wear me down while he's been drinking and relaxing with his friends.

His eyes narrow when I hesitate before taking his hand. You would assume he was doing this to be a gentleman, to help out his beloved daughter, but the look in his eyes tells me he's taking this last moment to insure my obedience. I have no choice but to slide my hand in his and get out of the car.

I'm happy that my knees do not shake and my lip does not wobble, the tears dried up. There is no sign of how truly afraid I am underneath the burning rage I have. I have to hold onto my rage, grasp it tightly with both hands, to stop myself from falling apart.

I will hold this anger to the very end.

"A good daughter does as her father instructs without the tantrum, Odette," he murmurs in my ear as he kisses my cheeks. The pilot is the only man watching us who hasn't seen my father hit me before. This seems like such an act for someone who will look the other way anyway, the money is too good to intervene for some girl.

I give him a tight, grimacing smile and nod my head, speaking lowly through my teeth as he steps away from me, "I hope you got a good price for me, enough to keep you high for many nights to come."

Knowing that it's going to happen doesn't lessen the sting of his hand cracking across my face. My vision whites out around the edges as I stumble back against the car. I wonder if my future husband will be as heavy handed.

I smile though the tears start forming in my eyes at the thought. This man will never lay a hand on me again. Though I don't know if my new husband will be any better, that thought gives me enough joy that I can turn on my heel and stride to the private jet. As tempting as it is to make them throw me over a shoulder kicking and screaming it's too ingrained in me to be a *good girl* so I walk, calm and steady, up the stairs and into the aircraft.

Anywhere would be better than here.

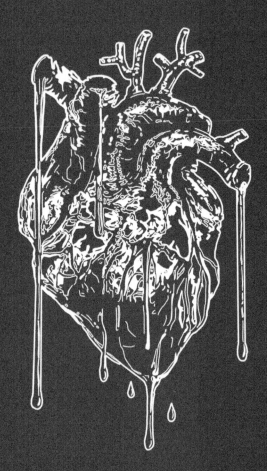

CHAPTER TWO

ILLI

Mounts Bay, California, is a fucking shit-hole.

I've hated the place my whole life, from the second my pops left me in a safe-place so I'd end up in foster care, I knew this place was the worst hell on Earth.

I have no fucking clue why I won't leave.

Probably because I've built a life here, a name, a reputation that precedes me and crowds part when I arrive anywhere. The money is also fucking good, I don't really have to work anymore but I have a taste for the blood and pain now. I have easy access to all the pain I need because of my office hours.

I guess being the Butcher has its perks.

But that's all besides the point. The reasons I stuck around don't matter, all that counts is that I stayed in the worst fucking city in the country. That's where I met my heart and had it ripped right the fuck out of my chest then had it parading around, as if it wouldn't fucking kill me to have her hurt. And she did get hurt, fucking brutalized, and I played a part in it.

I'm getting ahead of myself here.

The day I made the biggest fucking regret of my life thanks to my life in the Bay starts like every other day. I wake up, eat a balanced meal, workout for a few hours, then head down to the basement to check on the guy I'm torturing in the lowest level of my warehouse. I'd bought the place because of these basements. No one can hear you scream ten feet below ground in a room with cement walls a foot thick.

Great place to work.

I'd built an apartment in the upper levels so I could look out over the amazing views of the Bay. Psh. The docks aren't exactly a great view but the water beyond them is nice enough. Sometimes, after a long day of cutting people to pieces, I stare out at that water and wonder why the ever-loving-*fuck* I'm still living in the Bay.

So I'm standing there staring at the guy, well, the fucking corpse because the piece of shit went and died on me like a pussy overnight, when my security alarms tell me someone has tripped the sensors on the far side of my property. I have zero patience for houseguests when they haven't called ahead so I seriously fucking consider setting off a flash bomb or something to get them to fuck off, only the glimpse of the two motorcycles stop me.

I know these two assholes.

I know them well enough to give them a free pass because I'm a nice fucking guy, as nice as a sharp knife to your throat in the dark.

So instead I unlock the front door remotely and wait until I hear them cross the threshold before yelling out, "I'm in the fridge!"

Then I get to work hacking the dead guy to pieces. Nice, easily digestible pieces to ship off to a contact who enjoys using them as bait in his arctic fishing expeditions. Weird guy but he pays good green and the cops aren't exactly trolling the arctic nets for missing perps.

It's basically recycling.

I'm a fucking humanitarian, an eco fucking warrior.

That's enough to have me cracking a smile as I work, the knife feeling like an extension of my arm as I slice through the meat of his legs. I can get down to the bone with brute strength but it'll take the bone saw to get the limb off of him. He must have died shortly before I got down here because his blood hasn't pooled or started to congeal yet. Makes for a messier job but easier to get it done.

Footsteps break through the quiet of my haven signalling the bikers have made it down to me finally.

"What the fuck is this place?"

Harbin's voice echoes through the refrigerated room like a gunshot and I turn to face them both, the cooled blood still dripping down my face.

"This is where the meat comes to be processed. What the hell are you two doing here? Don't you know this is my sanctuary?"

Harbin smirks and walks in with the confident air of a man who has spilled a lot of blood and his best friend Roxas saunters in like he's the reason it's always spilled, like he's the center of the world and everyone should weep at his fucking feet.

He's an absolute asshole, but he's also the kind of guy you want having your back in a fight.

"What's this guy in for? Is he a job or personal?" Harbin says, leaning down to inspect the hanging man's lax, dead face. His eyes are nothing but bloody sockets and his mouth is open in a grotesque *silent* scream.

Thank fuck. I swear my ears are still ringing from the real screams he was letting out last night while I played with him for the information I needed. He took the torture like a little bitch, squealing and sobbing like a pathetic piece of shit. I've seen little girls survive with more dignity.

"I don't do personal. Life's easier without any of that bullshit, you guys should know better," I say, washing my cleaver under the water at the utility sink.

Harbin chuckles under his breath and walks farther into the room, his eyes on the wall of knives, saws, electric cattle prods, and all the other tools of my trade. Irritation creeps down my spine. I hate having people in here. It's my fucking happy place and I don't need people ruining it with their emotions and shit. I just need to get my work done and get my money.

He's not a bad sort of guy and I know he's not here for any sort of ulterior motive, despite his road name. He really is a Harbinger of the biblical sense; shit turns to fucking chaos when he arrives. The Unseen only call on Harbin to wade into a fight when they're pulling the big guns so having him here, in my space and poking around in my shit, means something's fucking happening.

I don't like it.

"Shit's going down, man. There's a whole lot of bad juju going on in the Bay and it all leads back to your boy," Roxas drawls, the Southern accent he just can't fully shake slipping out even though he's been here in Cali for-fucking-ever.

I give him a hard look and he shrugs, nonchalantly. "The Jackal is a fucking dickhead and I wouldn't piss on him if he were on fire, but you're a good man, Illium. Can't have you going down with him, can I?"

"If you think I'm a good man you need your fucking head checked, dude. What exactly do you need? If you're just here about the Jackal then you can walk your asses back out. My circle is small but tight." I grunt out, pissed they'd even fucking try to talk me into betraying D'Ardo.

Some things are a given and my loyalty is one of them.

I'd met little Matteo D'Ardo in the shittiest group home in all of the Bay, right in the middle of the fucking slums, and the kid had a strong stomach, pain tolerance like no other, and a nihilistic view on life that rivaled my own. True, I wish he was a little less ambitious and would stop recruiting dickheads to his little fucking gang, but that's his own business.

I'm not going to tell him how to own his shit.

Roxas stops beside me and leans his hip on my workbench. I quirk an eyebrow at him until he rolls his eyes and straightens up. "Look, we owe you for saving our asses in that shootout last month and cleaning it up with the pigs. I can't let this go on, not with all the shit I'm hearing, without saying something to you. He's fucking crazy man. He's building a fucking bomb! That's like homeland security, feds, national crisis levels of fucked up. Is being *the* Kingpin of drugs and firearms not enough for him?"

Clearly not. "He's obsessed with being the biggest player on the board, just pretend it's not happening because he'll never actually get the bomb built and even if he does, and that's a big fucking if, he's not going to fuck his business up by blowing us all up. He's not really suicidal, just a bit fucking unhinged."

Roxas stares me down, the silver-rimmed charcoal eyes of his are serious for once, all the sarcasm and shit-stirring gone. "Johnny, I'm saying this as your friend. Get the fuck out before he takes you down too."

They just don't get it.

All or nothing.

Ride or die.

With the Unseen's warning still ringing in my head I get the body shipped off to its watery tomb and then get my shit together for tonight's big fight. I haven't been in the cage for over a week and the frenetic energy buzzing under my skin tells me I've left it too fucking long.

I need to kill someone with my bare fists. I need to end them with brute force and grim determination.

And I need to do it now.

I flick a text to D'Ardo to meet me there for a drink after I'm done with the fight. If the Unseen are getting worried about what the hell is going on with him then I need to look into it myself. Last thing we fucking need is the Boar sniffing around in our shit.

He doesn't need to find out we took out the Hawk.

I shove my fight bag into my '69 Mustang Boss 429, a true classic and better than all the flashy suped-up bullshit overrunning the streets, and then pile in, letting the engine roar to life and the thrill of the horsepower under my control giving me the first taste of adrenaline for the night. That's the only real drug I need, the high of controlling something so fucking powerful it could kill me in an instant but owning it instead.

I'm almost pissed off that I make it to the Dive so quickly and I consider doing a lap of the entire block just to keep driving but the call of the fight lures me in. I know I'll be put against some cocky, ex-marine or some hardened ex-con and they'll think they'll be the first to take me down. Fuck, that sort of shit almost gets me hard thinking about taking them out. What can I say, I'm a complicated sort of guy.

I park behind the building, right next to the Viper where I know there's security cams watching my car, and then I head in, clapping the guard on the shoulder as I pass. He's the type that will survive this place, sees nothing and can move a body without breaking a sweat.

The place is overcrowded, clearly word has gotten out I'm fighting here tonight and I'm up against someone running their fucking mouth. I move to the bar, the private one, only to find a little lost girl sipping away at a glass of whiskey like a fucking pro.

"What are you doing here, kid? Way past your bedtime."

The bartender slides a glass over to me with a tip of his head and I eye him like I'm planning where I'm going to stab him, you know, just for shits and giggles. I might. I hate this fucking place enough to risk never coming here again. If the Viper cared about his bartenders enough to ban me from coming back that is, I truly fucking doubt he gives a shit.

Fucker doesn't care about anything except his fights and his money.

"I'm on a job," she says, her eyes never once leaving the crowd though the corner of her mouth lifts into a half-smile, something she gives me like it's a peace offering. Fuck knows why she wants to be my friend but no matter what I say to her she's always so fucking nice to me in return.

The worst type of nice too, the genuine type. Like she actually believes I'm worth the respect she gives me, not just that my reputation demands it.

"Oh yeah? You getting cash for that or still hoarding those diamonds like some rich bitch housewife?" I say, sipping at my own drink.

She shrugs. "I've got my own plans for them. Nothing like a safety net to get you through to retirement."

A snort bursts out of me, she's a funny little fucking thing. "Kid, if you make it to retirement you'll be the first fucking miracle to occur in the Bay. Is our friend here tonight or are you flying solo?"

It's a dumb question, even if D'Ardo isn't here tonight then one of his shitty flunkies will be keeping an eye on her for him.

She shrugs again. "He's doing business with the Viper over in the backrooms. Drugs and new girls for the strip joint, I think. I didn't bother with the details."

Bullshit. I don't think this kid misses a goddamn thing that happens around her. "Well, enjoy your night. Make sure you put money on me, the other guy hasn't got a chance."

That half-smile reappears. "They never fucking do."

I throw my bag down in the corner and unzip it, taping my hands securely. No need in busting them up so bad I can't work, not for a run-of-the-mill sort of fight like tonight. The jeering and shouting around me lets me know what my opponent thinks of this.

"Pussies strap up! Afraid of a little pain, *Butcher*?" The sarcasm drips from the dickhead's voice and I smirk back.

"No fucking point breaking my hands on your death, I have others to rack up this week." I glance up to take the cocky cunt in, the smirk never falling away from his ugly mug.

He's definitely an ex-con. Perfect, the rough and unrefined brawling on someone who's fought in lockup is exactly what I'm craving. I strip off my shirt and roll my shoulders back, pushing the tension out of my muscles until I'm loose and light on my feet again. It's like my body loses the tether it has on the Earth and I'm made of fucking air, quick and impossible to land a real hit on.

The doors at the end of the room open and D'Ardo steps through, with the Viper and a handful of their men following behind him. I jerk my head at him and he smirks back, stalking up to the little girl of his obsession and joining her for a drink as they get ready to watch me fight.

I stride into the cage like it's my second home, because it fucking is. This is where I grew up, learned how to become the man I am, killed for the first time, and made enough money to eat. This is where Johnny Illium became the Butcher, and there isn't a man in the Bay who could best me here.

Especially not some mouthy fucking dickhead who was

definitely someone's bitch in prison. You can always tell, it's the mouthy ones over-*fucking*-compensating. I keep that little fucking smirk on my face as the guy walks in after me, laughing and joking with his little buddies like this is a game.

The referee, someone who's just there to call the fights really, steps onto a small platform and shouts, "Last call for your bets. The Butcher verses Diablo, first blood or knockout."

Not fucking likely.

"I'm going to enjoy making you my bitch, Butcher," the guy calls out, blowing me a kiss and yeah, I fucking called it. Some guy wifed this guy up *good*.

"You won't be breathing in about three minutes dickhead, mark my words."

The bell rings and he pounces at me, all punches and elbows with zero finesse. He doesn't land a single one, his fists barely graze my biceps as I duck and weave. I just need a little opening, just that moment he's off balance and he's fucking *mine*. Mine to kill and add to the ever-growing tally of men who met the Butcher and become nothing but a leaking corpse in a back alleyway.

The shouts and jeering of the crowd melts away as I watch him, throwing a few punches of my own that land perfectly, and then finally he stumbles, my ankle hooking his and planting him on his ass.

Gotcha.

I throw my mass at him, straddling him and knocking him

senseless with a single hit to the temple. I snap a few of his ribs between my knees as I position myself on him, my thighs stronger than his feeble attempts to dislodge me. I can see the whites of his eyes as his spits out onto the mat, wheezing up at me.

"Blood. Th-that's fucking b-blood!"

I grin down at him, my forearm presses over his windpipe, pressing down slowly until I feel the muscles and cartilage give way under me. "Only pussies tap out. I don't fight for anything less than death. Who's the bitch now, *Diablo*?"

I push up and stand over him as he gasps out, his arms pinwheeling and his fingers scratching at the mat uselessly. Goodnight, motherfucker, I stomp on his chest, over and over again, until I'm sure every damn one of his ribs have snapped and all his internal organs are skewered with bone shards.

Nothing fucking better than listening to the man wheeze and scream, the gurgling sound of him choking on his own blood is like a balm over my fractured and fucked-up soul. Maybe someday this will feel less fucking soothing but when that day comes I'll have to put a bullet in my brain because there isn't much left living for as it is. I can't fucking lose that, too.

I look up to find D'Ardo grinning at me as I step out of the cage, motioning me over to the door to get a little peace from the shouting and betting of the crowd. The noise is fucking hell to my ears, even with the high of the kill still thrumming through my veins and I swoop down to grab my shit, pulling a jacket over my shoulders as I follow D'Ardo out into the warm, summer night.

His flunkies all spread out and keep watch over us as if we're about to be jumped by some street punks and I roll my eyes at them as I grab my cigarettes, lighting up and taking a lungful deep into my chest and holding it there for a second.

I feel fucking empty.

Way too soon after a fight to feel like this, fuck, maybe I am losing my edge. If I'm not the Butcher, riding the highs of the hunt and the cage, then who the fuck am I? D'Ardo watches me, quiet for once in his fucking life until the unease I'm feeling spills out.

"You ever get sick of all of this?" The blood on my hands soaks through the paper of my cigarette and gives off a fucked up smell. Even that doesn't make a difference.

D'Ardo shakes his head. "Nope. My man, you need a side project. Something just for you, something to keep your mind busy when everything else is sending you up the fucking wall."

Side project.

He's talking about the little girl he's stalking, the one still sitting up at that bar as if she's not afraid of what goes down in this place. Something dark settles in my gut about it but I brush it off. Doesn't fucking matter, nothing in this city does.

"And what do you think I should do, eh? Find myself some pussy to keep? What the fuck sort of side project does *The Butcher* take up, anyway?"

D'Ardo chuckles under his breath and shrugs, taking my cigarette and puffing away at it like he doesn't have his own pack in his back pocket. "Once I own my Starbright, I'll have her chained to my bed. Only place to keep pussy is on a leash."

I blow out a breath. Whatever the fuck his mother did to him, it was bad. I've never seen a woman climb out of his bed with her mind intact. I should care more about this, I should give a fuck about what he's doing, but I just can't find my fucking conscience.

"You'll get bored of her like you get bored of all the rest." I steal back the cigarette.

He shakes his head. "Nah, there's something about this one. I'm going to take my time in breaking her open because no one else will ever fucking compare."

I take one last deep inhale and flick the butt into a puddle to join the rest of the trash in the alleyway. "You're a sick man, D'Ardo."

He grins back at me. "So are you, Johnny-boy."

Butcher of the Bay - Part One

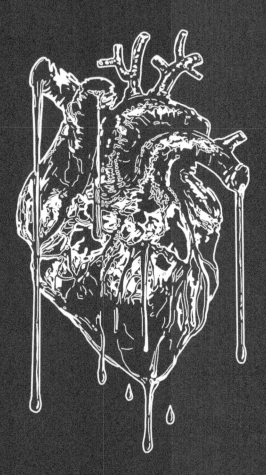

CHAPTER THREE

ODIE

The only thing worse than finding out my father is a spineless drug addict who has no sense of honor is being stuck in a private jet with him for thirteen hours.

I lock myself in the small bedroom and refuse to come out for the entire flight. I don't get any sleep, instead I stare up at the ceiling and try to convince myself that everything is going to be okay but my mind just keeps skipping back to my mother.

How could she do this?

My father had always treated me poorly but my mother... I truly thought she loved me. At least enough to keep me safe. How many times had she thrown herself in front of me when my father had beaten me? To take that pain for me, only to stand by when my father and his men had shoved me into the car.

After she started drinking too much, right around the time

my father began taking her jewelry to sell in order to pay for his habit, I was so angry about his abuse that I blamed her for staying with him. For being with him in the first place. She is a beautiful woman, even with the alcohol she's more beautiful than me. She could have had any man in the world and yet she chose him, a criminal who profits on the addictions of others. But my anger was never something I spoke to her about and it has long since burned out. I even felt guilty about how much of the hatred I have for my father had been diverted into being upset with her. But she can't have ever really loved me, not if she's let me go like this, without a single word! The grief climbs up my throat and bursts out as sobs that I can't contain.

It's a terrible feeling.

I have no one, nothing, what even is the point of being here? Why should I even continue breathing when every tether I have to this life has just snapped? If I had a knife I would carve my own heart out, just to stop the pain in my chest at this betrayal. The sobbing gets worse, the tears streaming down my face until I'm a wet mess.

I cannot think about my buyer, this man who will be my husband.

I've only ever slept with Louis, something that had come about from years of friendship. He had done his best to protect me from my father's rage, chaperoning me to the beach whenever there were large parties and gatherings at the cottages my father would hide us in. It was always after one of these that he would become violent, the alcohol and drugs mixing into a cocktail of rage in his blood.

How could I possibly have sex with another man? A stranger who values women as property?

A wail bursts out of me unbidden and I know what will happen before the door slams open, my father's face a mask of fury.

"Odette, you are making a spectacle of yourself! Pull yourself together!"

I can't. I can't stop the tears anymore than I can stop this plane.

He grabs a fistful of my hair and drags me from the bed, throwing me to the ground and backhanding me again. "I do not want to hand over damaged goods to Signor Mecedo but if I have to beat the obedience back into you then I will."

I look up at him through my fingers and but I'm hollow, no fear left in me to have at his words. I even consider fighting back for the first time in my life, the anger at this man, a living thing inside me that has consumed everything else, but the sobbing that just will not stop means I can barely lift my hands away from my face. I'm frozen, stuck in this position and this stupid airplane.

He only hits me twice more, this time with a closed fist and to the side of my head where my hair will cover the damage but my brain feels as though I've just stepped off of a merry-go-round, everything spinning and bright.

"You. Will. Obey."

No. The second he says those words to me I know that I really won't obey him. I'll lose myself in my emotions right now and I will bide my time but I will not go along with all of this plan of his. I will find a way out of this terrible mess he's thrown me into.

I clamp my mouth shut around my sobs, clenching my teeth so hard I think they might break, to stifle the noise enough that he will leave me where I'm curled into a ball on the lush carpet. I listen to the sound of his breath heaving until he finally grunts and walks away, the door snicking shut behind him. He couldn't possibly slam it, not with the pilot and stewardesses on board and listening to our every move.

I wonder what they think of the sounds of him hitting me?

I collapse back onto the bed, my head pounding and the tears still streaming from my eyes. I feel bile creeping up the back of my throat as stars dance in front of my eyes. No, it doesn't matter how low I feel. I'm going to make it through this and then I'm going to fight my way out of it too, I just don't know how yet.

Finally after hours and hours have passed with my stomach rebelling and the white of the ceiling burning holes in my eyes one of the attendants comes in to tell me that the plane is about to start its descent. I freshen up in the small bathroom, running my fingers through my hair and washing my face, thankful I hadn't worn any makeup so there's nothing running down my face. Then, deep breath, I take my seat out in the main cabin next to my father, facing my traitorous boyfriend. God, I guess he's now my ex-boyfriend.

I stare at a point above Louis's shoulder, where the stewardesses are sitting, a placid look firmly fixed on my face. I need to get off of this damned airplane without being beaten again.

Then I can plan how to get the hell out of this situation.

"Are you over your little temper tantrum?" my father murmurs, and I keep my stare on the stewardesses instead of him as I nod. I will choke on any words of platitude I try to give him right now so silence is my greatest asset.

"You must realize it's safer for you to be out of France, Odette. I have far too many enemies back home, America will be a better place for you to be."

America.

He's sold me off to an American drug lord. I will be stranded in an entirely alien country, with a language I barely have a grasp on, married to someone whose method of making money I despise.

My vision blurs again as I blink back more tears. They are as useless to me now as they've ever been.

"You will be a very rich woman, your husband has amassed a great wealth in his business," Louis says, and my father laughs.

"She will never see the money, she will live like a prized treasure in his palace. She will never work or leave the building, her every need will be catered for. Honestly, I've given you a gift many women would kill for and all you can do is cry over it? Pathetic."

Louis pulls out his phone and taps away at it. I've never been allowed a phone of my own, never been allowed friends outside of my father's specially-curated inner circle. Again, I desperately wish I could sit here and spill Louis's betrayal to my father. To tell him all about the secret meetings we've had over the last few months, how he taught me to pleasure a man, and all of the dirty things he's done to me, but I'm now certain my father would kill me for it.

Whatever he owes this Signor Mecedo, it's a lot and my virginity will be the only thing to cover the tab.

So I keep my mouth sealed shut as the airplane makes its descent and my fate comes rushing towards me.

My father's palm sweats where he's gripping my arm.

Signor Mecedo is *much* older than me, his jet-black hair slicked back like a cap and a fat cigar dangling from his lips as if we aren't standing on a tarmac in the middle of nowhere, the engine of the private jet still blistering hot at our backs as we stand here it what must be the desert... which desert, I have no idea. There isn't a building or customs for us to pass through, and I have no doubt the flight we've just taken was illegal. I'm tense as I wait for hordes of border control to burst out of the bushes like they do in the movies but there's nothing as far as the eye can see, except the large SUV's my new husband and his men arrived in and the airplane itself.

I can't understand the conversation happening in Spanish around me, only that *Signor Mecedo* doesn't look happy. I suppose I'm not to his liking, most men these days want rail-thin women and I have more curves than your average model. My figure is a perfect hourglass, perfect for a man who wants an ass to grip and breasts to feel heavy in his palms.

My father wrenches me around so I'm standing in front of my new husband, staring up into his black, void-like eyes. I fight to stop my lip curling in disgust. He is easily old enough to be my father, maybe even my father's father, and his eyes stay glued on the soft flesh of my breasts peeking out of my blouse.

"She'll do," he murmurs, and my father's hand drops away from my wrist finally.

God, I hope he speaks some English.

At the sounds of gravel crunching under feet behind me, I glance over my shoulder to see my father and Louis both walking away from me, without a single word of goodbye. I have no tears left in me, no emotion left in my hollow shell of a body.

Just pure outrage and fury at them both.

I don't let my gaze falter away from the man who has *bought* me, the man still standing in front of me eyeing me up like I'm a piece of meat and the men behind him openly leering as well.

The second man grabs me, his hands rough around the tops of my arms as he shoves me into the back of the large SUV. I stumble over my feet and fall onto my back against the hot leather of the seats, baking away in the hot summer sun. I've never felt such searing sunlight before, the heat is nothing like the summers back in France. I move to sit up and right myself when the car door on the other side opens and hands clamp around my arms again, holding me down. I gasp and try to squirm away but the man who just shoved me into the car grabs my thighs and holds me still.

The plane hasn't even taken off yet.

I take in a deep, gulping breath, ready to scream and fight them off, when a large hand covers my mouth. It stinks of tobacco and sweat and his fingers bite into my skin as he squeezes my jaw like he's trying to break it. I choke on my scream as I try to move away from him but the pain only gets worse until I stop fighting.

The men don't move any further, they just hold me against the seat like a pinned butterfly, all splayed beauty and death.

The only sound is the harshness of my breathing and then my new husband speaks.

"I don't want fucking leftovers and I don't trust her father. Check her."

I have no idea what he's said but both of the other men laugh and then the one holding my legs rips my blouse out from where it was neatly tucked in and he slips his hands into the waist of my pants, his fingers searching for the buttons.

A scream bursts out of my throat only to be muffled by the hand, tears leaking out of my eyes, as the button pops off of my pants when he finally gives up trying to open them, instead just destroying them to get them down my legs.

I try to rip my hands out of the sweaty hands of the man holding me but he only chuckles and tugs my wrists further up until I think my back might snap under the pressure. My eyes fly back to my new husband as he stands behind his men, the cigar dangling from his lips as he murmurs in low tones to them, none of the words making any sense to me.

Rough fingers pry my thighs apart and I scream again, my thighs tensing as I try to snap my legs shut but I'm not strong enough. Panic sets in and I can't catch my breath, the sobs stealing any chances I might have had at being rational. I attempt to kick my legs out but the fabric of my pants traps my ankles.

I hear a man spit and then two fingers thrust roughly inside me with no other warning.

My sobs turn into a wail as I try to get away from the assault, every fiber of my being violated by this treatment. I was wrong back on the plane, my father's wrath was better than this. I would relive every moment of his abuse to get away from this.

I know deep down this is only the beginning.

"She's definitely not a virgin. There's no seal here."

The sobs just keep coming.

"Vadim Archambault will be dead before his plane arrives home."

The fingers finally disappear and my legs are shoved closed. The hands around my wrists also drop away, only to be replaced by a fist curling in my hair, pulling me until I'm slumped onto the floor. Doors slam shut around me and the fist in my hair jerks my head back until I'm staring through my tears at one of the men.

He speaks in broken English, the words garbled and hard for me to understand. "Senor Mecedo does not want another man's leftovers. You should not have lied to us."

He slams my head into the seat in front of me, the sickening crunch of my nose breaking vibrating through my skull, and then he finally lets me go, slamming the door behind him.

They're going to kill me.

Bile creeps up my throat and I swallow it down, the metallic tang of the blood pouring out of my nose overwhelming me entirely. One of the men hops into the driver's seat and starts the car, cheerful Latin music playing loudly through the speakers like some sort of cosmic joke.

My eyes swim with tears and the pounding in my head only gets worse with the motion of the car until all I know is darkness and I pass out in a pool of my own blood.

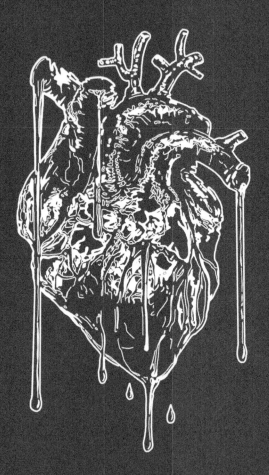

CHAPTER FOUR

ILLI

The docks are a stinking pile of rotten wood, dilapidated buildings, and homeless people sheltering in rickety old boats who see fucking everything and nothing all at once. The warehouses and boat sheds that house the parties and business rooms of the Twelve are nearby but the spot I've chosen for the meetup is away from D'Ardo's security cams and hired muscle. No doubt he's paying one of the bums to keep watch but they're far enough away that he won't know exactly what my business down here has been for, only that I was here.

I trust that man like a brother, but sometimes he oversteps and forgets I'm not one of his little flunkies.

I lean against my car, looking out over the sludge pile of seaweed and trash that makes up the shore down here. The water beyond is calm and still, the moon reflecting perfectly against the gentle ripple of the tide. It could be beautiful down here. If the Bay wasn't hell on Earth, if someone gave a shit about the place at all, it would be a fucking amazing city.

Instead it's overrun with gangs, crime, bikers, drugs, and murder.

That had always been perfect to me but fuck... something is wrong in my head right now. I still crave the blood and the burn of my work but something is missing and fuck me if I can think of what it is.

Maybe I am losing my fucking edge.

Lights hit me and snap me out of my shitty, reflective mood. I shake myself off and roll my shoulders back. Gotta get my head back in the game before I get taken the fuck out.

The car is fucking nice, a '67 mustang Shelby Sportsroof, that would look fucking perfect in my garage. Fuck, maybe I'll ask for that as payment for my next job. A smirk stretches over my lips at the thought of taking it, knowing just how fucking hard to come by they really are.

Two thugs get out and tip their heads at me with respect which I ignore entirely and then their ugly-ass boss steps out, adjusting one of the rings on his scarred hands as he looks around, not entirely trusting that we're alone and unwatched out here.

The Viper is my biggest client.

I don't trust the greedy fuck but from my time in the cage he knows exactly what I'm capable of and usually treats me with enough respect that I don't feel the need to peel his fingernails off with toothpicks. His crew are all dumbass meatheads, not worth the air they consume, and this means I make a lot of money out of this member of the Twelve.

He drops my payment at my feet without ceremony, the set of his jaw pissed off and on edge. I smirk back at him. "Bad day at the office? Having trouble finding fresh meat?"

"Someday you'll have to let me induct you, Illium. You'll be backed into a fucking corner and have no choice," he grunts out. I get the feeling he's still pissed at the hike in my prices. I deserve more, after every fight and every job I raise my rates a little, just enough that they all know I'm not some chump for hire. If you want me, gimme the fucking cash.

At this point, only the Devil out prices me and no one here is dumb enough to call him.

I light the cigarette between my lips and smirk at him. "Not fucking likely. Maybe you should find a different gene pool to skim, your new blood is kind of pathetic."

The guy I'd pulverized the previous night had apparently been the brother of one of the Viper's most trusted men. Fucking pathetic, the lot of them.

He gives me a look as he sets the leather bags down at my feet. A thrill runs up my spine. I fucking love cold, hard cash. Nothing safer than green packed into the walls of my warehouse, there's not a man, woman, or child in the Bay braindead enough to come steal from the Butcher.

Banks aren't so fucking trustworthy.

"I need the guy alive, y'hear me? No more accidents. If the Chaos Demons find out I'm looking around their business then it'll bring a whole new war to the Bay and I've been enjoying the peace," he mutters, leaning in as he slips me the paper so his men don't hear what he's saying. Huh. So he's completely fucking aware he's recruited mouthy trash who can't keep their mouths shut to fucking save themselves and yet he still keeps taking on more of the dickheads. Nice.

D'Ardo might be a merciless, evil fucker but at least his men know the score.

"Yeah, yeah. The last guy had a heart problem or something, he croaked too fucking easy. When I took him apart I found it looked a bit... fucked."

The Viper snorts out a laugh. "Of course you played fucking doctor on him. Did you package up his meat, too? How much do dismembered corpses go for these days?"

I smirk at him, all teeth, and enjoy the disgusted looks of his eavesdropping men. "I've got some rich cannibals on my speed dial. They pay by the pound."

They were sick fucks too, but that's beside the point. Green is green and I plan on dying a rich man. So fucking rich there isn't a fucking man in the Bay I couldn't buy, just for shits and giggles because a man without a plan is just fucking... bleak.

"I need to know about the supply tracks, Illium. I need it now so even though you're having a fucking laugh at my expense right now... I'll double the fees if you get me the information. I'll even get you some fresh meat for the cage, someone to really push your limits."

Hmm. That's fucking tempting but I won't tell this fuck that. "I'll get it done on my own time."

He nods and drops the butt of his own cigarette, crushing it beneath his heel. "You always do."

I take one last drag of my own smoke and then flick it towards the stinking water, blowing the smoke out in one deep exhale. "Anything else or can I go back to my business?"

The Viper rubs his hands together, his rings catching and making a small tinkling noise that sounds fucking weird as hell coming from him. "Just remember Butcher; the higher the man, the greater the fall. Someday you'll need me and when you do, I'll have your fucking loyalty. Every fucking penny I've paid you will come back to me eventually."

I'd rather fucking die. I'd rather get beaten in the cage and be bled out on the fucking mats than devote my life and freedom to someone else.

Never going to happen.

No matter how much D'Ardo and this fuck want it.

I smirk and give him a mocking salute, one that he sneers back at. Not many people treat members of the Twelve with such little respect but I think they all know I could rule them all if I fucking wanted to. I just couldn't give a fuck about the entire institution. They're all only on top for now, only until change arrives and if my life has taught me nothing else it's that nothing ever stays the same.

I watch as the car rolls away, lighting up again and holding the smoke in my lungs to feel the burn. Fucking perfect to kill some biker trash.

I look down at the slip of paper in my hands and frown.

Chance Graves.

That's fucking familiar but I can't quite place it. It doesn't fucking matter, money is money and as long as it's not one of my many informants on the paper I don't give a fuck. With one last look over the docks I get back into my car and start it up, the engine purring like a fucking dream under me. Time to find Harbin and Roxas, get more info on this Graves and get this job done.

I hope the fight is worth it.

I park behind the titty bar and kill the engine, flicking out a text and waiting for the reply. It doesn't come, instead the back door opens and Roxas saunters out, the hitch in his step betraying just how fucking wasted he is.

Perfect to get the goods from him.

"Illi, my man! Tell me you're here for a drink? Juliet is here, the tits on that girl! Perfect to stick your cock between." The grin is wide and fucking dumb on his face.

I shake my head. "Maybe later, man. How much do you know about the Chaos Demons? I'm having some teething problems with them. None of them squeal right."

Roxas roars with laughter, lifting the beer in his hands up to salute me with. "You have a fucking way with words. I know way too fucking much about the Demons. They're enemy number one to the Unseen, man, where have you been?"

The door opens again and Harbin steps out. Never too far away from each other, these two. He's steadier on his feet even with a beer in his hands. "Twice in one week, Illi, what's the occasion?"

I shrug at him. "You tell me, man. Everything leads back to the MC clubs at the moment. Were you warning me away from D'Ardo because your Prez is planning something big?"

I can't stand the Boar, more than any other fucking member of the Twelve. He hates that I'm friends with half his crew and does what he can to fuck with me through them.

Roxas had learned that the hard way years ago. I'll never fucking trust that biker Prez again, not for anything.

"What's going on, man? If someone in our club is stirring shit up with you we'll deal with them," Harbin says. Fuck, he's a decent enough guy but he should know by now decent guys don't survive in our world.

"Why are you guys warring with the Demons? I've got a hit on one of them and I need to know if I'm crossing you guys before I go in there, so we can work it out like men." I say, my smirk only getting bigger.

Roxas shakes his head at us both and stalks off to take a leak on the bushes at the edge of the parking lot, facing the road so every car that drives past cops an eyeful of what he's packing. I roll my eyes but Harbin's attention doesn't waiver from me.

"Demons are bad news. Stay the hell away from them, the money ain't worth it," he mutters, taking one last swig of the beer and throwing the empty bottle so the glass shatters against the side of the building. Zero respect for shit around here.

"I've taken the job, it's set in stone. Anything in particular you wanna warn me about?"

Harbin shrugs. "Stay the fuck away from Grimm if you can, and his original crew. If it's one of the younger guys you need then just lure him out by his dick and make sure you leave nothing behind."

Grimm. Fuck, that's where the name is familiar. Grimm Graves has two sons in the MC; Colt and Chance. Fuck me, I have a hit on one of his fucking sons. "Right. And if it's impossible to get the guy without Grimm being aware of it? What's your advice then?"

Harbin eyes me like I'm testing him and I stare back, unrepentant and unfeeling. Just because he's decided we're friends, doesn't mean I'm changing my business for him. This is a point of pride now, I never fail at a job.

"You should know before you go there the Devil is stalking Grimm. The psycho likes to play with his food before he eats it. Don't get caught up in that shit, Illi. In and out."

Well, fuck.

That's almost enough to keep me home.

Because my night hasn't been busy enough, I get a call from yet another member of the Twelve. I miss the days of dealing with mobsters and drug dealers, I swear it was fucking easier.

"If it isn't my favorite meat packer. I have a job I require your... expertise for."

My jaw clenches at the sound of the slimy bastard's voice. "How about you try that again before I tell you to crawl back into the hole you came from, Vulture."

He chuckles down the phone, his mouth way too fucking close so I can hear every little wheeze of his breath. Fucking disgusting. "Come on now, I'm offering a lot of money for the job I have for you. Let's just cut the bullshit niceties and talk numbers. I have a package I need picked up from the airport and delivered to the docks. Big client, big fucking package. There's more money in this than any other business transaction I've ever taken before so I knew exactly who to call to get the job done. I'll give you ten percent of my cut."

My eyebrows hit my fucking hairline. The Vulture is the richest, cheapest bastard out there. Skin sells for a pretty penny and yet he hoards his wealth like he's going out of business. Ten percent... that would be in the millions.

"When does the package get here? I'm on another job."

He laughs, his breath coming out in hacking gulps like a

fucking hyena. "The package is already on its way, you'll need to be at the airport by four in the morning. The package will be handed over to you by the seller."

I check my watch. Two hours, I'll have to shelve the Viper's job for tonight. "What security do I have to get past? Give me the rest of the details and I'll see what I can do."

I get off the phone twenty minutes later feeling creeped the fuck out but less apprehensive about the work. Security has been taken care of already, private jet, a long drive back to the docks. Probably the easiest money I'll ever fucking make. The Vulture is worried about the men who were outbid coming for the package and a larger detail would be an easier target for them but who else is there who could deliver the damn thing without needing at least a second person?

No one.

So I head home to my warehouse, change cars to my BMW with bulletproof glass and load up with a heap of more weapons. Knives and my beloved cleavers aren't great defense when you're also the delivery driver. Once I'm sure I have enough lead to sink a fucking ship I head out, irritated at the smooth handling of the luxury car.

Gimme a roaring engine any day of the week.

Parking is a nightmare as I try to find something close to the terminal with cover in case I need to take cover, but I find something tucked behind the building. I keep a close eye on my surroundings, nothing jumping out as suspicious except maybe the fact that none of the security look me in the eyes as I pass. I'm a big guy, covered in tattoos and clearly packing an arsenal. You'd think there would be someone the Vulture hadn't gotten to in the building, some lower level dickhead prancing around thinking no one was above the rules but nope, zero eye contact.

Guess it makes the job even fucking sweeter.

Waiting at the boarding gates isn't pleasant. The security staff may not eye ball me but the civilians all think I'm putting on a fucking show for them, especially when I get through to the First Class lounge. Fuck me, I've never looked so out of place in my life as I do in the plush lounge. Businessmen and their wives all stare at me with something close to horror on their faces, clutching at their bags and covering their rolexes like I'm a common thug. Pfft, I'm probably earning more right now than they're ever put on their tax returns.

Once the novelty wears off and I've got a little more privacy, I check my phone to see if there's any word from my out of state contacts about Chance. Nothing. God-fucking-dammit. I need to know more about this drug pipeline the Viper is trying to tap into before I hunt the biker fuck down. No use going in blind and finding myself in the middle of some turf war, especially not if the Devil is involved. Look, I'm a big enough guy to know when I'm outclassed and there's only one guy on this planet I'm not ever going against, and that's the Devil himself.

I shove my phone in my pocket just in time for the gate to open and the security to rush around as the private jet lands. I stand up straight and roll my shoulders back, expecting a high class hooker. The men who buy from the Vulture want very specific types of girls and for this one to break the record in price she's going to be either a virgin or a pro. I'm expecting her to be primped and waxed and painted to the point of not really knowing what fucking age she is, probably for the best because knowing the sick fucks who frequent the skin auctions she's probably underage. I stand there and make a thousand different assumptions about who is getting off that flight and not a single fucking one of them is right.

A fucking *goddess* gets off the flight.

My breath gets sucked right out of my chest at the sight of her long legs, ass for fucking days, and a rack that would make grown men weep. Naturally blonde hair down her waist, lush lips that would look fucking perfect around my cock, and a waist so tiny my hands would easily circle it. She's utterly fucking sinful.

My dick has never been so fucking hard in all my life.

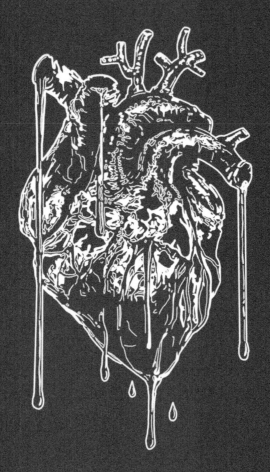

CHAPTER FIVE

ODIE

I wake up in pitch darkness, so complete I'm not sure for a second if my eyes have actually opened or not. I move my arms around until I feel the car seats around me and know I haven't been moved from where I passed out, even if the car itself has been. Panic settles into the pit of my stomach. What if the car has been buried somewhere? Would I know, is there some way to tell even if it's too dark to see anything?

Eventually my eyes adjust a little more and I can make out another car next to the one I'm stuck in. It's some sort of garage, possibly underground. The clock on the dashboard says six in the morning. We'd landed at two in the afternoon, how was I unconscious for so long? I rub at my head, finding the sore spot and wincing. When was I hit here? Is time slipping away from me?

Why can't I remember anything else?

I wish I had a light and a mirror so I could check my body over. Was I drugged? Beaten? There's a soreness between my legs as well, is that the pain of that man's fingers or was I assaulted further? If I had any tears left in me I would cry but instead I lay back down and try to think of what I should do but there's nothing. I am completely helpless.

I am left in the car for the rest of the day with no food or water.

I don't think I could stomach any type of sustenance even if I had some available, but the constant tears I've been in for the last few days and the heavy bleeding of my nose means I'm terribly dehydrated. My tongue feels both cottony and heavy in my mouth, like a dead weight, and my throat burns when I try to swallow.

A good side effect is I don't have to use the bathroom. For the first few hours I'm too scared to try to open the doors but eventually the thought of suffocating here has me attempting to open one with no luck. I don't know whether the car is sealed enough to take me out with carbon monoxide poisoning, but hours pass without any changes. I don't know if I'm glad or upset at not having the quiet death of slipping into unconsciousness and never waking.

The terror slowly leaves me and then, all of a sudden, I'm bored again.

I think my father may have broken that part of me that

stays scared. Maybe it was sometime after he beat me so badly I couldn't stand for a week, I remember suddenly becoming reckless after that, like I knew how little control I have over my life so it's all just become kind of... pointless. Yes, I have dreams and hopes. I enjoy my painting and walking by the beach, but I never really *do* anything. I could never get away with it.

The hours continue to tick on and my thoughts take a darker turn.

Is it possible to want to die without being suicidal? I want Odette Archambault to die a fiery death and I want Odie to take her place. I want the woman who is owned by the men around her to cease to be, leaving behind a woman who forges her own path.

I want so many things that will never be.

I lose all sense of time, even with the small blinking light of the clock on the dashboard, long before the door opens again with no warning and the garage floods with artificial light. My eyes water after being in the dark for so long, my brain sluggish to catch up to the fact that I'm once again in danger.

I sit up and look out, squinting against the light and trying to make out where the men are coming from, only... it's not a man.

A small, older woman with the gentle face of a grandmother walks towards me. Relief courses through my veins as she pulls keys out of her pocket and the car beeps as it unlocks. I swallow. Should I get out myself?

I have no chance to decide, she moves quickly to the car

and pulls the door open, peering down at me with her big, warm brown eyes behind the glasses. I let out a deep breath. Maybe she will help me get home? Wherever that is now, Paris maybe? Anywhere but here with that man who *bought* me.

We stare at each other for a minute and then she clicks her tongue in disdain as she grips my chin, turning my head to get a better look at the mess my face must be.

"You look like a cheap whore. What man would pay for you, eh? How am I going to get my money back with *this*?" her voice is warm and low, as if she's comforting me. I sigh even though I do not understand her words, so glad I'm finally being treated with some sort of respect.

"Come, girl. I need to clean you up for the photos." she murmurs.

I stare back up at her blankly, no idea of what she's saying. She clicks her tongue again and motions for me to follow her. My legs shake as I stand, my hands trembling as I clutch at the waist of my pants. I'd completely forgotten the button had been broken off and now they won't stay up. My shirt is covered in blood and the red dirt from the desert of the airstrip. I let out a shuddering breath. It would be good to be able to clean up a little, maybe she has something I can cover myself with?

"Uhm, do you speak the English? I do not know any Spanish." I murmur, and the woman huffs under her breath.

"Of course I speak English. We're in America."

I swallow again, wincing at the dryness of my throat. It

was worth a shot even if disappointment now burns through me. I swallow and hitch my pants up a little higher from where they've slipped.

She leads me through the door and into a tunnel-like room without windows. The air feels different here, heavier. Definitely underground. I try not to panic at the thought of the walls closing in on me but then that's all I can think about. Deep breath in, keep walking, this is hell, how on Earth do I get out of here?

The older woman stops and pulls open another door, ushering me in. I smile and nod at her in thanks when I see the shower. The room is clean enough, very dated and roughly put together. This is definitely not her home, at least I hope not. The thought of this little old lady living underground... makes my skin crawl.

She closes the door behind herself and motions to the shower. Oh. She wants me to shower with her in the room? I glance at the door and there's no lock on the door. I guess I'd rather her be in here with me than to be naked and vulnerable with those other men. At least one of them is here, the man who broke my nose and drove me here.

I smile at her again and let go of my pants to let them drop at my feet. The woman nods and bends to grab them, holding them up and frowning at the damage. "Idiot men. Damaging my merchandise."

I smile and lift my shirt over my head, careful to not catch my sore nose on the fabric. I catch my reflection in the mirror over the sink and see the bloody mess my face is in, grimacing. I look as though I've bathed in blood, as disgusting as that sounds.

The woman starts clicking her tongue at me again, startling me back into moving. I slip my bra and panties off, dropping them to the floor and starting the water in the shower, stepping in once the water warms up. The soap doesn't smell very nice, like the type a man would use to cut grease, but I soap up and scrub with it anyway. Washing my face is harder but I make it work, swiping gently with my fingers until I think the blood is gone.

The woman watches me carefully for a while and then moves to open the cupboard under the sink, pulling bottles out and handing them to me. I recognize the English words, shampoo and conditioner, and smile at her in thanks.

They smell a little better, floral enough to hide the smell of the soap, and I give my long hair a good scrub. The sore spot at the back of my head is still tender but getting clean helps to wash away what happened yesterday… enough that I can take a breath.

The woman starts poking around in the cupboard once more, pulling out a hair dryer and some make up. I frown. I don't want to use another woman's makeup and I certainly do not want to be fussing over my injuries.

Why would I even need it?

She stands up straight again and shuts the water off for me, motioning me to step out as she plugs the hair dryer in. There's no towel, so I stand there awkwardly as I drip water all over the floor and she dries out my hair. It's so strange, not something I've ever experienced before, but what can I do if she cannot understand my questions? And now I am naked so I can't just flee the room, run screaming through the underground halls when the men who assaulted me will probably find me there.

Once my hair is dry, she starts to style it, fussing and primping it carefully. She hums under her breath, happy in the work and the tension again eases out of me. All must be okay, she couldn't stand here with me like this if it wasn't.

Once she's satisfied, she moves me back over to the mirror and starts to do my makeup, just a quick coverup of the slight bruising I have around my nose. It still looks straight and I can breathe the same so I must have gotten lucky and it doesn't need to be reset. I watch as she carefully lines my eyes with a dark kohl and then paints my lips in a deep, blood red. I always did look good in that color.

Finally, she packs the supplies up and bends down to stash them away again. I stand there, still a little awkward in my nakedness, and hope she's about to pull out some clothing or at the very least a towel.

She doesn't.

She pulls out a camera.

A *camera.*

Dread thrums through me once again. There's only one reason she would need a camera, my makeup done, and my naked body. My brow furrows and I shake my head, trying to stop myself from screaming. Water still drips from my body but she doesn't care about that.

She starts taking photos, none of them of my face, and she murmurs under her breath to herself. I raise one of my hands to cover my breasts and her face completely changes.

There is nothing about this woman that is a sweet, little old lady.

She slaps me across the face, harder than my father had ever managed, and stars burst across my vision. I stumble and catch myself against the tiles.

She leans forward and speaks slowly but in perfect English, "Your father stole a lot of money from me. You are going to get me every penny back. Do you understand me now, whore?"

A different man escorts me onto the airplane.

It makes no difference to me, I have learned my lesson. I do not try to speak to him or argue with with as he grips my elbow, only following his every direction promptly.

After the photoshoot with the cruel old woman, she left me in that bathroom for hours. Completely naked and without food. I'd been able to drink some water but my stomach had begun to feel as though there were claws digging inside it with hunger. How many days had it been since I last ate?

The old woman had returned with clothing for me, throwing them at me and clicking her tongue at me to hurry me along. I took my time in putting the scant lingerie on, then the cheap, but sensual, dress on. The heels she threw at me didn't fit and the look she gives me is one of censure, as if my feet had grown overnight in spite.

I consider gouging her eyes out with my bare hands, but I was raised to be a *good girl*. Good girls don't attack other women, even disgusting ones who work as sex traffickers.

Once I'm dressed and ready for my new buyer, she walks me back out to the garage, shoving me into the back without ceremony. The new escort shadows her the entire way, the gun strapped to his hip in clear view as if to subdue me.

It works.

I sit silent in the backseat with nothing to look at outside my windows but the same red dirt of the desert. I am careful with where I look while my escort is watching me, but I never stop looking for a way to escape him. I try the locks on the car doors but they do not open from the inside. I grit my teeth with frustration, the plan to roll out of the car into oncoming traffic an appealing escape. The death would have been quick that way, only we do not pass any cars and short of breaking the window, there's no way out of here.

After an hour of staring at the same nothingness, we finally start to see life.

The road gets busy quickly, as if I've blinked and suddenly

we're in a city. Maybe it's not that way and the bump to the head has me forgetting things. I secretly hope I have a slow bleed that will take me out but no, I stay conscious as we slow and begin to weave through traffic and into some large city. The man escorting me switches the radio off and hums under his breath as he navigates the road, completely at peace with the work he is doing.

These people are sick.

Finally, we pull into a real airport and leave the car with the valet. He grips my arm in a firm hand and directs me into the building, bypassing the security with a simple jerk of his head at the workers there.

Despair settles deep in my stomach.

So they all know him, know what he does, and probably know I'm here against my will. The chances of finding someone who can help me are not great here, better to be silent and cooperative until I reach my destination. Maybe an air hostess or someone at the next security gate will help.

Maybe if I scream and make enough noise as I run away from him, someone will notice and help me.

We walk through to the first class lounge, the man showing our boarding passes and my passport as we move through. I didn't even know I had a passport. I barely catch a glimpse of it but my name and details seem to be correct.

I need that if I'm ever going to get home.

The flight is commercial but with only four other people in

first class. The air hostess who shows us to our seats is pretty and smiles at me a lot, complimenting my dress. I try to smile back but I'm too aware of the man's firm grip on my arm to react as I should.

She doesn't seem to notice, probably used to rude and entitled women in this section, and she moves away quickly.

I settle into my seat, clicking the seatbelt and glancing around as if there's going to be some big sign lit up; 'help is here'. No. There's nothing but the air hostesses and businessmen around me.

So I wait until we're in the air before I press the call button, ready to start a very public fight with this man to get the hell away from him and out of this sale. He angrily jabs at the button to stop the call and I turn on him, opening my mouth to speak when his hand slides between my legs to cup me intimately.

My entire body freezes.

"Do not attract attention, little whore. I have been paid well to get you to where you're going but no one told me I couldn't sample the product if you give me trouble."

I can't breathe. I barely manage to jerk my head into a nod and he chuckles under his breath, sliding his fingers over me once more before moving away. The hostess walks up and speaks, but the terror is still pumping through me too hard to understand a word of what she's saying. My escort speaks for me, dismissing her and then turning back to his drink.

I sit frozen for the rest of the flight, too scared to move or smile or even think.

Maybe my half remembered assault did more damage than I originally thought.

The flight only lasts an hour, thank god, and when we've landed I stay seated until my escort tells me to move. Adrenaline shoots through my veins even as I walk off of the plane on jelly legs. I need to get out.

I need to escape and find someone to help me.

My escort tucks his hand into the crook of my elbow again, guiding me as we both step into the airport terminal and past the staff. I'm ready to jerk away from him and run the second I can. My eyes scan over the entire first class lounge, only to find myself staring at the most terrifying man I have ever seen.

A shiver runs down my spine as I take in every terrifying inch of him. The tattoos and weapons strapped to his body, the sheer mass of his hulking body, he is like no man I've ever seen before.

He is a monster, only worse because he is flesh and blood.

And he's here for me.

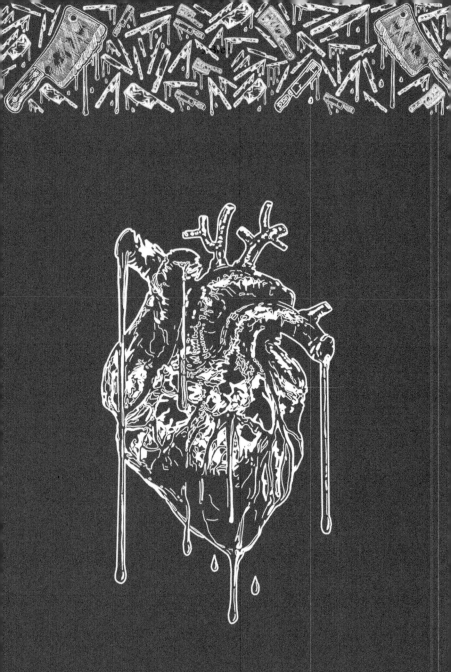

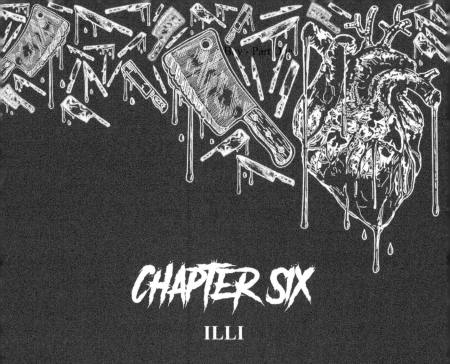

CHAPTER SIX

ILLI

Her eyes burn brightly and her body is fucking perfection.

No wonder she went for such a high price.

The cartel who escorted her over doesn't utter a word, just holds her elbow to direct her over to me and then turns on his heel to get back on a plane home. Huh, no fucking love lost there. Maybe he's an ex, pissed she's moving on to greener pastures.

I'm glad she isn't quaking in her fucking sexy heels, I'd have to get her the fuck out of here if she was being trafficked. Fuck, to go for such a high price and be willing... she must be fucking legendary between the sheets.

I can't get my dick under control.

"We're this way, baby girl. Do you have any luggage?"

Her eyes flash at me as she shakes her head and, fuck me,

that only makes the situation in my pants worse. The anger there is enough to know that she'd be fucking unreal. Those lips wrapped around my dick... fuck, I need to get her moving out of the airport before I bend her the fuck over something.

Fuck this is it.

This is my fucking side project.

I'm going to do whatever the fuck it takes to get her warm and willing and fucking fiery underneath me, on top of me, wrapped around me... fuck. I'm just standing here staring at her like a fucking dick because she's knocked the brains out of me with all that she's working with.

She's working with *a lot*.

I could afford her. Even double the price, I could make it work. Fuck, it's so tempting to offer her the money to come home with me right the fuck now instead of the rich dick who has already paid for her time. She's sex on legs that go for fucking miles. But I don't want to insult her by offering her the money. She might be a pro but, fuck, you meet someone like this? You fucking keep her, whatever it takes, and I'm not sticking my fucking foot in it so quick.

I'll take her to her job, look her up, and do this shit the right fucking way.

Even if the thought of some other guy touching her makes me see eight shades of blood red and my fingers itch for my cleaver. Fuck. Okay, it's fine. Don't rage out and murder half the fucking city in a jealous rage, no matter how bad you want to own her.

Fuck me.

Her eyebrows raise a little at me and I try to relax my jaw a bit so I don't crack my fucking teeth. I offer her my arm and she stares down at it like it's a weapon. I mean, it is but I don't want her thinking I'm some thug, so I wrap it around her waist instead and walk her through the building, safe at my side from whoever might be dumb enough to try and take my girl.

Fuck.

Not my girl.

Nah, fuck it. My girl. She's going to be, whatever it takes. Fuck, I'll have to call the Vulture and get more details about her. Enough that I can take my time in seducing her. I feel like some horny teenager again, except I skipped over the fumbling part and went straight to banging anything with a pulse that looked hot in heels. Fuck. I can't think about her heels and those legs, not with her pressed up against me, all warm and soft.

She doesn't make a sound the whole way out.

I try to keep my attention on the tasks ahead, triple checking there's no one following us or so much as glancing our way. She follows my lead perfectly, pausing when we need to and ducking her face away so she attracts a little less attention which is great because she's a fucking showstopper.

When we get to the main doors I pause to check out how things look outside and I see some anxiety in those sexy, fuck-me eyes of hers. Well, that won't fucking do.

"It's okay, baby girl. I'm the best in the Bay, there's no one who can get past me. I'll get you to where you're going without a hitch."

She swallows and nods. I feel fucking cut she won't speak to me, what kind of pussy am I, but I keep my word and get her to the car so fast her feet barely touch the ground. I open the door for her like a fucking gentleman and help her into the backseat. That dress of hers rides up a little and my soul leaves my fucking body.

I need those fucking thighs wrapped around my head.

Right the fuck now.

If she wasn't sitting there, all class and perfect fucking ass, I'd just drive her home but something tells me I need to impress the fuck out of this woman to get her attention and pulling a caveman isn't it. Just drive her to her fucking job and then look her up later.

That same mantra is on repeat in my head as I get in and start the car, letting the engine warm up as I unstrap a few of my weapons so they're close if I need them. I hear a little gasp in the back and meet those eyes in the mirror.

"It's okay, I know how to use them. You're in capable hands."

She nods again, swallowing, and something not quite right hits my gut. I shake it off, I'm just being a jealous fuck, and I pull the car out and into the stream of traffic. I check my mirrors a whole lot more than I usually do, this job being the most important one of my life, and also because I get to look at her every time I do.

The silence starts to grate on me.

"What do I have to do to get you to talk to me, baby girl? I need to hear that sweet voice of yours for myself."

She shrugs, and looks out the window. "*There is nothing sweet about what I have to say to you, monster.*"

Holy.

Fucking.

Shit.

I nearly nut myself.

I didn't know I had a thing for breathy, low tones in some other language and yet here I am, panting over her a little more. I mean, the legs and ass, tits and lips, that was enough to have me hot for her but the voice... fuck me, she's it. She's definitely the side project I fucking need.

Maybe I understand D'Ardo a little more now.

But no, I don't get him because there's nothing about this woman I want to break... except maybe her brain from coming too long and too hard at the end of my dick.

"Do you understand what I'm saying, baby girl, or is this all just noise to you?"

She nods again without looking at me. Instead, she stares out at the streets of the Bay, the dirty and the broken. There's nothing beautiful about this place. She's probably wishing she hadn't taken the job.

I wouldn't want to be here either.

"You've probably never been to a city like this before. The Bay used to be the playground for the young and rich, the coast line was always a big drawcard," I say when I wait for the lights I'm stuck at to turn green. My phone buzzes in my pocket but I ignore it entirely. No way I give a shit about anything else right now.

"Well, the same way it always happens, drugs took hold of the city and crime started getting pretty bad. There's a lot of kingpins in this place. Do you know which one you'll be... working with?"

She frowns out of the window and shakes her head a little.

If it's D'Ardo I may kill him, rip his throat right out with my teeth. Deep breath. "Well, there's a lot of them here. The Bay is... not the kind of place you want to stay long term. Not without someone to hold you down, keep you safe. You hear me, baby girl?"

She nods, chews on that lush lip of hers and I'm jealous as fuck. I want it between my teeth. Fuck. I need to stop thinking about it before I take the wrong turn and drive her back to my place but it's all I can think about.

I need a distraction.

I flick the radio on to some rock song, way too much talk about love and loss for me but the bombshell in the back relaxes into the seat with a sigh. Right. I'll keep it on this then, even if it is some bullshit boy band.

I slow my driving down, not giving a fuck about making it to the docks on time, just enjoying the sight of this gorgeous woman relaxed in the backseat of my bulletproof car. Safe and secure under my watchful eyes.

There's only so many times I can circle the block before I have to admit we've arrived at the docks and take her in.

I think about offering her extra, here and now, but I also don't want to start shit with her that way.

I get the feeling once I get her in my bed... she's never fucking leaving it.

I pull the car up and park it carefully, more to keep my passenger resting than anything to do with the car. The Vulture is already here waiting and, surprise surprise, D'Ardo and his flunkies are standing around with him. I'm about to rage out and shoot someone, sure that D'Ardo bought my girl to break apart, when another car pulls up alongside mine. The guys who get out are obviously cartel and they nod at me respectfully as they peer into the backseat. Fuck.

At least it's not D'Ardo.

"End of the line, baby girl." I murmur low and smooth so I don't startle the sleeping beauty, and her eyes flutter open in the back. She looks peaceful for a second, the edges of her mouth quirking upward, and then she glances out of the window at the men and her face drops.

I don't like that.

Not one fucking bit.

"What's that face for, baby girl?"

She glances back at me, all wide eyes and pursed lips, and for a second I think she's going to speak to me. Then she shakes her head and the fire is back in her eyes.

Hm. Maybe she just wasn't looking forward to the job. I open my mouth to tell her she doesn't have to go with him, fuck I'll put a bullet in all of their heads right the fuck now just for shits and gigs, when her car door opens and one of the men motions her out.

Still, she doesn't say a fucking word.

I'd think she was mute if I hadn't already heard those sexy breathy tones of hers at work.

Irritation prickles down my spine and I blow out a breath. Here I am, sitting in this car with blue balls, pissed off like some chump. Fuck that, I just need to find some other chick to fuck tonight, burn this one right out of my system by burying myself in some quality Bay pussy.

I get out of the car and look back over to where she is, standing by the cartel with the curve of her ass making me weak at the fucking knees.

There's no way in hell I'm getting her out of my head.

She glances up at me and her shoulders roll back, her eyes taking me in one last time, flaring wide with the fire she has, and then she speaks.

"Thank you for delivering me to my rapist, Monster. I look forward to seeing you in hell, because helping these men will certainly get you there."

I have no fucking clue what she's saying but, fuck, my dick likes the sound of it. Fuck, I'm going to pay for a week with her. As I walk over to D'Ardo and the Vulture I do the calculations in my head and I think I can afford a couple of months with her if she's not interested in anything else.

I'll fuck her right out of my head.

The Vulture smirks at me and kicks a duffle bag of cash towards me. Fucking cockhead. I ignore it and jerk my head at D'Ardo, glancing down at the kid by his side. She's glaring at the ground, scuffing those big boots of hers against the cracks in the road and the weeds sprouting up. D'Ardo leans down to murmur something in her ear and the change is instant; the glare is gone, her face is that perfectly blank mask that she wears around him.

I fucking hate it.

Tugging at my jacket, I pull a cigarette out and light it. I've never given a fuck about the kid before, why would I suddenly give a fuck about D'Ardo's mind games with her? Today is messing with my fucking head. I glance over my shoulder at the car again, as if the bombshell is a magnet and demanding my attention.

Fuck I want to give it all to her.

Every fucking second of it.

"She sure is something, isn't she, Butcher?" The Vulture says, and I turn back to him with a sneer.

"We're not friends, I'm not here to flap gums with you, Vincenzo."

His lip curls, and he slicks his hair back like some two-bit, slimy gangster. "Zero respect. I don't know why you keep this guy around, Jackal."

D'Ardo shrugs and slings an arm over the kid. She shifts away from him, so minutely that no one else probably notices, but I didn't become the best of the best because I miss shit.

Fuck, am I finally growing a fucking conscience?

Is that pro's power so fucking good to a man's soul that you only have to sit in a fucking car with her to become a changed man?

I need a drink.

I need some violence and chaos. I need blood on my hands and a man screaming at my feet and I need it fucking now.

The Vulture leaves with his men and D'Ardo steps forward to finish his business with the lucky fuck from the cartel with the hottest woman in the world in his backseat. I stand there, looking out over the water and try to contain my jealous, bloodthirsty nature.

The kid just stands there with me and stares at me like I'm a pile of shit.

I frown at her. She never does that shit, she always treats me better than I deserve, especially considering how fucking badly I treat her. The bad feeling only gets worse.

D'Ardo finishes up with the cartel, a shake of their hands and the deal is sealed. If this guy can drop high seven figures on that amazing piece of ass for the night then I can only guess how much he's just sold to D'Ardo. His business is getting fucking huge, big enough that he's taking out the other dealers in the state.

He's probably going to be the biggest player in the damn state at this rate.

I already hate the idea of that, he's a fucking dick half the time as it is, but he's a grown man and that's his own business. I'll just stick to my own shit and refuse to drink with him if he brings all of his fucking posse with him. There's eight men here now for this little meeting, for fuck's sake. It's pathetic.

I crush the cigarette under my boot and light another one, watching the car drive off with my girl.

Fuck.

I need a drink.

Or maybe I need to wade my ass into the mess that is the Chaos Demons and find that kid. Piss his daddy off. Start a war and keep myself real fucking busy with blood and pain for a few months, clear my head some before I go after this girl.

I glance down at the kid and pure *loathing* is rolling off of her in waves.

Not having that, not today and not with the mood I'm now

in.

I catch her arm and pull her into me, murmuring under my breath where D'Ardo won't hear us, "Why do you keep looking at me like that, kid?"

She shrugs like it's nothing but her voice betrays just how fucking pissed she really is. "I always knew you were a killer, Butcher, but I didn't know you were a shitty human being as well."

This little girl has watched me torture men, kill them, carve them to pieces as they beg me to stop. She's seen me in the ring and knows no man ever leaves those fights with me alive. She's seen me bend chicks over barstools and fuck them in the middle of raves.

One sentence from the bombshell and she hates me?

Something is fucking wrong here.

My fingers tighten around her arm. "You speak her language?"

She nods. Fuck. "What did she just say?"

The kid tries to pull away but my fingers tighten even more around her arm, enough to leave marks but bruises mean nothing to this tiny little slip of a kid.

She huffs and rolls her eyes at me. "Don't act innocent now, Butcher. You did the deed, you got your money, all is right in the Bay. That's how you work right? No lines, green is green, *fuck everyone else.*"

D'Ardo turns to see us both glaring at each other. I see the jealousy from a mile away, he doesn't like me touching her, but I ignore it. Too much is at stake here.

The kid doesn't like that jealousy at all though, and leans forward to snap, "She said 'thank you for delivering her to her rapist. She looks forward to seeing you in hell, because helping her rapists will certainly get you there.' Nothing too out there, right? She was pretty generous with her words, if I'd been sold off to the cartel at a skin auction my speech would have been a little more fucking colorful."

No.

Absolutely fucking not.

I did not just deliver her to someone against her will.

She didn't run, she didn't ask for help, she was calm the whole fucking way. There's no way. No way.

My hand drops but I don't step away. "She was there for a job, not against her will."

I don't know if I'm trying to convince myself or the kid but she scoffs at me. "Whatever you say, Butcher. She seems to think otherwise."

D'Ardo saunters up, ready to start shit because there's nothing he hates more than being ignored but fuck him, I don't care. "Why didn't she say something to me? She understood what I was saying, kid. She knew English, she could have—"

D'Ardo snorts at me, cutting me off and I straighten up, reminding him that I could kill him without fucking sweating if I felt the need.

I'm kinda feeling the need.

"So you delivered a piece of ass to the cartel here, who gives a fuck? She'll be dead before dawn, Gabriel doesn't like them being around for too long. Fuck, she might be dead already! Word is he likes fucking them once their cold too, sick fuck. So there, all over with. Let's get a fucking drink."

We have been as close as brothers since foster care.

That means sweet fuck all to me when I knock him the fuck out, right there at the docks, surrounded by his twitchy, blithering flunkies who don't make a move to stop me.

The kid just watches as her little stalker crumples to the ground, then glances back up at me. "You really didn't know?"

My chest starts to heave as I suck in air to try to contain the rage in me. I'm such a fucking idiot! "Kid, there was no fear in her. Nothing until she got into that other car and spat those words at me. Nothing fucking like it. What was I supposed to think? Not once did anyone say she was bought against her will."

Fuck.

Now I need D'Ardo conscious and awake to tell me where the fuck the cartel were heading. I can get her back.

I can fucking get her *back*.

Butcher of the Bay - Part One

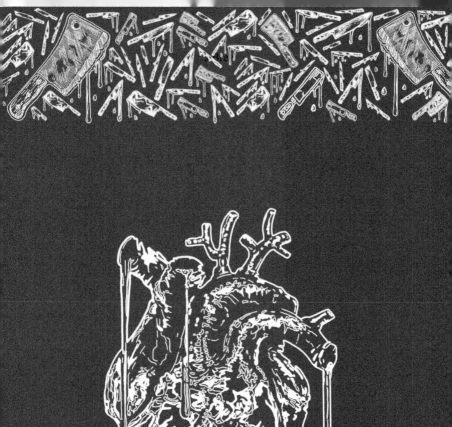

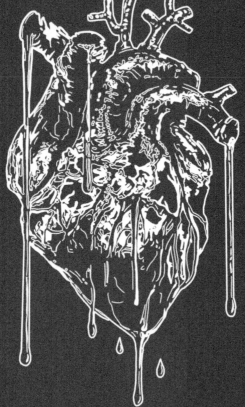

CHAPTER SEVEN

ODIE

The car smells of cocaine.

It's one of my father's favorite party favors, something I grew up around and know a lot about, so I know the second I sit down what it is I'm smelling. I try not to breathe too deeply, not wanting to get high accidentally.

I watch as the man who delivered me here, the biggest monster of all, glances back at me as if he wants to come speak to me. I couldn't possibly take that. I could barely handle him talking to me in the car, his soothing voice and pet names for me like a balm over the wounds I've endured over the last few days. To know that he was here to help in my capture and sale… it was too much for me.

I look away.

Better to put him out of my mind and lock him away with

the older woman who had betrayed our entire gender where his voice and gentle arm cannot cut my soul anymore.

He had held me as if I meant something to him.

I could feel it in every inch of his muscled arm wrapped around me, the care he was taking with me, the protective force that he was as he moved me to the car. I wonder how much he was paid to pick me up and deliver me to these men?

I wonder how he'll sleep tonight.

I curse myself for thinking about him and focus myself on not breathing too hard, my lungs starting to tingle and protest at the shortened breaths.

There's a small delay and then the car doors open all at once and three large men all take their seats, two up front and one in the back with me. I stiffen in my seat and he chuckles, running a finger down my arm without a care over my reaction.

I pull away without thinking.

I wonder if I'm to be married to one of them or if I'm being taken somewhere to be killed instead.

I cut the thought off as soon as it flits across my mind, my chest aching to breathe more, deeper, longer, just more.

They ignore my obvious panic and start to discuss their business venture, with enough veiled details that I'm confused. If they were completely open I'd know I was going to be killed, witnesses can't spill secrets if they're dead. My mind whirls into a panic and I fight to keep the keening cry from spilling out of me.

I lose myself in the panic as we drive.

The trip may have taken hours or maybe just minutes.

I have no clue.

It's only when we arrive at the gated community that I come back to my senses, fear pulsing through my veins and depriving my brain and limbs of the blood it needs, making me lightheaded. Car doors open around me and then my door is opened for me, one of the large men moving to grab and get me out by force.

I act on instinct, barreling into the chest of the man opening the door and catching him off guard. My placid demeanor so far has lulled them all into thinking I'm accepting of what they're doing, that I've decided to lay down and take their abuse and rape.

That's not who I am at all.

I might not know how to get myself out of this, but with every fiber of my being, I want to be out of this.

I run across the pristine lawns and let out a scream that could wake the dead, praying that there's someone around me who cares that these men want to hurt me.

It's late at night, I must be waking people up with all of this noise, and yet not a single light comes on in any of the windows.

They ignore me.

It doesn't matter, I keep running through the street, flinging my heels off of my feet and ignoring the pain in my feet as I cut them on glass and sharp rocks. Nothing will stop me from trying to get away, nothing except-

Hands clamp around me and lift me into the air as if I am *nothing.*

I kick and scream, another hand clamping over my mouth that I try to bite but he's too strong for me, whoever this man is. He carries me the short distance I managed to run in a handful of strides. Still no lights come on, no one looks out of the windows to see what it is that's happening out here.

This is not a normal suburb.

These people have been trained to see nothing, to hear nothing.

And I am nothing.

A sob once again takes over me until I'm trembling in my captors arms. He grunts and snaps at the other men, talking too quickly and in a mix of English and Spanish so I can't keep up.

I feel a mouth press against my ear and then my captor whispers, "You will stop fighting, little whore, or I will slit this pretty throat and use your corpse. Eventually you will start to stink, it'll be a shame to lose you but I'll burn your body until there's no trace of you left on this Earth."

My whole body freezes.

I really am nothing to these men.

Nothing but a way to release violence and need into a vessel. My entire body begins to tremble but the screams fade into nothing and my limbs grow heavy, dropping away from where I was fighting back.

Maybe I do want to live.

The hand moves away from my mouth and strokes my hair away from my face. "Ahh, so you can be trained? Too bad. I like it when my whores fight back."

The tremble gets worse. Does he not want me to follow his instructions? Is there truly no easy way to do this? My mind continues to cling to hope that this is something I will endure and then move away from.

He drags me forward, past the men crowded around the door, all of them watching me as though I'm some prized piece of meat. My skin crawls and bile creeps up the back of my throat.

What if they all rape me?

What if I'm here to *service* them all? That's what whores do right?

The man marches me forward as I panic until we step into the house.

It's like a tomb.

There are no windows or natural light, if I hadn't walked in from outside I wouldn't be able to tell what time of day it is. The windows are all covered with metal sheets, the walls are all too thick, as if we're in some sort of bomb shelter. My prospects of escaping are looking worse and worse the more I look around.

The front room is smokey and full of men talking and packaging drugs as they talk and laugh amongst themselves. They don't bother looking up at us, busy in their work instead.

We move through and past several more rooms filled with

men, drugs, and one with piles and piles of money. Floor to ceiling, there's cash everywhere and two large dogs with spiked collars sleeping in the doorway, their muzzles stained red.

My feet stumble and the man holding me chuckles in my ear again. "Pretty, aren't they? They have a taste for human flesh. I wouldn't go sneaking around the house, little whore. They'd leave nothing but bones behind."

I've stumbled into a nightmare.

That's what this must be, I must have passed out from one of my father's beatings and now I'm trapped in this hell-scape.

We make it to a dining room, overly formal and ornate considering the mess of drugs and smoking men that exist outside of this room. An older man sits and eats dinner at the head of the table, a bottle of tequila and a shot glass sitting in front of him and a cigar smoking between his fingers even as he chews. His hair is white and thinning, strange looking when his mustache is still dark and bushy under his nose. The suit he's wearing is tailored though I can't see if it's a designer. He obviously cares about how he looks, even if he doesn't care about the state of this house.

He glances up and his eyes are black voids, no emotions or humanity in them as he looks me up and down.

The arms fall away from me and I tense, forcing myself not to crumble into a pathetic pile and weeping woman on the ground.

There's silence for a moment, no one speaking or even

breathing, and then he picks up the tequila, taking a long sip before setting the glass down.

My heart starts to pound in my chest. I don't want to be fed to the dogs. I don't want to be hurt. I don't want to fucking be here!

Finally he speaks, his voice dark and in perfect English.

"Chain her to the bed. I'll play with her later."

Dear God, no.

The room I'm left in is filthy.

The sheets are stained with blood and other questionable things, and the second I'm shoved down I feel as though bugs are crawling over me. Tears start to slide down my cheeks as the men laugh, ripping my legs apart to secure them in cuffs to the end of the bed. They wrestle my hands into a set of handcuffs, snapping them shut so tight they bite into my skin and my hands start to go numb immediately.

They leave my panties on.

Small mercies, though my stomach revolts at the idea of what's to come. That man... he's coming to me. He's the one who truly owns me.

The lights are turned off as they leave and without a window, the room plunges into pitch darkness.

The tears streaming silently down my cheeks slowly turn

into sobs and they come harder than before, my body wracked with grief and fear and loathing of every last one of these people. Every fucking person I've ever known. Not a single person I've ever crossed paths with has ever seen me as anything more than my face and body. No one sees a human being worthy of respect when they see the packaging I come in.

I lay there, chained to the bed, legs splayed open and wait for what's to come.

The walls are so thick I can barely hear any life outside of it, only the panicked beat of my own heart to keep me company. I'm so used to being abandoned for hours now that it barely registers to me when I finally fall asleep, countless hours later.

I'm startled awake when the door opens.

The room is still dark but I have no way of knowing how long I was asleep. I guess time doesn't matter here anymore. Do I really want to know how much time is passing while I'm captive?

Then he speaks, that flat tone still dark but he speaks in Spanish so I don't understand what he's saying at all but I can tell by the tone of his voice that he's not happy at all. The light flicks on and blinds me, my arms jerking to cover my face but the handcuffs only dig further into my tender skin. I can barely feel my hands now, the numbness almost completely removing all sensation.

I wish my entire body was that numb for what's to come.

My eyes adjust to see the older man standing by the bed,

slowly removing his clothes, folding them neatly and placing them on the chair besides the stinking bed. I watch him in silence, my face a mask of disgust and loathing.

He doesn't like that at all.

The sharp sting of his palm snaps my head to the side but I barely even notice it. I've been at the mercy of my father's temper for so long that this kind of pain doesn't even register.

I'm more concerned about how quickly he's getting to taking his pants off.

His face gets angrier and angrier the longer I go without crying out in pain, and then he hits me again, this time a closed fist that makes my vision white out. My head snaps back against the pillows, groaning softly under my breath and I hear the sound of his belt unbuckling.

Oh God, no.

I squeeze my eyes shut. I don't have to see the assault. Feeling it will be bad enough, I don't need the image in my head as well. He laughs at me, the sound weird and disjointed in my dazed head, and then he climbs on top of me. I choke on my own vomit and at the sound of my gagging he grabs my throat, squeezing as if he'll be able to stop my body's reaction to him.

His skin is hot where his presses into mine.

I want to die.

He rips my panties off and laughs again as he strokes my intimate flesh. The laughing messes with my head until I want to cower away from him, duck my head and hide but I still can't move.

I think I pass out until he settles back down over me and shoves himself inside me.

He's not wearing a condom and I've never been less aroused in my life so the pain is *unbearable*. I can't help the scream that bursts out of me and my arms tremble as if I can heave myself out from under his weight. He groans in my ear, chuckling as I whimper, and his hips begin to move.

My mind scrambles to find something else to think about, for some kind of escape, but I'm present for the entire, horrific act.

The only blessing is it lasts all of three minutes before he groans again, the hand around my throat tightening until I think he's trying to kill me now he's had his fun.

I can't stand the wet feeling of his come dripping out of me. When he finally moves off of me he laughs again, murmuring under his breath as he grabs my face and squeezes my jaw as he inspects the bruise that's coming up from his fist.

Then the door opens and another man steps in.

Oh God.

Please *no*.

Butcher of the Bay - Part One

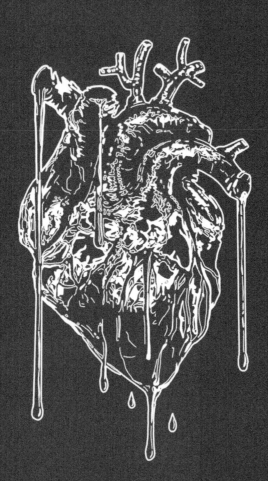

CHAPTER EIGHT

ILLI

There is no getting her back.

I get the name of the buyers off of the Vulture and quickly find out the cartel she was sold to is a fucking *ghost* operation. No word of where they are, where they do business, fucking *nothing*. I try every fucking one of my leads and then I start breaking down doors, pissing drug dealers and their momma's off trying to find her… nothing.

Fucking *nothing*.

I get really fucking wasted.

Next level, can't-even-piss-straight, fucking *trashed*.

I didn't even drink this much when my mother died at the hands of the fucking Twelve when I was a kid. Not even when my old man left me at a safe place so he could run from them, get away from his debts that had already cost him the woman of his dreams. Would cost him his life too but he did his best for me.

Fuck.

Fuck, it's bad if I'm thinking about that bullshit. It's really fucking bad if I'm drinking and reminiscing about all of the reasons I became untouchable.

It's pathetic and not at all like me. I never get this messy and never in public with no one to watch my back. Doesn't matter though. One look into that siren's eyes and she sucked my fucking soul out and made it her own.

I need her like I need air, and now that she's gone, I'm drowning. How the fuck did I think my life was complete before her? How had I not known that something so vital to me was missing?

D'Ardo won't answer my calls, still fucking pissed at me for knocking him out down at the docks like a little bitch. I'd piled him into his car with his little flunkies to go back to the vaults to sleep it off and the kid had split, taking off and scurrying back to whatever little job she had for the day.

She still wouldn't look me in the eye.

It shouldn't fucking matter but now that I'd lost her respect... I thought less of myself.

Fuck, it shouldn't be possible with how fucking badly I think of myself for my part in the rape, torture, and, *fuck me*, murder of that stunning woman.

Because I'm fucking wrecked but not a braindead dickhead,

I go to drink at the biker bar down the street from the docks and my warehouse, where I have more friends than enemies and people I know will watch my back while I get fucking messy. I like being around bikers because, for the most part, they don't give a fuck about the Twelve.

I have a lot of complicated feelings about the entire institution that runs the underworld of Mounts Bay.

My father was once a respected businessman. A butcher in a good part of town and we lived a white picket life until I was ten. My mother was a classy stay-at-home mom who tucked me into bed every night with a bedtime story about good men who saved the princesses. I wanted for fucking nothing, knew nothing about the horrors of the city, always had a belly full of good food.

I didn't know my father had a gambling problem until his debt collectors came knocking.

He didn't know how dangerous those men were until they hacked my mom to pieces.

My belly was never full in the foster system.

Fuck me, there isn't enough whiskey and bourbon in this fucking bar to get me through tonight if this is where my mind is going. Never even had the fucking woman and yet I've failed her just as badly as my old man failed my mom. I'd sworn I'd never be like him and yet there I was, handing the French dream over to her killers last night.

I'm a fucking joke.

I empty my glass and pour myself another one, ignoring everything around me in favor of the oblivion the drink beckons to me with. There's three different clubs here tonight, like there are most nights, but the crowd is a little rowdier than it usually is. Fuck, all I need is for a fight to break out so I can carve some guys up. If anything could ease the ache in my chest, it would be that.

The chair in front of the booth I'm in pulls out and I sigh, already fucking knowing which asshole isn't going to let me wallow in my misery in peace.

Harbin takes the seat and whistles a low sound at the state of me. "Who the fuck died? I didn't think you had family left. Fuck, did someone skin your grand-momma alive or something? You look pretty fucking grim, man."

I down another shot and give him a glare, hoping he gets I'm not in the fucking mood. He raises an eyebrow and stays put, sipping at his own beer a hell of a lot slower than I'm working through my whiskey.

"I'm struggling to find a cartel I need. No one knows where the fuck they are and I'm about to start knocking down every fucking door in the Bay to get to them."

He stares at me for a second, rubbing his chin with his scarred hand. He's just as busted up as I am, just as tattooed too, and though he's not built like me, he's not the type of man you should underestimate in a fight.

The man feels no pain and has no conscience.

He's a good man.

"Right. Who is it then? I can help out. Don't know why you'd be this gutted over a fucking job but—"

"It's not a fucking job." I hiss back at him, and his shoulders roll back. Fuck. I've gotten his attention.

"Well, fuck me. I thought you didn't do personal?"

I gulp down some more whiskey so I don't wring his fucking neck. "This is exactly why I don't do personal. This fucking… misery. The cartel is run by some scumbag called Alvaro Alcatron and the whole business is made up of his family. He's got like fifty nephews and cousins on his books. The closest I can get to him is one of his buyers but D'Ardo won't tell me shit. I'm about to break down his motherfucking door and start some shit."

Harbin nods and scrubs at his chin some more, his eyes following a couple of the Silver City Serpents in the room. They're usually allies so I'm not sure what his fucking problem is today but I also couldn't give less of a fuck.

"I know a guy, might be able to help. Fuck man, I thought going after Grimm's boys was bad enough, you sure are in some deep fucking shit at the moment. Maybe you need to take a break, hit up a titty bar, blow off some steam."

My teeth clench together. I can't think of anything fucking worse than going to the titty bar right now. The only one on this side of the city is owned by D'Ardo and it's full of vacant-eyed girls, half of them underage, and all of them doped the fuck up.

None of them want to be there.

My stomach turns.

I can't ignore that shit anymore. I can't stand by at all now because, fuck, I'm part of the problem. Not once have I given a shit about the skin markets. Yeah, I've never bought because it's not my thing, but not once have I tried to stop D'Ardo from doing them.

Fuck, I've stood by and watched him stalk, torture, and groom the fucking kid.

I'm a fucking disgrace.

"Jesus fucking Christ, you're having a life crisis here, aren't you? Fuck, we need more whiskey, man!" he shouts out to the bartender, lifting my empty bottle. I've got fucking nothing left.

Roxas appears out of the crowd with a fresh bottle in his hands, slapping a few backs as he passes some friends and shouting out barely veiled threats to guys he wants to knock the fuck out. I size them up and decide quickly they're not worth our time at all.

Fuck tonight and fuck this entire city.

"Oh great, here I was thinking we were going to be having a good night celebrating!" Roxas laughs out as he pours us all drinks.

"What fucking news?" I snap, and Harbin makes a face at his best friend.

"Man, he isn't up for it tonight. Let's save it until after he purges his mood from his system. Maybe we should pick a fight with Tank, he's been a secretive cock lately. I'm sure he's planning something shifty."

I peer out over to the enforcer for the Silver City Serpents. He's a long way from home, out here for some shady shit his MC is taking part in with the Boar, which only makes me trust the guy less. I mean, I don't really trust anyone except D'Ardo and even he is getting pushed off the fucking list these days because his power and inflated self-importance is pissing me the fuck off.

Roxas slides a bundle of fabric across the table to me and when I move to grab it he says, "Look at it once you're sober. It'll help you out with the Viper's job. It can wait until after we're done drinking you into an early grave anyway."

Fuck.

Maybe I can count these two as friends, too.

The boys drop me back to my warehouse sometime after dawn.

I pass out on the floor in my kitchen and don't exist again until well after dark. My head is pounding, my mouth tastes like something died in there, and I smell like a trash can that's been set on fire.

I'm a fucking mess.

I strip down and take a cold shower to wake myself the fuck

up, scrubbing my sins away but leaving behind a man who's rotten to the core. I shave, wincing at my own reflection. I look a hell of a lot older than twenty-four right now. I look fucking forty, shot up to hell and riddled with scars, the puffiness from the hangover only makes it ten times worse.

The shave at least makes me feel human again.

The hair of the dog down the hatch eases the pounding in my head enough that I can focus on fixing myself something to eat without throwing the fuck up all over my eggs. It's only once I'm sitting and eating that I remember the small bundle Roxas had handed over to me at the bar last night, long before we'd been stupid enough to start a fight with the Serpents. Fuck, I was looking for a way to hurt myself and destroy someone else that if we hadn't taken on some of Tank's guys I would have turned all that loathing onto Roxas and Harbin themselves.

They knew it and deflected it fucking perfectly.

I finish my food and go to find the little bundle of fabric, fishing it out of my jeans and carrying it back out to my kitchen counter.

Wrapped inside a raggedly cut square of black fabric is a USB drive.

I grab my computer and boot it up, plugging the drive in and waiting for it to load. While the spinning wheel does its thing I flip the fabric over in my hands.

It's a Chaos Demon patch.

Well, fuck me.

I wonder who the hell Roxas took out to get this to me? I might owe the guy something stronger than a whiskey and a decent bar fight. The Serpents we'd gotten into with had been down in the Bay sniffing around the Unseen's business. The fight had been about reminding them of exactly who runs this fucking city and it's not some fucking hillbilly biker gang from Louisiana.

If you're not born in the Bay then you don't really know what it takes to survive here.

That reminds me, I grab my own whiskey and sip at it, just enough to keep the headache from coming back but not enough to get my next binger started.

The screen finally switches over to the files and I set the patch aside for now. I'll keep it, just in case. You never know when you need to show off some credentials to get into some seedy biker bar in another state. The Chaos Demons are big enough that no one would fucking notice a newly patched in guy with a Cali accent. Fuck, they'd take one look at me and try to convince me to patch over to their branch.

I can't think of anything fucking worse than joining an MC and answering to some two-bit, drunk Prez with ideas bigger than his fucking needle dick. Nope, that's just not the life for me. I'd rather be a loner alcoholic stashing money in my walls and carving dead bodies up in my basement.

I take one last sip and then get to looking over the files. Fuck knows what I'm looking at though, just a bunch of times and coordinates. Nothing makes any sense until I start punching them into a separate browser.

Well.

Fuck me, Roxas is fucking good at this shit.

I have before me the pick up and drop off zones for the Demons, all of their movements for the last three fucking years. It doesn't take a genius to crack the code, to figure out that it's a rotating roster of places that switches up during winter and the high traffic peaks of summer.

I now know exactly when and where Chance will be.

Problem is I have zero fucking motivation to go find the little biker dickhead. I need the kid alive enough to talk but if he gives me fucking lip right now… nah, I'll hang him from a hook and drain the blood right out of him, sever him limb from limb, cut his tongue out and sell it off to the local cannibals on the black market.

Actually, that sounds like what I need right now, fuck the Viper and his plans.

First, I've got to get my head together.

I head downstairs and spend an hour beating the shit out of a boxing bag. You don't stay as big and as quick as I am without putting in the work. Guys who slack off get sloppy, that's not what I'm about.

Once I have my workout done and dusted, another punching bag torn to fucking shreds and leaking sand all over the place, I head back upstairs to get my shit together to head out. I have a few more places to try for my girl before I'll admit she's really gone. Roxas and Harbin had said they would help out but there's only so many places bikers can get their information.

I have some other avenues.

Fuck, if D'Ardo wasn't such a fucking dick to the other members of the Twelve I could hit up the Coyote. I'm sure that little ferret could find fucking anything. Problem is he's gone underground after D'Ardo went postal on him over a missing drug shipment. He lives in a fucking bunker and there's no way in if the little fucker doesn't let you in.

He fucking despises me.

There's no way I could get his help now.

Not unless I call the Crow and I doubt that dickhead would even take my calls. All of these problems lead back to D'Ardo but he's been like a brother to me for too long to get shitty about it.

If I don't find her tonight, I'll fucking kidnap the Crow and force him to take me to the Coyote. The smug dick thinks he's safe in his little concrete palace, I've had the plans to get in and out of that place for fucking years. I just never gave them to D'Ardo because he's a little… impulsive. Unstable.

Fucked in the head.

Doesn't matter, I'll side with him any day of the fucking week. The Crow is some fucking suit who walked into the Bay one day and decided to become a crime lord. Nope, not going to give that man respect until he earns it but, instead, he builds a fucking fortress and hides there while he wines and dines senators to do his dirty work for him?

Hard fucking pass.

Again, I know little girls with more guts than him.

Fuck.

I can't think about the kid without sees her face down at the docks and the feeling of my guts being ripped out as the realization of what I'd fucking done hit me. I don't know when I suddenly started respecting the kid enough to care what she thinks and yet... and yet here I am, thinking about how much she hates me now and feeling even more like a fucking monster.

I need more whiskey.

Instead, I head out to try and find some more leads.

I find nothing.

She's really gone.

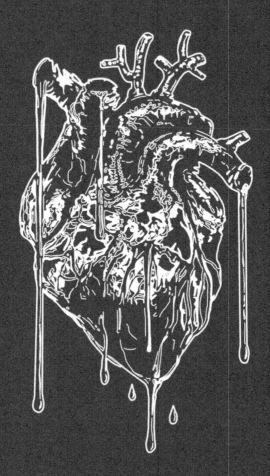

CHAPTER NINE

ODIE

I have no way of knowing how long I have been here, but I do not want to exist any longer.

If I thought I was broken before, I am shattered to pieces now.

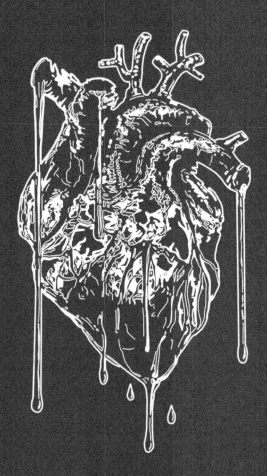

CHAPTER TEN

ILLI

I go to my usual fight on Thursday night at the Dive.

I arrive sober but with the fog of my hangover from my bender still hanging low over my head, so the fight itself is particularly brutal. My opponent doesn't die of internal bleeding or suffocation like they normally do. No, I rip his throat out with my bare teeth until his blood pours down my face and neck and the entire bar is silent.

Yeah.

Sometimes they need to be reminded of who I really am.

The Butcher of the motherfucking Bay.

I don't bother to wipe myself down or clean up in any way, I just step out of the cage and head right for the bar, barking out my order to get the bartender moving. They're all standing there in shock, struck dumb at the sight of me doing what I do best.

I'm downing my fourth straight bourbon when the Viper settles into the chair next to me.

Not today, dickhead.

I shoot him a look which he ignores entirely, fuck him. He lifts a hand to his man behind the bar and the guy leaves the bottle and a clean glass behind.

He pours the drink himself and clicks his tongue at me like I'm an unruly child. I plan out exactly how I'm going to rip his tongue out of his head. "I didn't think I'd have to chase you around, Butcher. Where the fuck is my information?"

I tilt my head at him without looking over. "You said you needed it as soon as possible… well, I'm working on it."

Lie, I hadn't thought about it since the moment I'd arrived at the airport and fucked my entire fucking life up by thinking with my dick instead of reading the fucking situation properly.

That's the part that's killing me. I know better. I know exactly what happens at auctions, why the fuck would she sell herself there? I was led by my dick straight into hell and now she's probably dead, killed in the worst fucking way.

That lands with me.

"I'll have the information in next week. Nothing is going to change between now and then in your shitty business. Fuck off and leave me to my victory drink." I snap and he smirks at me, topping my glass up with a smirk.

"I told you, it's only a matter of time until I own you. Keep being a sloppy fuck and it'll be sooner than I thought."

Own you.

Own.

Own.

That word rings around in my head until I think I'm going to fucking *scream*. I fucking delivered her to hell while I was too busy thinking about how I could pay for a slice of her ass. The terror in her eyes... I helped fucking put that there.

I'm a fucking *monster*.

Worse, I'm worse than a monster. I always have been the thing in the dark you should be scared of but fuck... now I'm every little part of the Bay that's fucked up and that shit doesn't sit right with me. Not at all.

I turn in my chair slowly, ready to beat the life out of him when the crowd parts and D'Ardo walks through. Predictably, there's six huge flunkies with him as well.

I try to push the French dream I'd let slip through my fingers out of my mind around D'Ardo. I can't handle him saying she's dead by now. I can't think about it or that she might be a fucking shell of herself.

The Viper gets up from his seat to shake hands with him and they talk about their bullshit business together. I zone them out and work on my drink, needing some inebriation to get me through this fucking night.

There's no one here to blame but myself. I know what happens to women who are traded and sold, growing up in the Bay it's a fact of life, but it's never really bothered me until now.

It's *really* fucking bothering me now.

Unfortunately, D'Ardo knows me well enough to pick it up a mile away.

"Are you just going to keep on being about as cheerful as a kick in the balls or are we going to carve some meat today?" he asks, cheerful and obnoxious. I really struggle to not rip his throat out and have him carried out of here as a corpse and through into an incinerator with the chump from the cage fight.

"Have you got a job for me or not? I don't want to sit around while you lord it over your pathetic kingdom tonight. I'm not in the fucking mood for it."

His eyes narrow at me. "What the fuck has gotten into you? You've turned into a miserable fuck and no pussy is worth all this. Is Harmon back in town or something?"

My blood boils beneath my skin. He's really fucking set on pissing me the fuck off. "How about you shut your fucking mouth before I shut it for you. Fuck, I might just carve you a new one, see if you keep your fucking peppy attitude then."

He scoffs and shrugs at me. "You need to get your head back into the game. You need to let it go, hot blondes are a dime a dozen around here."

The stool next to me slides out and the kid sits down, nodding at the bartender when he drops a whiskey in front of her. D'Ardo's eyes flare as he watches her take the shot, his lips parting as she shakes herself off a little. Fuck, I forget how fucking sick it is he wants her. She's a fucking kid, living through all of D'Ardo's sick games.

Fuck it, I wait until she gets busy on her phone with a job and murmur to him, "Who's head needs to be in the game? You moon after her like a fucking lovesick puppy."

He doesn't though. He watches her every move, killing and torturing anyone who dares to look her way for longer than a second. I don't know how the kid has survived, I'd have fucking suffocated by now under the scrutiny.

He ignores me and leans over her. "I thought you said you weren't coming out tonight, Starbright? I would have picked you up if I'd known you were coming, too."

Hm. They didn't come together. That's out of the ordinary, she never comes without him. Usually, he signs her out of the group home pretending to be a family member.

Fuck. She's still in fucking *foster care*, she's that young and yet here he is panting after her.

She shrugs. "I got a call for a job. I'm just here for my supplies."

He wraps an arm around her shoulders and she suddenly looks even fucking smaller. "Who has hired you for the night? Johnny-boy and I are going to paint the town red."

I narrow my eyes at him, nothing I fucking hate more than him treating me like he's my fucking boss and not just a friend. We need to sort this new-found dick attitude of his out and *soon*. He must be still pissed I knocked him out but, well, he can get the fuck over that and quick.

The kid shrugs. "I'm going to see the Vulture, he has some runaway debts he needs taking care of. It looks like the Butcher is done for the night, I thought I could grab a ride over with him, is that okay?"

She directs the question at me and I frown at her but there's something in her face this time that makes me nod.

"Sure. I'm about ready to call it a night. I'm on a job that needs me clear tomorrow."

D'Ardo frowns at us both, his eyes seething with his usual dose of jealous insanity. "I'd join you both but I have my own problems to deal with tonight."

The kid nods and pulls away from him, sliding over the bar and grabbing a bag stashed somewhere amongst the bottles. She slips it over her shoulder and walks out, not bothering to check if I'm following her. Gutsy little thing she is. I put my glass down and move to follow her when D'Ardo grabs my arm.

"She's mine. Just so we're clear, don't fucking touch her. No matter how tempting she is."

Tempting? She's a fucking *child*.

He's all sorts of fucked in the head but I've always known that. I pull my arm free and smirk at him. "I don't take orders from anyone. I'll do whatever the fuck I want, but you're in luck. I don't stick my dick in anything under the age of eighteen because I'm a deranged killer not a fucking pedophile. You might want to get your fucking head checked, brother."

He smirks. "Mounty pussy doesn't count and we both know

it. Stay away from her and we'll be good."

That's it, I'm finding somewhere else to fucking drink until he gets over his bullshit and I forget about the bombshell I fucked over.

The car ride is mostly silent, the kid just stares out of the window with a blank face. Eventually it gets under my skin.

"Is there a reason you wanted me to come? Is there some guy you don't think you can handle down here? We both know you've been collecting favors not cash, kid. I'm too fucking expensive for you to pay."

She huffs at me, way more attitude and fire in her now D'Ardo isn't around. Interesting. "I'm not working for the Vulture tonight. Well, I mean, I have done a job for him but it took me like a half hour before I came down here. We need to go to the auctions tonight."

I give her the side-eye of her life. "And why the fuck would I want to go there? I think we both know that isn't my kind of scene."

Just to remind her of what had gone down last week, of my error in judgement and her smacking me in the fucking face with reality. My fingers tighten on the steering wheel. Fuck me, I need a drink.

She quirks her head at me with such fucking sass and it

occurs to me *again* that maybe I've underestimated the fuck out of her. "Because there's an auction on tonight. A big one, I've heard that there's a stunning, blonde from France being sold. She's been beat the hell up but there was so much interest in her last time that they say she's still going for a pretty penny. I'm willing to back you up if you need it."

My cold, dead, worthless heart stops dead in my chest. "How the fuck do you know this, kid? I've been kicking down doors for days."

She grimaces. "I knew about the guy from the Jackal. I might've... pulled some strings to get her back at auction. I offered him something to put her up again."

I stop the car, veering over off the side of the road and slamming on the brakes, ignoring the sounds of horns blasting around us. "What the fuck did you do, kid?"

She finally turns to face me, looking me over properly and then gives me a wry smile. "Did you know that the Alcatron cartel have been supplying the Jackal with cocaine since the very beginning? No other dealer would buy from him before the Jackal. Did you also know they're pretty pissed off the drug of choice in the Bay has shifted to ice? I offered to help him get rid of the ice supplier, buy him some time to get his own manufacturing business up and running."

Well, fuck me. I stare back at her like this is the first fucking time my eyes have even really seen her. "Why would you do that? You fucking hate drugs, I know exactly how you ended up in that group home."

She smirks at me, slow and fucking murderous. "We both know his business can't be run from the grave, Butcher. I'll find where he sleeps someday and he'll wake up to a cleaver at his throat for touching her."

I think I see it.

I see exactly what D'Ardo wants so fucking badly from her.

She's still a fucking kid though and he's still sick in the head for wanting her.

I pull back out onto the road and put my gas pedal to the floor, the force of my acceleration whipping her back against her seat. "This isn't a rescue and send on her way, kid. She's mine. I'm finding her, I'm taking her home with me, no matter what. If you don't want a part of that you should say so now and I'll get you home safe."

She shakes her head. "No. There's a lot of bad shit I can't help with around here but this I can do and you might have failed her once but you won't make that mistake twice."

Fuck. I don't know what the fuck I've done to get this sort of trust from this girl but today I'm desperate enough to take it. Fuck, I might just drive her back to my warehouse after this and hand her my life savings, get her right enough to leave this fucking city and start fresh somewhere cleaner.

As the auction house comes into view I slow my roll, we don't need to attract any attention right now. I'm not going in there to buy my girl... no, I'm going in there to paint the fucking walls red with the blood of every man who's so much as fucking looked at her.

The whole fucking underworld if I have to.

"Have you been in there before? It's disgusting but I can run you through the entrances and exits, best places to lay low, whatever you need." The kid murmurs again.

I park the car and stay seated for a second, thinking it over. Her spot in the Twelve might just come in handy for me tonight. "You follow my lead in there but I'll listen if you have a better plan when things go south. Have you got your shit? I have a spare piece under your seat."

She shrugs. "I'm more of a knife girl."

I smirk at her. "Good kid. What's your real name? I can't remember it from the home and D'Ardo never says it. Unless it really is Starbright."

She grimaces. "Don't call me that. I go by Lips. Eclipse is just as fucking bad."

"Well, Lips, let's get a few things straight. Don't ever walk in front of me, if I throw a cleaver I don't want it hitting you because you're darting around like the little ninja-shadow thing you are. If we get cornered leave it to me, you've already done enough for me. I'll handle the rest."

She rolls her eyes at me, stripping off the oversized sweater she's wearing and pulling on a leather jacket instead. The scars all over her make me feel sick.

I helped D'Ardo trap her.

I helped him get her exactly where he wanted her so every last one of those wounds has my name on it, just as much as him.

She catches me eyeballing them. "Don't worry about it. My life isn't so bad."

I snort. "Kid, I know exactly how bad your life is. Better than anyone else. Once we're done here, you and I are going to have a long talk about D'Ardo and his plans for you. Then we're going to get you clear of him."

She chews her lip nervously. Fuck, tonight is like stepping into *The Twilight Zone*. I've never seen so much… humanity on her. "I know exactly what he's doing. I also know that I don't ever want to get caught in his traps. I'm working on something. Maybe… maybe we can talk about it. Later. I won't sleep until we've got your French girl home safe."

Home. Right. *My* fucking home, where I'll never let another goddamn thing touch her and I'll pay penance for my sins and stupidity to her every day until she's sick of fucking having me. And then another lifetime after that.

Fuck, I'm gone on this girl and she's only ever spoken one line to me.

I step out and go to my own go-bag in the trunk, loading myself up full of weapons until I think I could take out the entire fucking auction house if I need to. There's five above ground levels and a basement. If she's in the basement, I'm bombing the whole place. Leveling it.

The worst of humanity ends up dragging their prey into the basement.

I mean, that's what I do. Except I'm not some sick, depraved rapist who wants to chain girls up and fuck them unwilling and screaming.

The only screaming I force out of girls is consensual.

The kid... fuck, okay, *Lips* watches me strap an extra cleaver onto my thigh with shrewd eyes. I raise a brow at her. "Do you think I'll be up to it, Wolf?"

She scoffs back. "I was going to ask you to show me how you throw them, but now I think I'll pass."

I triple-check both of my pieces before holstering them. "Look kid, I'll train you up on whatever the fuck you want after this. You wanna throw knives around? Sounds fucking peachy to me."

She grins, a real one, and ducks her head. Fuck, that makes her look even younger. "I like learning new shit, having tricks up my sleeve in case of emergencies."

I grin back and pull my own leather jacket on. "You and me, both. Maybe you can show me how to choke a guy out with my thighs. Never know when I might need to sail through the air like something out of the old kung-fu movies."

She laughs back, smoothing a hand down the old, ripped up band tee she's wearing. The kid has taste, they're not half bad. "Some of that was luck, you know, but I'll show you some stuff. Fuck, the Bay better watch out if we're swapping tricks of the trade."

Then we put one foot in front of the other to step into the gates of Hell together.

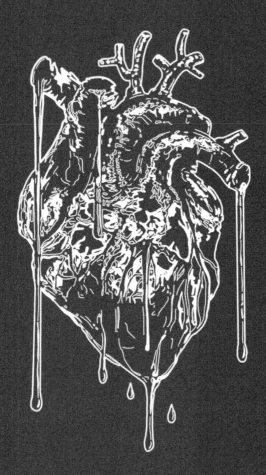

CHAPTER ELEVEN

ODIE

I don't know how many days I lay there in the stinking and filthy bed wishing for death.

A maid would come in twice a day to take me to the toilet. They don't ever look at me properly, never inspect the damage done to me by the men they work for. I've been beaten and raped and tortured every few hours for days on end and yet none of the maids will look at me or make a comment at all. They just quietly do their work and leave. There is no escape.

They undo the cuffs at my feet and then attach one of my hands to a small length of chain so there's never a time I'm not attached to something in the room. On my fourth trip to the bathroom I consider snapping my own wrist to get my hand out and make a run for it but then I remember the blood-soaked dogs downstairs.

I'll never get past them and the men alive.

I haven't decided which death I'd prefer yet, so I bide my time and do the only thing I can do while chained to the bed in solitude while my rapists aren't here.

I think about it all and plan out their deaths in my head.

I have no way of ever making those things come to fruition but it doesn't matter. I plan them down to the finest detail. I imagine exactly what I'll say and where I'd stab them first. I think about how I could possibly ensure they die screaming.

I think about how to kill them in the most unspeakable ways.

I grow weaker by the day. I'm only given a slice of bread here and a glass of water there to keep me alive. I start to think maybe I'm going crazy when white dots dance across my eyelids but really it's just the hunger setting in and turning my world inside out. I can feel my organs start to cannibalize themselves, my stomach a tender thing to the touch.

I do not want to think about the mess between my legs.

I wash myself as best I can each and every time I am taken to the bathroom, but the burns on my arms from the cigars start to grow red and weep, hot to the touch. I begin to pray they will cause blood poisoning and I'll die in my sleep.

It would be a kindness to escape this new life I'm trapped in.

Anything but this.

I continue to think that for what feels like days, right up until there's a loud bang somewhere in the house.

My entire body freezes.

I can barely hear anything else going on in the house, the concrete walls doing an amazing job of muffling everything. I never hear footsteps until the door to my room is opened. I never hear the maids cleaning or the guys packaging drugs downstairs.

So this noise terrifies me.

I'm laying naked on a bed, legs tied so I'm splayed open, with no way of protecting myself or getting out if the entire house is being raided or set on fire, or a list of other things my mind conjures up.

Then there's silence.

Silence for long enough that I start to shake with adrenaline, my body quaking with the need to *run*, and *leave*, and *flee*.

My door opens.

A maid steps through the door, her eyes on the ground, but something is different. She has a length of chain in her hands, one end chained to her own wrist. She's shorter than I am but curvier, larger than me.

When she moves to undo the cuffs on my ankles I decide I'm going to try to run away from her. I can't break the chain without a tool but I'll snap my own hand if I have to. It sickens me to think about but if I can get her on the ground I can stomp on her hand until it breaks. I would do anything to get out of here.

She moves around the bed to undo one of my wrists and finally she makes eye contact with me. She speaks in broken

English, "If you run, Señor Alcatron will cut you to pieces and fuck you bloody. He has been kind with you so far, puta. You cost him too much money so he is dragging it out."

I swallow, wincing at the scratching feeling of my dry throat. She gets me attached to the chain, pulls me up so I'm standing with rough hands, and then moves us both to the door. My head spins and I struggle to stay upright, the fatigue and starvation so much worse now I'm upright.

"Move, puta. We can't keep him waiting!" She hisses at me, yanking the chains and scowling at me as I stumble.

We walk back through the house, down to the dining room I'd first met my rapist in. The house is quiet, no sounds of life and I'm glad. I'm still stark naked, the burns weeping on my battered body. The maid hadn't let me clean up before we came down so I can feel the dried fluids crack on my thighs as I walk. Bile climbs up my throat at the thought of how I must look, shame riding me hard.

Instead of cowing down, I hold my head up.

I will not break.

I will not.

The dining table has men sitting around it, all of them dressed well and smoking cigars, and they turn to look at the maid and me as we walk in together. A few of the men start to jeer and laugh, throwing comments around that I don't understand but know intrinsically must be about me.

"Mira esa panochita tan deliciosa. A qué la puedo hacer

gritar más fuerte que Alcatron cuando le destroce hasta los órganos a esta hija de puta."

"Ya quisieras pendejo con lo que te llevas cargando la vas hacer gritar, pero de vergüenza ajena. Mejor ven aquí y ponte de rodillas donde debes de estar y empieza a chuparme el pito pinchi arastrada, quiero escuchar que te estes horcando y no te atrevas a usar tus dientes."

"Por eso son pendejos, somos tres y tiene tres hoyos para rellenar. Apuesto que entre los tres va a terminar tan destrozada llena de sangre y meco que ni su padre la reconocería. Pero eso si, quiero estrenar ese culito."

My rapist ignores them and the maid entirely, his eyes boring into my skin like a brand, but he flicks his hand at me.

I refuse to move.

It doesn't matter what I want, the maid pulls me forward with a hard yank of the chain until I'm kneeling at his feet like a dog. My jaw clenches but I keep my face turned so I'm not looking at the ground like all of his invisible women. I loathe this man. If I die here then I pray for another life where I can find him and kill him in so many terrible ways.

"Stop staring at me like that, puta. I will carve your eyes out of your head just for the fun of it," he murmurs, his fingers biting into my skin as he turns my head away from him and towards the door.

There's another man here.

His eyes widen as he takes me in, the sternness of his

appearance softening a little with the shock. He is definitely not a member of my rapist's cartel, for one he is caucasian. He's dressed too scruffy in a dirty pair of jeans, a black tank, and a leather vest on. His hair is dirty and curling around his chin but he's the first person to look at me in this house like I'm a person.

That's the real reason I know he doesn't belong to the cartel.

"What are you doing in my house, Unseen? I don't do business with the Boar."

The man shifts on his feet, his hands flexing at his sides. All of the cartel watch that movement carefully. Ah. He's armed and they're watching for him to reach for his gun.

I hope he does.

"You know the Butcher is after the girl, right? He's torn down half of the Bay already looking for her. I caught wind she was here and thought I'd pay you a courtesy visit. You don't want to be on that man's bad side."

None of his words make sense to me but I don't like the sound of them.

Señor Alcatron chuckles under his breath. "Why would I care about that man? He is under the Jackal's thumb. It does not matter to me. You should not have come here, Roberts."

The man looks around. "I shouldn't have ever come here but I guess that's what drugs do. Look, you gotta let the girl go. Whatever it fucking cost you to get her, it's not worth the death the Butcher will give you. It's just not."

Señor Alcatron chuckles again, flicking his wrist, then

watching as four of his guys pounce on Roberts. He doesn't bother to struggle, sure he's just being thrown out of the house.

But he's seen me, knows where I am, could tell this other man where I am.

So instead, I'm forced to watch as they chain him to the floor.

Still he doesn't struggle or fight it, just tells them over and over again, it's not a good idea.

It's only when they wake the dogs he knows what's coming but by then it's too late to fight back.

I vomit over the carpet at Señor Alcatron's feet, mostly just stomach bile. I can't think about what exactly happens, my mind tries to blank most of it out, and when my rapist notices what I've done he punches me so hard I black out.

I wake again tied to the bed, legs splayed open and a soreness that tells me I was again raped while I was unconscious.

I can't close my eyes without hearing the sounds of his screams and the dogs growling over the pieces of him as they ate.

I don't think about running again.

I retreat back into my mind, trying my best not to fall asleep and become consumed by the darkness that lurks there now. The maids all continue to work efficiently as if their boss hadn't just killed a man by feeding him to his dogs. Their eyes always stay on their work and never on me. I begin to feel so bereft of life. It's as if I've lost the tether holding me onto the Earth and now I'm cast out into a different solar system. It's terrifying, isolating, and frustrating.

I want to go home.

I can never go home.

Time blurs once again. I know I've fallem asleep due to exhaustion twice since the dogs, waking with a raw throat from screaming in my sleep, when another of the maids comes to get me with the chain once more. I'm smarter than the last time I tried to leave the room and I ask to use the bathroom before we head down. I relieve myself, washing away what I can of my assaults and I try not to look in the mirror at the shadow of myself that stares back at me.

The girl staring back at me is gaunt and hollow looking but, curse my damned genes, I still hold some of my beauty. I wish more than ever I was born plain as I splash water onto my face to clean up, any pride I once had in my looks long since torn from me. I will never again look at my appearance as anything but a curse.

"Puta, *Señor Alcatron* is waiting for you," the maid hisses, snapping me out of my little moment of misery.

"*Of course, I couldn't possibly make him wait.*"

She frowns at my use of my mother tongue. I don't care.

My legs tremble as badly as the last time I was forced to

walk down here, though I'm sure it's about the dogs more than my physical state. Once again, there's no sound as we walk through. I look a little closer this time though and each room we pass is empty, even the room that once held mountains of cash.

Are we leaving?

Or are they leaving and feeding me to the dogs now they're bored of me?

The tremble in my legs gets worse but I force them to keep moving and I keep looking around for some sort of clues about what is going to happen to me now. The the rest of the house is as darkened as my room, the lamps making it look as though the cartel was going for mood lighting, when really I know this is just the way the they choose to live; in a series of dark, secretive rooms, connected by winding hallways filled with blind, subservient maids who obey without flinching even when a man lays dead at their feet, his bones snapping under the jaws of the drooling beasts eating him.

The tremble in my legs is a full blown shake as we step into the dining room and I'm not sure if it's pain, starvation, or the fear of being ripped apart by the dogs. I'd very much like to be put out of my misery but being eaten alive... being ripped apart by those beasts is not the death I would wish on *anyone*.

I take a seat at the table at the maids direction and stare over at my most brutal rapist.

Maybe I would wish that death on this man. And the other ones who visit me.

He's here alone, nothing but a drink in front of him for once. I'm glad to see his usual cigar missing, I don't need anymore burns littering my body.

I stare down the table at him, meeting his eye so he knows that he might own my body right now he won't fucking break me, and I imagine the death I would give him. I fantasize about snatching that steak knife away from his disgusting hands and slashing his throat with it. I imagine his blood pouring out over us both, hot and thick, and the satisfaction I feel from that act… god, I would give anything to be able to do that now. Even the show of making me watch the dogs devour that man who came here about me, that hasn't stopped me from having a spine.

The room is silent as we watch each other, me with utter contempt and him with that same deranged *possession* he always has.

"There's my beautiful puta. You're causing me a lot of trouble, you know? What am I supposed to do about that, eh?" He says, sipping at his glass of amber liquid. He drinks many different things, all of them have been breathed on to my skin before and all of them now make me feel sick to my stomach.

I don't speak. I learned that lesson well from my father, better to keep your mouth shut than to enrage him further and triple the rage he hits you with. He stands slowly, walking over to me. The maid holding my chin ducks her head even more and takes a half step back in subservience.

I keep my eyes trained on him.

He can cut them out for all I care now. Maybe then he'll stop thinking of me as a beauty and I'll finally be put out of my misery.

"I got an offer for you, you know," he murmurs, stroking my hair away from my face. I force myself not to flinch away from his hands, even as he starts to stroke my cheeks with his fingertips. "I didn't think there was an offer I would take over you. You're a very pretty toy, my brother and I enjoy playing with you. Fucking you raw. Leaving this pretty white skin with our marks. That pussy of yours... it might have been fucked before but it's still as tight as a fist. I had so many plans to destroy you."

I hold my breath as my heart stutters to a halt in my chest with something cruel, something far too close to hope for me to handle.

It's too much to hope that he's going to let me go, but maybe my father had a change of heart and wants to buy me back? Maybe Louis planned this all along as a way to get us both away from France? I will never forgive him, not ever for the treatment I've had, but I'd take that over this hell.

"You're heading back to the auctions, puta. That's all you're good for now but this way I get my business and I'll get some of my money back. A fair trade for a used up pussy."

My heart drops at the word auctions but then my eyes catch on the dark stains on the carpet. Maybe the next man to buy me won't have such ways of keeping me here. As long as it's not the salivating jaws of the dogs, I'll find a way to get out.

Anything but the dogs.

He watches the decision happen, it being written all over my face, and he smirks at me again. He strokes my jaw with those evil hands of his again and works his way up until he can take a fistful of my hair, squeezing tight until a gasp rips out of me unbidden.

"One last ride, puta. No point in sending you back to hell whole."

And then he rapes me, one last time, bent over the dining table, staring at the stain on the carpet while the maid holds my chain tightly for him.

Her eyes never leave that stain either.

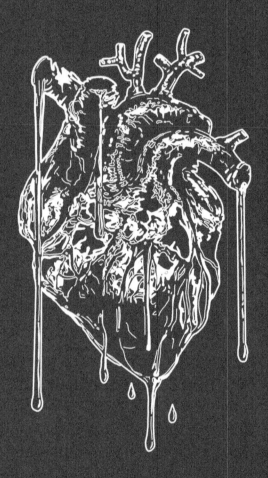

CHAPTER TWELVE

ILLI

I stand off to the side with the kid, hiding in the shadows so all of the walking wallets don't get an eyeful of little old me. Something about me scares the shit out people and it always has worked in my favor.

Lips looks out over the crowd with a fierce glare, her lip curling as she takes the men and women in. Oh yeah, there are women buyers here too by the dozen. I didn't get a look at the buyer's guide on the way in but there must be some prime meat up for grabs tonight.

I jerk my head at the stage. "We should burn that fucking thing to the ground, kid."

She smirks back. "Gimme a time and day and I'm here for it. This place is a fucking cesspit."

It really is.

There are hanging cages from the ceiling with girls in it that are due to be sold later in the evening. Some of them are sobbing, some of them don't even have tits yet they're so young, and my fingers start to tingle at the thought of cutting the Vulture's fucking head off.

How long has this place been here and I've ignored the depravity because it wasn't on my radar? How many fucking children have been stolen and sold off?

I'm not just going to burn the place down, I'm going to find the sales ledger and work my way through it. One by one, I'll take them all the fuck out for doing this fucking disgusting shit.

The lights finally dim and a woman in a sexy looking skirt suit walks out on stage and up to the podium. The crowd quietens down to murmurs and the clinking of glasses together, a refined crowd despite the zip code.

Residents of Mounts Bay can't regularly afford skin at these auctions.

Millionaires and billionaires from all across the country and even the world come here to buy their skin. The Vulture has made a name for himself, that's for fucking sure. There isn't a fetishist or a serial rapist who hasn't been down here to sample the goods.

I glance around again and yep, there's pretty much a full spread. Girls and women of every color, age, body shape, and fucking flavor are represented but there's only one here tonight I can save.

Her photo nearly fucking kills me.

She's naked but I'm not looking at her goods. She's at least fifty pounds smaller than when she'd arrived in the Bay and her body is covered in bruises and burns, cuts and scratches, until there isn't a single patch of unmarked skin. Her eyes are hollow and empty, too big in her gaunt face.

Fuck.

Now I know for sure she's taken my soul and made it her own.

I feel nothing but rage and misery at what's been done to her. I need to get her home and safe, heal her up, and then I'll walk my ass back down here and start gutting men in her name.

Lips glances at the photo for a second and then away, not lingering on it for even a second. "Do you think you can get her back? Like, save her from the demons she'll have, not just get her out of here?" she murmurs.

I grit my teeth. "Don't doubt it for a second, kid."

She shrugs. "I don't doubt you. I just don't think I'll ever get over what's happened to me. She's clearly had worse, she's going to need a lot."

My eyes flick back down to her and I size her up for a second. To anyone else it looks like she's standing there confidently, ready to take anything on, but I've honed my own skills at being able to pick this shit from a mile away.

She favors her left side, the right one being the side D'Ardo smashed to pieces. Told her he was doing it as training when really it was to try to stop her from getting so fucking good at killing people, sneaking around, and running. She was starting to get better at it than he was and he can't fucking stand people being better than him. It's like a fucking poison in his brain, he only takes it for me because we've been as close as brothers since the group home.

She's covered in scars from him and her fucked-up druggie mom and all of the jobs she's been on, but I know she's not talking about that shit.

"You've both survived shit. Different shit, but it's still shit. You'll figure it out, kid."

She shrugs, her eyes never leaving the stage, and we stand there in silence as we watch the girls slowly get marched out, one by one. None of them cry, thank fuck. I think I'd lose my cool if they did. I'm a heartless bastard while fully grown men scream and cry, and even when D'Ardo pulls his twisted shit I've never really noticed, but now?

Now I fucking care.

I grew a fucking heart and if anything, it's made me even more fucking dangerous.

The prices the girls go for start in the low six figures and climbs quickly. We hit seven figures well before my girl's number gets called. The Vulture's men drag her onto the stage by the shackles around her wrists. There's a fucking gag in her mouth and she's fighting them off, kicking and screaming.

I'm a fucking sick man, but that just gives me hope. If she

has the fire left in her to try to fight them off then maybe she's not as broken as the photos made her out to be.

I expect a drop in the amount she goes for this time around but once again, I've underestimated the fucking depravity in these suits. The moment the woman in red starts calling out for bids eight paddles hit the air, no one dropping them and the price just keeps climbing. Lips blows out a breath when the number surpasses her last price and it shows no sign of slowing.

My teeth clench but I hold myself still, memorizing their faces instead. They're all dead. Every last man who has touched my girl is fucking dead.

The kid nods at me without even looking at my face. "Agreed. They're all dead."

I huff under my breath, my eyes glued to the stage. "You fucking psychic or some shit?"

She shrugs. "I've spent a lot of time around murderous men. I can read you all pretty well now."

Nah, she's too fucking smart for this world. She sees fucking everything, D'Ardo has bitten off more than he can fucking chew with her, not that I'd ever say that to him, better to let the asshole find out for himself.

She goes to move now the entire crowd is captivated in the bidding war and I stop her. "No. I wanna see which assholes want her. I need a full list of who has to die."

She shrugs and nods, and I find myself impressed again. The longer we wait around the more that can go wrong and yet here she is, ready for fucking anything.

D'Ardo has *definitely* underestimated her.

My girl goes for nearly double what she originally sold for.

The auctioneer makes some fucking joke about the fee as the men drag her back off of the stage, screaming and kicking for all she's worth. Lips chuckles under her breath when my girls heel manages to connect with the dick of the guy's holding her, his cussing a shout that's loud enough for the whole crowd to hear.

A few of the suits around us chuckle and make a comment about punishing her and breaking her of that behavior and I have no choice.

I have to cut their throats where they stand.

Lips is quick on her feet, grabbing one as I grab the other, her skinny little arms no match for his bulk on their own but the knife she has is sharp and his breath gurgles out of his slit throat like music to my ears tonight.

"A little warning would be nice," she snarks, all talk because she doesn't look even remotely concerned with the blood on her hands.

"Like fuck. Did you hear them? *Break her*. I'll be fucked if I'm letting that shit go. If you're not up for it, kid—"

She cuts me off. "I already said I'm in, let's get moving. I don't need the Vulture finding out I'm taking out his clients, he'll be on me in a hot fucking second."

The shudder of repulsion goes through her and I know the

feeling. The creepy fuck is bad enough for me, I can't imagine what he's like for her. He probably had a number in his head for her the second he laid eyes on her, all girls are nothing but a dollar amount to him.

I drag the corpses to a dark corner behind us, where they won't be found until the light's go back on when the night is over with, and then I give Lips a nod to push through the crowd to the back.

Time to get to work.

The backrooms are a dark pit of despair.

Cage after cage, I can't help but look around at the girls here and clench my jaw so hard it might fucking snap. There's only two reactions I get from them all; they either shy away away, terrified I'm their buyer, or they stare out at me blankly like it doesn't fucking matter what I do to them, they're already broken inside.

Burning the whole fucking building to the motherfucking ground might not be enough. We'd need a fucking cleansing, an exorcism, zone the entire place radioactive to keep people away from the evil juju. It's beyond fucking evil.

Lips knows the guy on the door and with a nod he disappears.

I give her a side eye. "He cool or are we about to be stabbed in the back?"

She smirks as her eyes dart around the cages. "He's solid. I think my real skill is knowing enough people to go places unseen because there's no way he'd ever nark on me."

I hope she's right, only because I don't want to have to clean up tonight. I just want to grab my girl and get her the fuck out of here. I'll deal with everyone else later, once she's clean and warm and calm.

I keep seeing her battered body every time my eyes fucking shut, flashes as I blink. I can't stand it. I want to crawl out of my fucking skin at the thought of it.

My fault.

The whole fucking lot of it lands at my feet. I took the money to land her in that hell.

We pick up the pace, aware we're on borrowed time, and move through until we get to the cages at the back. Great. The cages with pick-proof locks and an electric current running through them at random intervals.

"Fucking perfect. Do you bring a fucking lock pick kit or do I need to go find the keys?" I mutter and Lips gives me a smug-ass look. It looks good on her.

"Please, this shit is my specialty." She says, all sarcasm and cutting wit, and then pulls a little metal box out from her bag. Three wires attach to the code panel and then she fucks around with it for a second.

I let her do her thing and crouch down to look at my girl. She's lying on her back in the corner, her clothes nothing but dirty rags hanging off of her. There's a bump on her head, already bruising up, and her eyes are dopey looking as she stares at the ceiling in a daze. Fuck, I can spot the concussion from a mile away. They've flung her brain around in her skull so hard she looks like she's taken a hit of heroin not a fist to the head.

There's a quiet beep and then the door swings open, the electric that sang and zapped in the air disappearing at once. My girl's head lolls around on the ground but she still has enough sense to blanch when she spots us, a vicious stream of French streaming out of her.

The kid crouches down to her level to talk to her, low and coaxing, from the open door of the cage. It's clear my girl isn't expecting the French, sitting up too quickly and turning a little green at the movement, but she listens intently, a little frown over her brow. I stay crouched where I am, watching over them both but ready to leap to action if any asshole tries to sneak up behind us. I trust the kid knows her shit, but I don't trust any man in the Bay not to stab us in the back.

My girl starts to murmur back softly, slowly, and the sound still has my blood singing. Lips nods and creeps forward slowly, like she's approaching a mama tiger that might rip her face off.

I leave them for a second longer and then whisper, low and gentle, "We've got to get a move on. It's not safe here, kid."

The kid nods at me and then looks back at my French siren, hesitating for a second before wrapping her arms around her shoulders and pulling her into a hug.

My girl stays still for a second and then crumbles in her arms, just fucking falls apart and that gets my blood boiling, the rage pumping through to my heart until I'm ready to rip some heads clear off of bodies until there's nothing but a trail of corpses left in my wake.

Lips looks so fucking uncomfortable at the hug but she kneels there and offers her what little comfort she can. Ok. I might just like this kid. I need to talk to her about D'Ardo before he fucking kills her just to see what she looks like on the inside.

The kid gets my girl standing up, helping her stay upright until they make it out to me. I shrug my jacket off and carefully drape in over her shoulders to try to cover her battered body up a little and keep her warm against the cool, seaside night. She flinches away from me but Lips murmurs to her again, helping her to tuck her arms in properly and zipping the jacket up. She looks fucking *tiny* in it.

I'm getting her a fucking burger on the way home.

The greasiest, cheesiest fucking thing I can find.

"Stay behind me, I'll get us through no problem," I murmur, and Lips nods again. My girl's big eyes take every inch of me in but her eyes are still glazed over so I'm not sure how much is really going into the sore brain of hers.

I want to reach out and pull her into my arms, hold her tight and tell her all about what I'd do to keep her safe, but there's no way I'm scaring her off. Not after the hell she's been through.

So I get us moving, watching every last inch of the building on our way out. Lips directs me with quiet words as we stalk out. I notice the cameras on the way out and curse but she laughs at me, low and sassy. "You think I forgot them? Have faith, Butcher."

I shake my head at her attitude and push through the crowd. We make it out of the cesspit, into the alley, and over to my car before two of the Vulture's men step out.

"Stealing the merchandise, Butcher? It's not smart to go against the Twelve."

I move so I'm blocking the kid, I don't need her getting fucking killed just for helping me right a wrong, and I palm two of my cleavers.

One of the guys glances down but he doesn't look anywhere near as worried as he should be. "Look, if you pay the price you can have the pussy. No one cares that you killed the suit."

Pay the price, so the filthy fuck wants to double his money on her? Over my dead, rotting corpse will I pay him a fucking penny.

The only thing he's getting from me is a shallow grave.

I let a slow grin stretch over my face. "Well, tell me which account to pay it in then."

The guys both relax and grin, absolute fucking amateurs.

My cleavers are still held tight in my fists.

I wait until they both take a step towards me before I move towards them. My face still has that lazy grin on it, a predator they should be able to recognize but they're too fucking stupid to see it.

"Have you purchased from us before? Let me give you the details. She went for a pretty penny, Butcher—"

I cut him off.

At the throat.

A red haze takes over me and I don't stop hacking away until they're both in pieces all over the alleyway. I forget that the girls are both watching me, all that's left of me is vengeance and retribution. Make them hurt like she has. Make them less than nothing.

Finally, when they're unrecognizable, I turn back to the girls and find them both blinking up at me. Lips doesn't seem too concerned, more that she's watching and taking notes. Where has my brute strength come in handy and where are the weak points that sliced that little bit easier. I really could teach her a thing or two.

I can't look at my girl until I get her safe in my car and clean myself up a little. She still looks too shell-shocked to grasp what's gone down and I don't need her figuring it all out and being fucking scared of me. I couldn't take it.

Lips gets her settled in the front seat, quiet words and soothing tones, and I wipe up quickly. I have no doubt there's about to be backup arriving and I need out.

Ten seconds later we're speeding the fuck away, driving away from the docks and over to my warehouse. It's a short trip, barely enough to get settled into my seat, and then I'm pulling into the garage. I've never had the kid here before but the second I park she's out of the car and opening the door to my girl, murmuring quietly to her where she sits with her eyes shut. I shut the alarm off and by the time I turn back to the car the kid is turning to leave.

I stop her. "What's to say you didn't just rescue her from one monster and deliver her to another? I am the fucking Butcher of the Bay, kid. You should stick around long enough to get her settled and... fuck, calm at least."

She smirks at me, a feral light in her eyes. "You think I don't know who the real monsters are around here? You're bad and you're ruthless but she's safe here. If I'm wrong about that then... well, I guess I'm already heading to Hell, how much worse can it get?"

I shrug. "She needs a friend, stay."

Lips winces and checks the time of her phone. "It's almost time for the bed check at the group home. If I miss it and Matteo has to square it, he's going to have questions."

Right.

Neither of us want that. He's a fucking jealous dick and his attitude problem will be even worse if he knows we've been out on a... job together. I give her a nod instead and she smiles a little ruefully back at me.

"See you 'round, Butcher," she says, and stalks off into the darkness. No fucking fear in the kid, it's not safe here at the docks at night but there isn't many men I'd wager would win against her hand-to-hand. She's made of tough shit, the type that gets you through Hell no matter what.

"Hey, kid!" I call out. She turns and I swear she's so fucking skinny she damn near disappears into the shadows when she turns side on.

I need to feed her sometime.

"My friends call me Illi."

She smirks, all white teeth in the dark. "I didn't think we were friends, Butcher."

I run my hand through my hair, tugging a little at the length of it. I'm due to cut the shit off. "After tonight, kid, we're more than friends. You need me, I'll come. No matter the cost."

She curls forward a little, ducking her head down and grinning at her shoes. "Ride or die, huh? I'm honored. Same goes to you, you know? And that beauty you just killed half the Bay for."

Then she turns and disappears into the night like she really is nothing but a shadow.

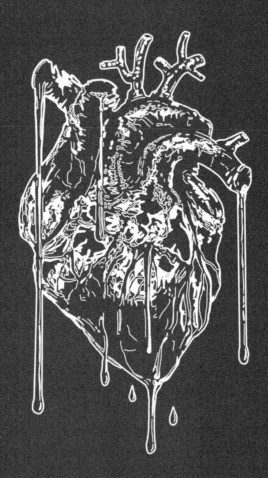

CHAPTER THIRTEEN

ODIE

The auctions are much worse to be at than I thought.

All of the men touch me too much, their hand roaming where they're unwanted, pinching and squeezing as if I'm a prized piece of flesh. I didn't even have time to feel relief at being away from Alcatron and for the rags they had dressed me in, finally some sort of coverings.

I am kept in a cage that sings with electricity.

The other girls in the room are all silent, some of them wear shock collars as if they are dogs and every so often they'll fall to the ground in spasms. I don't understand why they would be shocked like that, they're not attempting to escape or anything but I supposed evil men don't need an excuse.

After I had fought being dragged out onto the stage, one of the men had hit me and left me dazed, so when I hear the cage door open and find a beautiful girl staring at me I decide I have finally found peace.

"*This is it then? I am dead?*"

She shakes her head, speaking in low tones to me. "*No. We're here to get you out of here. There's nothing to be afraid of now, we won't hurt you.*"

That can't possibly be true. Everyone has hurt me. Every man I have met here, the little old lady and the maids. The woman who had auctioned me off hadn't ever flinched, even when she watched one of the men punch me.

"Have you purchased me?"

She shakes her head again. "No. We don't buy women, this place is evil and we're getting you out. Do you think you can stand?"

I look down at my legs, covered in bruises like fingerprints. My lip trembles and I blame the blow to my head for the weakness. I can't speak, if I open my mouth again a sob will come out and I don't want to scare the beautiful girl.

Then I hear his voice. "We've got to get a move on. It's not safe here, kid."

I know that voice. That's the monster's voice, the man who looked more terrifying than any other since I've arrived here in America. He didn't hurt me though, not physically, it was only the care he took with me that burned me because I knew it was because I was *valuable*, not that he cared about who I am.

I stare at my feet so I don't see her creep forward until

she's wrapping me in her little arms, gently folding me into her embrace. I startle, scared of what she's going to do to me, but when nothing happens I deflate, letting her take my weight.

She murmurs under her breath softly, rubbing my shoulder carefully. I should be embarrassed at the state I'm in, I haven't had a real shower since I was back home in France, but her arms never falter.

"We're going to move now, okay? Don't worry about anything, just focus on staying upright and we'll take care of everything else. We need to go as quickly as you can manage. Are you... sore?"

I know exactly which soreness she is referring to and I swallow. "I can do it. If we're leaving here, I can do anything."

She helps me stand with a little squeeze to my shoulders. "Of course you can. I never doubted it."

We get out of the cage and the monster gives me his jacket. I don't want him touching me but... he never tries to, his eyes never touch me for long and it's a relief to not be watched for a moment. Every man I've been around all this time has watched me with possession in their eyes and it's like a balm to my soul for him not to.

I cannot let my guard down though.

He is still a man, and one I truly could not get away from. He's twice the size of me easily. There's dozens of weapons strapped to his body and his arms look like weapons of their own. I've never seen a man like him, not ever, and I wonder how much money it had cost to hire him to rescue me.

Who had paid it?

We make it to the car out in the alleyway only to be found by two of the men who had dragged me out to the stage. My entire body gets overtaken in a tremble at the sound of their voices. We were so close, so close!

"Stealing the merchandise, Butcher? It's not smart to go against the Twelve."

The monster moves in front of the girl and I, his large frame easily covering us entirely. He doesn't say a word, just grips a meat cleaver in his fist. What a strange weapon, I glance at the girl but she doesn't look worried. No, she looks blank and as if she's about to get up and help him.

How could she possibly help?

"Look, if you pay the price you can have the pussy. No one cares that you killed the suit."

My jaw clenches. God, I wish a violent and blood-soaked death to these men. For them to call me that, to only see the body part they wish to own, I wish for them to choke on their own blood as they die screaming.

The monster speaks. "Well, tell me which account to pay it in then."

My breath catches in my throat but the little girl squeezes my shoulders again, shooting me a warning look. He's going to buy me. He's going to be my next owner.

"Have you purchased from us before? Let me give you the

details. She went for a pretty penny, Butcher—"

I hear the gurgle over my internal panic and glance up again just in time to see the blood begin to spray out from the man's throat. He goes down, clutching at and convulsing on the ground but the wound is so deep it's a matter of seconds before he passes out from the blood loss.

We sit there and watch as he gives the men the exact death I wished for them, my eyes round and my stomach calm. He doesn't offer any of them a swift death except the first man. No, on the rest he aims for places of their body that will take them down but keep them mostly awake as he hacks their limbs off and slowly the alleyway looks as though it's had a visit from Jack the Ripper.

Not once do I feel anything except relief. Maybe he's not a monster, maybe he is the angel of death and war, sent here to avenge the wrongs done to me. I am not a saintly being though, I do not know why he would be here for me.

When he's done, he stalks around the car to wipe down his face of the blood without a word.

"He just killed those men," I murmur, and the girl looks at me, dead in the eye.

"He just saved you. He just killed the men that sold you at auction to your next rapist. He did that to protect you."

I nod, placidly. He did. I don't know why but I'll be grateful regardless.

"I'd like to go home," I murmur, and she nods.

"The Butcher will take you home."

Why would a *butcher* take me home to France? Is that their slang for a pilot? Or maybe it will be an illegal flight and that is their way of saying that. This country is so confusing! There is no other place on Earth quite like it. Their language and all the words with two meanings, I will never figure it out.

The girl covers my hand with her own. "Slow your breathing down, you're starting to hyperventilate. Everything is going to be okay, we'll take you somewhere safe and you can... heal up there."

A dark, twisted sound claws its' way out of my throat. "You cannot heal what was done to me. There is no coming back from being used in such a way. But I will survive it and whatever else is to come."

I rest my head back against the leather seats and shut my eyes as we drive. The monster is definitely speeding, the road laws cannot be so different to the ones back home that this is legal, but it's either a very short trip or I once again lose time because I startle awake in a bed.

A very comfortable, plush, clean bed.

Where the hell am I?

Panic sets in.

I'm not chained to the bed.

There's a little wooden table by the bed with a towel and some clothes on it and a pair of slippers on the floor. I stare at them all for a moment and then glance around the room to take stock a little more. There's a bathroom at one end of the room, the light on in there casting a glow that helps me see what else is here. The bed I'm in is massive, the biggest I've ever seen, and the bedding is all very high quality. Whoever owns it is a very rich person and someone who values their sleep highly.

The dresser against the wall at the end of the bed is made in the some dark wood as the bed and tables, and it has a small photo frame on it but that's the only personal touch in the entire room. There's no art or other photos, no rug on the floor, nothing to say who owns it.

But there is a window.

My heart sings at the sight of it and I stand on shaking legs to walk over and pull the blackout blinds up. The sun shines in and blinds me but the tears that stream down my face have nothing to do with that.

I haven't seen the sun in weeks.

Weeks.

When my eyes adjust I see the ocean and sand as far as the eye can see, gulls flying overhead and calling out. It's stunning, so beautiful that it feels like a dream.

I stand there for as long as my bladder can hold on, but eventually I have to move to the bathroom. I remember to grab the towel and clothing, desperately wanting to get out of the rags. I hate that I wore them in that beautiful bed but the alternate option isn't any better.

I would have woken in a panic if I was naked.

The bathroom door has a lock and a bolt, making it impossible for someone to get in here while I'm naked, a luxury I also haven't had in weeks. I take my first real deep breath since I stepped off of that private jet in the desert, where my father had abandoned me to my unwanted husband.

I strip off and step into the shower, wincing as the water touches all if the cigar burns that cover me. I use the body wash there and scrub around them, over and over again until my skin is pink and raw to the touch. I might never feel clean again. I wonder idly if I can have six showers a day here, until I really do feel clean again? Maybe I'll be brave and ask... whoever it is that now has me.

Does he own me?

Is it a he?

I don't see how that beautiful little girl could have possibly bought me but then... I had been stolen, hadn't I? Secreted out of the auction house like a stolen treasure.

I don't feel at all like a treasure.

I find a medical kit under the sink and clean all of my open wounds, some of them already hot to the touch and weeping. I'll have to be careful that they don't get any worse. If I'm not going to be abused here then I don't want to be taken out by blood poisoning.

I pull the clothing on, relieved to find warm and oversized clothing that will cover every inch of me except my face. They smell quite nice, like a man but nothing like any of the ones who had taken me.

It takes me a long time to come to terms with unbolting the door and coming out.

I tell myself over and over again that the beautiful girl wouldn't lie. She was pure and honest, I'm sure of it. There's no way she would lie to me, I understood her every word.

Eventually, it's my hunger that moves me. I need to eat something so my legs can stop shaking and my vision can stop whiting out.

I make it out of the bathroom and four steps into the bedroom, only pausing to look at the photo on the dresser. It's old. I can tell by the hairstyles it's fifteen to twenty years old, and there's a woman grinning at the camera with a little boy standing at her feet, grinning that same grin.

It's a sweet photo but my heart clenches at the sight of it. I know exactly who that little boy is.

I slept in the monster's bed.

I have to take a deep breath before I can step out of the room and into what I'm expecting to be a hallway but is actually a large, open-plan living area. There's a huge kitchen with marble countertops and high end fittings in one corner and a large living area with leather couches and a big rug on the floor in front of the biggest television I've ever seen. There's a dining table and a little office nook, but the best thing in the entire room in the giant wall of glass that showcases the ocean beside the apartment beautifully.

It knocks the breath out of me again.

Well, maybe it's that or the hunger pains again, but the sun shining and the rolling waves calls out to my soul, owning me in a way I actually want to be owned.

"It's a beautiful view, right? Worth staying in the Bay for."

I startle at the sound of his voice, my body tensing as I look up to meet his eyes. There's no way I'm going to lower my head now, not after all I've already gone through, but meeting his eyes is more terrifying than any of the other men so far.

He's standing in the kitchen, I don't know how I missed the giant wall of man at my first inspection but there he is, leaning against the counter with a pan in his hands and a calm look on his face.

I can't speak. My voice just dries up in my throat.

He doesn't notice my silence, grabbing plates and pouring piles of fluffy scrambled eggs out onto them.

My mouth is too dry with dehydration to water but my stomach comes to life at the smell. I need those goddamn eggs. I might just die right here in this perfect apartment if I don't get them.

"Do you want bacon too, baby girl? I've cooked enough for us both."

Bacon.

Mother-fucking-bacon.

My legs nearly give way at the thought of it and a slow smile stretches across his face. "Perfect, my girl likes bacon. Come sit down and let me feed you up. We've got to get you back to healthy."

I can't even feel the appropriate amount of suspicion at his words because all I can think about is the bacon. I stumble over to the barstools at the end of the breakfast bar, wincing as I climb up to sit down but I think I'd walk over glass and hot coals right now to get that bacon.

Bacon.

He piles it up onto the two plates, pushing one over to me and handing me a knife and fork. I try to thank him, I'm not a savage, but the words won't come to me.He doesn't take notice, just smiles in satisfaction as I tear into the plate. I try to slow down and savor every bite, but the void in my stomach gnaws at me until I'm inhaling the food.

He sets his own plate down next to mine and then fusses with the coffee machine, coffee, before bringing us both a cup each.

I drink it all in one gulp.

It tastes awful but I'd love four more of them right now.

He chuckles and immediately moves to make me another one, handing his own cup to me.

"I'm going to keep feeding you until you either puke or pass out, baby girl. And then when you're up for round two, I'll order in some pizzas or burgers or something."

I swallow a mouthful of eggs and force myself to choke out, "Thank you, Monsieur."

His eyes flare as he places the third cup of coffee in front of me. "Ah, so you can talk to me. Good, baby girl, good work. I'm also going to call you a doctor to make sure you're okay."

I blink back tears and he curses under his breath. "I mean that those wounds aren't going to cause you anymore trouble. I know you're not okay, baby girl."

I swallow roughly again, the delicious food in my stomach roiling with nerves now. There's so much a doctor could say to me that would make me much less okay. "And what do I do if I am pregnant or have some incurable disease? Hm? None of the men who assaulted me used protection. You will throw me out and I'll be stuck in this country with no passport, no money, and no way to return home. I'll lost here."

I look back up at him try not to cry at the sight of him because tears are useless.

The monster looks looks furious, so unbelievably angry that I feel dread stroke down my spine like icy fingers.

He turns on his heel without a word and stomps out of the room, slamming the door and then it sounds as though he's kicking walls on his way down the stairs.

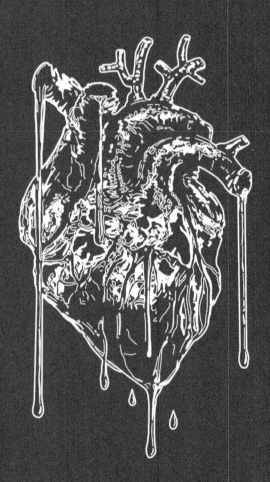

CHAPTER FOURTEEN

ILLI

I head down to my gym to workout because I can't fucking think about that shit around her.

She walked out of my room with her head held high and that fire in her eyes and for a second I forgot how fucking bad her situation was. I forgot that she was a sex trafficking victim and that she was raped, over and over again.

By multiple men.

I need blood.

I need gallons and gallons of blood, spilled in her name and my penance for what I've done to her. I need it now.

I destroy two more punching bags and my fists because I don't bother wrapping my knuckles. I don't deserve to wrap them, I need the pain. I grab a shower down here so I don't freak Odie out.

Yeah, I had to call the kid to ask her what my girl's name actually is.

Now I have her dad's name too and the fact he sold her to pay his debts. The little fucking cretin is on my list. I'm going to just keep taking down these names until I have them all accounted for, ready for the day I can come bleed them out.

I need to focus on my girl first.

I call Doc and put in a home visit request. He doesn't usually do them but we go way back and I'll pay him whatever it takes. He gets back to me straight away but he's on another job, fuck it.

I'll have to wait it out.

I text Harbin for an update on his search for more info on the guy who had Odie. The tears in her eyes tell me I need to fucking gut him, slow and careful, at her feet. I mean, if she's into that sort of thing. Maybe my butchering last night scared her so bad she couldn't speak to me this morning? But she hadn't spoken to me in the car when I met her either, maybe she's just quiet?

Fuck, I don't know much about her... except that she owns me and I would paint the entire city red for her.

I will do that, just as soon as she's healed up and secure here.

Right. I need to go talk to her. Apologize for raging out and leaving. Fuck, I can't remember the last time I said sorry to someone. Probably my mom, so about fifteen years ago.

Fuck me, I can't think about her right now either.

I throw my spare workout gear on and stomp back up the stairs, taking a deep breath before I walk back into that room. Right, don't look angry or blood-thirsty. Think calm thoughts, don't think about her getting hurt. Right. I can do this.

I step into the main apartment quietly, closing the door behind me and checking the security camera by habit. It's clear like I knew it would be. It screeches like a fucking bitch if there's someone coming, we're good here.

I look around and find her sitting in the oversized leather armchair by the window, staring out over the water. I wonder if it soothes her like it does me? I made sure I could look out over it every day and night without ever having to get curtains because of neighbors. I mean, if I ever get neighbors I'll just kill them rather than obscuring this view.

Probably why no one ever moves down here.

I walk over carefully, sitting down on the big couch so she has some space. Fuck, how long will she need this space? I need to ask Doc.

"I'm sorry I got angry. I would never hurt you, I just can't fucking stand to think about you being hurt or upset."

She snorts at me and my lip twitches as I fight the grin at the little noise. It gets knocked right out of me at her answer. "I'm sorry to tell you, Monsieur Boucher, but I don't think I'm ever going to live without pain and anger curled in my gut again. They are now a part of me."

Fuck.

But I guess that's true about me too.

I give her a nod but my eyes stay glued on her hands. She has them clasped in front of her on the chair, her fingers long and fine. Fuck, am I sitting here all captivated by fucking hands? I need to get a grip.

She stares out of the window at the circling gulls, her face calm and peaceful again. I don't want to take that peace away from her but I need to fucking say my piece. "If you have some disease we'll get you medicine. If there's a baby in your belly then we'll sort that out too."

She startles at my words again and, fuck me, tears fill my eyes. "And if I want to keep the baby? What if I can't imagine playing a part in the baby's demise, hm?"

Fuck. That didn't even occur to me. That she'd want to keep it or that she'd expect me to order her to get rid of it. This is a fucking mess and I don't deal with this shit well. I need the kid back here right the fuck now.

I shake my head at her. "I'm not telling you we'll get rid of it, I'm saying we'll sort it out. Get you whatever you need. If you want to keep it then we'll keep it. Whatever happens we'll sort out together."

It's her turn to shake her head at me. "Do you collect broken things? Or do you own me now? Why else would you be helping me? My father cannot pay you, if it's money you're after. He can't even pay his own debts, let alone mine."

My jaw clenches. "No one owns you, except you. You're safe here for as long as you need and we're getting you healed up. That's it. I don't expect any-fucking-thing from you. Nothing. Sleep and eat and sit here and look at the water all fucking day. That's it. That's your job."

Her eyes narrow at me, her head held high and her back so damn straight I'm kind of thinking I might get shanked by her at some point today if we keep talking like this.

I must be a sick man too because my dick gets hard just thinking about it.

"Monsieur Boucher, you need to tell me why I'm here. Saying all of these things... it does not make sense."

Her words are a little hesitant, like she's not sure she's saying them right. Fuck, I'm obviously confusing the shit out of her after all of the shitty treatment she's just had at the hands of the cartel, but I can't exactly lay it all out to her. Hey, that hour you spent in my car changed the entire course of my life now and I won't hurt you or treat you bad but I'm also never fucking leaving your side again, 'kay? Cool.

But her words are right and clear enough so I nod, motioning for her to keep going.

"I would like to know what is going to happen to me, are you sending me back to France?"

Her eyes are clear and her hands are steady. Fuck, I'll try some version of the truth, one that's a little more palatable. "I'm not sending you anywhere. You're here until you decide you want to go somewhere and then I'll be going there with you. That's how this is going to work."

She frowns. "I do not understand you. Why would you come with me? Are you being paid to protect me? Who would do that? Louis?"

Okay, who *the fuck* is *Louis*? "I'm doing this because I was wrong to take you to the cartel. I'm righting my wrongs and you're the biggest fucking mistake I've ever made. So you're here until you're ready to go somewhere else, and I'm with you."

Her frown deepens. "That does not make sense. I have no money, Monsieur. I have no way to repay you."

"I don't want your money."

She recoils from me. Fuck. "You want my body then? I'm afraid to tell you, the goods are soiled. Broken. You would be unhappy with your payment."

Soiled fucking goods, I'm going to tear the cartel to fucking pieces. There won't be a fucking single person left in the Bay by the time I'm through.

I try to relax my jaw but my words still come out through my clenched teeth. "I don't want your body unless you want to give it to me. There's no payment, nothing owed, you being alive and safe and happy is what I want."

I get up from the couch again before I rage out, fighting to keep my face resembling something sane and normal. Fuck, I'm all Butcher right now.

Which reminds me.

"My name is Johnny Illium. You can call me Illi. The Butcher is my job title here in the Bay and, baby girl, there isn't anyone fucking stupid enough to try and hurt you now you're with me."

I feed Odie three more times before I have to head out for the night. I'd leave it entirely but the Viper is now sending a constant stream of bullshit messages and threats to me. I'm going to pick a time, grab the biker boy, and take out some of my anger on him until he squeals on his daddy.

I'm going to do all of this without letting Odie know about it either. She doesn't need to know what happens in the basement, at least not right now. She hasn't once mentioned the scene at the alleyway and she doesn't have a problem arguing with me about why I'd want to keep her. I don't know if she's seen a lot of that kind of business or if the knock to the head has her forgetting all about it. Either way, I'm easing her into this life of mine. Dipping her toes into death and destruction, having them come back ruby red the same way I'd paint the world for her. Fuck it, I'm a goddamn poet.

I call Roxas and he's happy to fuck around with his bike in my garage for the night, just to have that extra fucking layer of protection for my girl while I get shit done. I don't even consider calling D'Ardo, not with his obsession for breaking girls. It makes e fucking sick to my stomach thinking about it now but my code says I stick with him. Fuck, I have no idea how to reconcile who he is with the man I've become while he hasn't noticed.

I'm still pissed he's ignoring my calls.

I tell Odie I'm heading out. I explain the security alarm, Roxas downstairs, and leave her a phone with my number programmed in but she is happy enough to stare out at the water without my hovering around her like a whipped bitch.

I'm not sure if that's a good reaction or a bad one but there's nothing I can do about it until I get Doc here to look her over and he's not due until well after midnight.

I tear away from my place in my Mustang, ignoring the dread in my gut over leaving her. I can't keep her safe if I've got the entire Twelve coming at me at once and even though I know the kid would side with me... D'Ardo's radio silence has me doubting him. Fuck, I feel guilty even thinking it but he's never gone this long without coming to find me and talk shit about what's happening on our turf.

The lookout over the city is probably the second most dangerous place to be in all of the Bay. The cops know better than to ever come here and the Twelve have enough of them in their pockets that it's become a safe haven for deals and pickups.

The fact that the Chaos Demons picked here to do their trade off's tells me they know nothing about how the Bay works. Too many eyes here, too many transient addicts who don't know the score.

Which is exactly how I know to come and it's how I know to come now.

You see, the Demons send a scout in first. Someone without a record, who knows to keep their mouth shut if they get picked up, and someone who will happily plant a bullet through some fucker's head if they start shit.

Grimm's sons are exactly the right bikers for the job.

Colt stays closer to home though, not sure why. Chance on the other hand, that little fuck loves the thrills of going on runs and is always the first to volunteer to scout. Dumb fuck probably thinks going first makes him important, calling the shots and shit. It doesn't, it's the exact opposite. He's the fucking bait. Throw it out and if you catch a bite you don't lose your shipment.

So I park my car and flash my toolkit at the homeless guys skulking around it so they know exactly how I'll kill them if they touch it. Then I find a good vantage point and throw the hood of my jacket over my head to blend into the shadows a little more, and I wait.

And I wait.

Fuck me, I'm an impatient dick but the wait is fucking terrible, they're definitely late. I check my phone three times to make sure Odie hasn't called before I finally see the headlights come up from the bike. They hit my Mustang and slow down. Perfect. That's exactly what I'm after.

He rolls to a stop in front of my car and climbs off of his rig, leaving it running. He's a tall guy, leaner than I am, but bigger than I was expecting from a seventeen-year-old kid. Helps me feel a little less guilty about what I'm about to do though.

I walk on silent feet behind him while he's busy checking the empty interior of my car out, the rumbling purr of his bike covering any sounds I might make well enough.

The kid doesn't see what's hit him as I pistol whip him hard enough that he drops like a sack of shit, out like a light, kiss your mama.

I don't have time to fuck around, his brothers won't be far behind, so I lug him into my trunk, secure his wrists, tie his own dirty bandana around his mouth like a gag, and shut him in.

Three minutes later I'm back on the highway and heading home to my girl. I pass by the rest of his little crew as they're on their way out of the city and I salute them, fucking dickheads.

If that doesn't put a fucking pep in your step.

Roxas is a fucking peach and helps me carry the fucker down to my basement, securing him to a chair down there without much trouble thanks to his unconscious state. I then give the biker a slap on the back as he jokes about some hot bartender he tag-teamed with Harbin last week. They have a fetish for sharing women and, while I don't get it at all, I can see why it works for them.

The two of them are like brothers. They're never going to be happy finding a woman each because women in their world have a tendency of driving a wedge between men.

At least fucking them together means their friendship stays intact.

I triple check the security alarm is set and check the cameras. Odie is lying on the floor in the living room on the rug, her arms splayed out as if she's trying to fly off somewhere and I take a screenshot of it with my phone like some lovesick asshole but fuck, she looks perfect. Even beat up to hell, misery clinging to her skin, and her bones poking the hell out everywhere she's fucking stunning.

The attitude only makes her hotter.

Then I get my tools all laid out and ready, change into my work clothes, hum under my breath as I prep everything to carve the guy to pieces, slowly, carefully.

I hear a groan and smirk, turning around to meet his squinting eyes as he finally gets a good look at me. Shocks and horror just about sums it up, and then the guarded look snaps into place. Wonder if his daddy taught him that?

"Good of you to finally join me. We have a long night ahead of us."

He doesn't say a word, just stares me down with that unwavering look of his.

Fucking familiar but I just can't place it.

I've never met this kid before, or his big, biker daddy. I know all about them both though. All about their twisted fucking MC trying to take over the fucking world. He might look young but he's one of the heirs to a fucking empire, the kind built in pain and blood, so I feel fucking *nothing* about torturing what I need out of him.

"I'm sure you already know this, Chance, but I'm the Butcher of the Bay and you're not here for a good time. Your daddy is carving up our country into a whole new set of states, boy. We can do this the easy way, where you tell me what I need and then I kill you quick... or we can draw this shit out."

I lean forward in my chair, the cleaver in my hands catching the light and shining it across his face. He doesn't flinch or say a word, the only movement in him is the clenching of his jaw.

A slow smirk stretches across my face. "Gonna make me work for it? Fine by me."

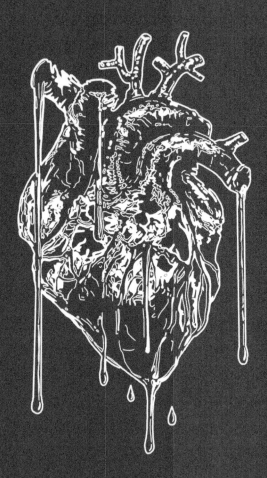

CHAPTER FIFTEEN

ODIE

The monster… Illi, he makes no sense.

I'm expecting this to all be a game to him. I assume he's waiting for my guard to drop and then he'll chain me to the bed, but as the day goes on… nothing.

I'm left alone.

At first I think I'll go out of my mind after all the time I've spend alone during my time with the cartel but things are *very* different here.

The view keeps me busy. Well, that and eating and drinking as much as my stomach will allow me to. My stomach is still tender to the touch and I have to pace myself so I don't feel sick, but I find myself munching on food slowly throughout the day.

The fridge is always full and everything in it is so different to what we have back home. The bread is terrible, but pizza here is amazing. Coke tastes the same but juice is sweetened and pulp free.

After he leaves to go work, and I shudder to think about what it is he's doing, I wander around the house and look for clues about him. Signs that this is all a trap or something else about his life. The only personal item I can find is the childhood photo of his mother in the bedroom.

The bedroom.

I can't find another one. I don't know if he slept in there with me last night or if he slept on the couch but my stomach roils at the idea of what we'll do tonight. That will be when I find out this entire day has been a trick and he'll rape me on those perfect sheets.

I get up and start looking through the cupboards and shelves again.

I find two very important things. I find paper and pens, just the plain type you make notes with but I can draw and sketch with them to help pass the time. I can't figure out how to turn the television on and I don't understand half the slang that has been used around me anyway so that just seems like a futile task.

I also find that he hasn't locked up the knives. I have access to them, presumably for cooking, but I could take one and slip it under my pillow. If he tried to rape me, I would have some chance of fighting him off.

He's huge and skilled at hacking people to pieces, but a weapon has to help me in some little way, right? Even if I can't really do anything with it against him, I could kill myself and stop the next cycle of abuse starting.

I stash the knife under the pillow in the bedroom and then take another one and hide in in the pillows on the couch in case I sleep out here and he comes for me here. I memorize where I've put it so I know to always sleep where it's within reach.

Then I spend a few hours sketching the circling gulls I'd watched during the day while I munch on fruit. Fresh, juicy fruit. I don't think I'll ever get tired of eating fresh food. Even if the bread was good, I don't think I could stomach another slice after my steady diet of moldy pieces. That and alcohol are strictly off the menu.

I watch as the sun rises again, drawing it as best as I can in a single color. I don't want to go to to sleep, too afraid that this has all been a cruel dream and I'll wake on that stinking bed again, but eventually I have to go to bed.

I decide to go back to sleep on the bed.

Illi isn't home yet and when he does arrive, if he wants to sleep, I'll go out to the couch. If he lets me and this hasn't been a ruse. I take another long, hot, soapy shower. Loving every second of it. I have no other clothes to change into but the sweatshirt is still clean enough. I don't usually wear pants to bed but I have no underwear and there's no way I'm sleeping without them. Not ever again, so I put the pants back on and fuss with the thermostat before I climb into bed so I don't overheat.

I'm asleep almost instantly, the demons in my head coming

out to play. I can feel the hands on my skin and the pain of the men raping me. I feel their breath on my face as they laugh and sneer at me, burning me until I scream.

I scream out loud, the sound bouncing around the room and waking me up with a start.

The light switches on.

Oh god.

Oh god, oh god, oh god.

Illi stands in the doorframe, filling it entirely with the width of his chest. He's wearing dark clothes but his hands are cut up and bleeding, the blood running up both of his arms as well.

He's been hurting people, killing them.

The panic left in my system from the nightmare takes ahold of me at the sight of him there. I need to stab myself in the throat right now because he's so much bigger than the other men and clearly so brutal, whatever he wants to do will be ten times worse, oh god.

I'm shaking too hard to do a damn thing.

So I shut my eyes and try to block everything out, but I still hear him exhale and walk into the bathroom. The water cuts on and he washes his hands. Okay, at least he'll be clean. That's a mark up from the cartel. If he breathes on my and smells of alcohol I will definitely vomit but if he's taking the time to... oh, now he's brushing his teeth.

Monsters brush their teeth.

A giggle bubbles in my stomach but I squash it down, this

is no time for hysteria over monster dental hygiene. Curse him, that's what this wonderful day of rest and calm and food has done to me. My guard is down.

"I can see the knife, baby girl."

Oh god.

Oh god, oh god, oh god.

If I open my eyes now I'll do something terrible like cry in front of him and I can't afford to show any weakness. Well, more weakness, so I keep them shut.

"Have you ever held a gun before?"

My eyes fly open, meeting his. He's standing there in shorts and nothing else and, my good god, he's huge. *Huge.* Tattoos cover every inch of his torso and his nipples are pierced, the little silver bars catching the light.

He smirks at me and blood rushes to my cheeks. "It's okay, baby, you can look. But that knife isn't a great idea. I don't want you getting hurt in your sleep, you thrash around some with your demons. I'll give you one of my guns but only if you know how to use it."

I blink at him, forgetting the sight of his chest altogether. "Why would you do that? What if I shoot you?"

He stalks over to the far wall and presses the panel. It pops out to reveal built in shelves that I would have never in a million years guessed were there.

I'm going to check every wall tomorrow while he's gone.

He chuckles at me and says, "There's two of these in the

kitchen as well, have fun finding them, baby girl. You can come look through my shit here if you want? We can do it now but I've gotta tell you, I'm fucking beat."

He knows I was snooping around.

"Do you have cameras on me?"

He looks over his shoulder as he grabs a gun and shuts the panel. "No. I have security over every inch of this place because it's my home and I take care of what's mine. I checked in on you while I was gone to make sure you were doing okay. I was twitchy about leaving you but a job's a job. I had to take care of it."

Oh.

He walks over to me slowly and then holds out the gun. I stare at it like he's trying to hand me a venomous snake. "I've never even touched a gun. It's... it's not safe."

He hums under his breath and step forward to grab the knife, setting it on the small table. "I'll leave that there for you and tomorrow I'll take you downstairs so you can learn the basics about guns. We can switch them out once you're comfortable."

I nod and realize I'm sitting here discussing me learning about how to kill him. He watches me carefully and laughs at the face a pull. "I'm hoping you won't shoot me but I also know I'm not going to give you a reason to shoot me. I want you armed and capable so if something ever happens you will know how to put the guy down. At least enough that I can get to you and finish the job for you."

There he goes again with his crazy talk again. "You will grow tired of me, Illi. That is what all men do, they grow tired of the pretty little women they own."

He frowns at me and stomps back around to the other side of the bed, laying the gun down on his own little table and sliding between the sheets. I throw the sheets off of myself, ready to go find the couch but he stops me.

"I won't touch you. Not until you beg me to, Odie. Lay back and get some sleep. I may not own you, but you're mine to protect so I swear to you, nothing is going to hurt you here."

He won't let me sleep anywhere else.

No matter how hard I push, he stands firm that we'll share the bed. It's so large that he never once touches me, not even when I wake screaming and thrashing about. When that happens he turns the light on and speaks to me, low and commanding until the demons clear and I'm aware of my surroundings.

He tells me all about his plans to kill the cartel.

I think he does it because he thinks I can't remember what he says once I'm awake but those plans of his... they trickle into my dreams until I find myself daydreaming about his cleaver rending them limb from limb.

I want to watch it happen.

I think he's private about his work because he never talks

about it around me, only ever talking about mundane things like the weather or what he's cooking us for dinner.

He does take me downstairs to learn how to use the gun. It's then I learn that we're not in an apartment building like I originally thought, but a large warehouse. The apartment is on the top level but there's two others, the ground floor with the garage filled with expensive cars and the middle floor which has a giant gym and a shooting range.

He owns a lot of weapons.

He laughs at the look I give him when he opens the weapon safe, but I've truly never seen so many different guns, knives, batons, throwing stars, and a wide array of his trademark cleaver.

I can't stop looking at those. He grimaces a little and says, "So you remember the alleyway then?"

I nod. "I do. I was… relieved to see them… dealt with."

He rocks back on his heels like I've struck him. "Fuck. Here I was hoping you wouldn't remember it. I thought you'd end up with more nightmares from that shit."

I look down at my toes. I don't want to speak about the cartel, I don't ever want to think of them, but I don't want him thinking of me as so… breakable.

I'm stronger than my face makes me look.

"I saw a man… get eaten. By dogs. It was… it wasn't very, uh, good. He tried to help me. He warned the men who had taken me that the Butcher, uhm, you were looking for me."

It takes me saying it to remember what that poor man had

been saying. The Butcher was knocking down doors looking for me. No man in the Bay was safe. Illi frowns at me, turning so his entire body faces me. "What man? I had people looking for you but I didn't know any of them were missing?"

Oh no. "I'm so sorry he's dead. It's all my fault—"

He reaches out and carefully takes my hand, the first time he's touched me since he first picked me up at the airport. I don't hate the feeling and that surprises me. I look down at his hand and then squeeze his fingers a little in thanks.

"I'm not ever going to put that on you, baby girl. It's all on me. I picked you up, thinking you were a pro."

I frown at him. I don't know what that means and he blows out a breath before he continues. "I thought you were a hooker, a professional. I took one look at all of this and thought you put yourself up for sale. It happens. Rarely, but it does. You weren't chained up or scared, you stared at me with this fucking fire in your eyes and I made a bad call. A fucking terrible call. I should have asked you, but I was too busy trying to keep my dick calm because you were the most fucking beautiful woman I've ever seen."

Oh.

Well.

That's not at all... what I was expecting. "So you do... want me."

He squeezes my hand again and then lets it go, stepping back. "I want you the normal way people want each other. I want whatever you want to give me, whenever you want to give it."

Right. Okay.

He steers me away from the weapons and then with gentle but firm instruction, he teaches me everything there is to know about guns. How to assemble and break them down, how to clean them, how to shoot them, and how to not shoot yourself. He doesn't ever get frustrated with me, just murmurs praise and carefully adjusts my stance as he needs to. When I get the hang of one he pulls out another and slowly they get bigger and more powerful until I struggle to keep my footing under me when I fire them.

I focus myself entirely on learning this new, life saving skill and I do not let my thoughts come out to play. Not until we've cleaned up and made our way back upstairs, Illi nudging me towards the couch to rest while he gets started on our dinner.

The moment I sit our conversation comes flooding back to me in an all-consuming wave. Panic claws back up my throat because there's no way I can give him... anything. I can't even get in the shower without panicking at the thought of being naked. I triple check the locks on the doors. I can't sleep through the night without waking us both up with my screams.

I don't want to be breakable but in reality, I'm already broken.

I've been safe with Illi for a week when his doctor finally arrives to visit us.

I'm writhing with nerves, terrified I'm pregnant or have some disease, but Illi's entire demeanor changes when he opens the door to the small man.

"I needed you a week ago, where the fuck have you been?"

His voice is cold and harsh, nothing like how he speaks to me. I'm instantly on edge and ready to lock myself in the bathroom until Illi decides to get rid of the man.

The doctor scoffs at him, brushing past and setting his bag down of the coffee table. I scoot away from him and swallow hard.

"Your good friend has started a hunt for something he should never have. I've been sewing his men up but they're coming in faster than I can fix."

I pick at the loose threads on the hem of my sweatshirt. Well, they're Illi's. Everything I wear is his and it doesn't matter how much I ask him, he doesn't want me in anything else.

The room is silent again and I glance up to find Illi staring at me. "What is it?"

His jaw clenches and he struggles with his words for a second. "The Doc is the best in the Bay. The kid... Lips, she swears he did good by her when she needed help with her shit.

If you don't want to see him, I'll take you somewhere else."

I look back over at the doctor. He's rummaging around in his bag like we're not discussing him. "What did she need? Does he know about what happened to me?"

The doctor straightens. "The little Wolf needed help with her reproductive organs and I know that you were sold at auction. She called me herself and asked a favor of me. The little Wolf does not ask for favors, not ever. So here I am. I will examine you, run some tests if you need them, and if there's a baby, I will give you your options."

Illi takes a threatening step forward. "She knows her options and you'll fucking leave them to her."

The doctor doesn't look worried about Illi's threatening stance. "They're her options, not yours. Do you own her? No? Then I will speak to her about them. Men do not own women's organs, not even the Butcher."

Well.

That's kind of sweet and not at all what I was expecting from an illegal doctor. I meet Illi's eye again and nod. "He can... examine me."

The doctor makes me test a urine test to check me for pregnancy. It comes back negative and I almost cry in relief. Then he takes a few vials of my blood. Illi's jaw clenches the whole way through until I think his teeth might just break in his mouth.

When I show the doctor one of the cigar burns he frowns

and clucks at it, snapping on gloves and prodding at it. Most of them are healing, there's only two that are still inflamed and both of them require me to take my clothing off for him to see.

I try to talk my way out of it but the doctor insists, so I have to remove my pants. My hands shake as I do it but Illi's eyes stay on my face and the doctor doesn't touch me, just asks me to move my legs as he needs me to and then lets me know once it's over.

He finds me a different cream and tells Illi what medication I need. He can't write me a script but when I question Illi about it after the doctor leaves he shrugs.

"I can get you anything you need. I have a guy for everything, baby girl."

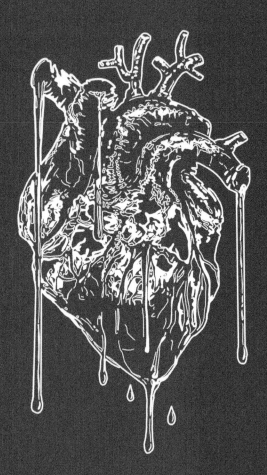

CHAPTER SIXTEEN

ILLI

The biker doesn't talk, no matter how much I carve him up.

I stick to superficial cuts, things that will heal, because I don't want him dying before I get the information I need. I don't want to have to find someone else and leave Odie again.

She's starting to trust me. She talks to me, and gives me these little smiles that fucking tear at my heart, and there's no way I'm going to go out for jobs right now when I can be staying closer to home. Closer to her.

They also sing to my dick but I'm used to the permanent blue-balls now. Fuck, I never knew celibacy would come so fucking easy to me but all I have to do is shut my eyes and think about the cigar burns on the inside of her thighs and my dick just settles the fuck down. The rage in my blood can't fucking take it though.

I might have a fucking aneurysm at twenty-four if this keeps up.

I wake up next to her and for the first time since I got her here she's slept through without screaming the place down. She looks peaceful and happy in her sleep, her face buried in my pillows. She's taken to switching them before I get in here, thinking I haven't noticed but I notice everything about her. Every-fucking-thing.

"You know I can go on like this for days, right? This isn't my first rodeo, I always make my corpses squeal," I say as I wash my tools.

He's covered in blood but he hasn't screamed or begged me to stop once. He's sweating, definitely in excruciating pain, but he's fucking resilient for a guy who can't even drink legally yet.

Kind of makes me pissy I have to kill him, but a job's a job and I'm fucking *great* at what I do.

I leave him chained to the chair and lock up my fridge, catching a quick shower in the bathroom in my gym before heading up to see what my girl is up to.

I unlock the apartment door right as my phone pings in my pocket with another pissy message from the Viper. Fuck, I hate that dickhead.

I need to get him off of my fucking case, and it's clear the biker isn't going to give me shit. Guess I will be heading out for the night.

But first I'm seeing my girl.

I find her on the couch with the Food Network on TV, some show about America's best burgers playing and she's watching that shit like it's the answer to all of her problems.

"I'm just going out on a job, baby girl. Do you have your gun? I'll lock up and have my phone on me. No one is getting past my security, either."

She blinks up at me with a slow smile stretching across those full lips of hers. Fuck, I could just spread her out on the couch right now and feast on her for fucking days but there's still some shadows in those big eyes of hers, I'm not fucking pushing her yet.

I can be patient for now.

It'll be so fucking worth it.

"I have it under my pillow. Should I go get it? Will you be gone a long time?"

Fuck, that breathy voice she uses on me now goes straight to my dick like the best and worst fucking torture. "I'll be back by dawn, baby girl. You're safe here, I just wanted to make sure you have it."

She smiles again, pushing her hair over her shoulder and out of her way as she stares up at me. Fuck. I want to wrap it around my fist as I fuck those lush lips of hers.

Fuck.

I need to leave before she gets an eyeful of what's happening in my jeans and freaks out.

"Call me if you need me. The kid's number is in your phone

as well so hit her up if you need some company."

She nods and focusses back on the TV, sighing as she collapses back into the plush leather cushions. I need to finish this fucking job so I can spend a week at home with her, coaxing her into my bed naked and wet and willing.

Fuck.

I leave before I let my dick get me into trouble. If I followed it where it leads I'd end up in hell. I triple check the alarms and then take the Mustang out for the night, the rumble of the engine soothing to my shot nerves.

I'm going to find the Twelve tonight.

There's a meeting being held by the Fox over some bullshit about the supply levels of drugs to his parties, and he's holding it in one of his regular party venues out in the woods. It's a decent drive away so I call Roxas to get some answers on something that's been grating on me for days.

He answers the phone with his usual brand of confident asshole. "Did you get that boy to squeal like a bitch in heat yet?"

I scoff. "The rumors are true, the Graves are a tough bunch to crack open. I'm not calling about him anyway. Odie told me something and it's grating on me. Have you had any of your men go missing lately?"

He covers the mouthpiece of his cell and mutters something, then I hear Harbin's muffled voice come down the line. "Now's not the time or place. Come see us for a drink later."

Obviously their asshole Prez is around, or one of his most

loyal brothers. Frustrating but I let it go. "I'll come grab a drink after the meeting is over. Is your Prez there or is it his little bitch VP getting pissy about you talking to me."

Roxas chuckles and says, "The second option. Look, I know you're solid but your friend isn't. Things are tightening up around here, if you catch my drift."

I do. "No problem. Just a warning that you need to check all of your guys and make sure they're all accounted for. I'll catch that drink with you later."

I hang up and light a cigarette, needing something to take my mind off of the situation. How far can I let D'Ardo go without calling him out on it? How far can I let him drag me down with him?

I don't fucking know because I've always lived my life by our motto and to know that he's turning his back on it... I'm not sure I can live with myself if I don't try to talk him out of the shit he's getting into.

Starting with the kid.

I burn through three more cigarettes and am ready to spill blood by the time I pull up at the old sawmill where the meeting is being held. There's at least forty cars here already, each member bringing enough of their men to duke it out over who has the biggest dick.

My money is now firmly on the kid.

That backbone of hers is something to be admired and respected, no matter her size or age. Fuck, if D'Ardo didn't want to own her he'd be trying to kill her for it. He can't fucking stand the Crow, and he's the only other member who has the backbone and drive to stand up to D'Ardo's tyrant ways.

Even if he is some bored, rick playboy who wandered into the Bay one day, just for shits and fucking giggles.

I get out of the car but I wait there for the meeting to be over, no point in dealing with the posturing bullshit of these dickheads and their flunkies. I burn through two more cigarettes and all my damn patience before they finally start making their way out of the building.

The Boar and his bikers leave first, glaring at me like I give a fuck about their opinions of me. I give them all a sarcastic as fuck salute and run my hands over my cleavers. The Boar ignores me, the staunch fuck, but his men all follow the movement and grow wary. Yeah, I could throw it at them and my aim is good enough to hit their throats with ease.

Next is the Lynx and her family, her husband holding her arm and ignoring her when she licks her lips at me. Never in my fucking life would I fuck a mobster bitch, not even before I had my girl. The Lynx's pussy probably has teeth, she eats through men that fucking fast.

Hard pass.

The Tiger is useful enough and I nod my head at him with as much respect as I can muster. The Ox is a cunt, so are the Bear and the Fox.

The Viper leaves with D'Ardo and the kid follows behind

them with her head held high and her eyes on her watch. Yup, she has that terrible fucking curfew to get back to. I give her a subtle jerk of my head and she gives me one back when D'Ardo stops eyeballing her to come over to me.

I'm still fucking pissed at the fuck.

But last to come through, the Crow and the Coyote leave together.

I brush past D'Ardo, ignoring his grunt of annoyance, and head toward the tech-wiz dickhead.

Can't ignore me now, asshole.

I fucking hate the Coyote.

Yeah, our business relationship didn't start off the best thanks to D'Ardo fucking him out of hundreds of thousands of dollars, but I had very little to do with that. All I did was go to visit the new blood in the Twelve, I had no idea D'Ardo wanted to play with him.

It was impressive too. D'Ardo had spent months and more money than most Mounties see in their entire lives trying to find the nuclear shit he was after, and yet a few hours of this guy on his computer and bam, there's all the info he needed wrapped up with a bow?

I need that sort of reach in my arsenal.

"Nope. No. I'm not fucking helping you, man. I've got a

strict 'No shithead' policy these days."

The problem is dealing with the little fuck's mouth. "Name your price, I'll pay it in advance."

That gets his attention. The Crow scoffs at us both but keeps walking, his eyes on the Jackal like they always are. Those two circle each other like sharks in bloody water, always wanting to be the biggest predator. I have on occasion been drunk enough around D'Ardo to tell him they should both just whip their dicks out, it would be quicker to just measure them.

He didn't take it well, the moody fuck.

"What if I want seven figures for it? Still gonna pay?" The Coyote says, the smirk on his face making me lose my calm a little.

"The job isn't worth that. Let's say you're not a little cocky asshole and charge fairly, I'll keep the jobs coming. All of them with prepayment."

D'Ardo is outright seething over by my car. I ignore him the say way he was ignoring me while I was looking for my girl. Payback is a bitch and all that.

The Coyote gives me a slow look up and down rubbing the non-existent scuff on his face. The guy definitely couldn't even work up a patchy excuse of a beard and yet here he is trying. "Are you also building a bomb? I don't have the heart to keep helping with that kind of shit."

I give D'Ardo a proper fucking glare at the reminder. "No. No bombs. I need a lead on some biker activity. Nothing to do with the Boar so you're not going to get spanked at your next meeting for it either."

He smirks. "Like I give a fuck about old, dirty bikers. Fine. Come see me. Bring the Wolf, she had a job for me too which is a little strange. She's usually doing everything she can to pretend I don't exist."

I don't fucking blame her.

She already has one psychopath stalking her, she doesn't need any more. Plus this guy would hack into her shit and follow her every move. She doesn't need that going on at all.

D'Ardo stalks over, snapping at his men as he pushes past them, "I'm taking the Wolf to see you tomorrow, you little fucking creep."

Great.

A pissing contest over a kid who doesn't fucking want it. "Get in my car, Coyote. I'll drive you back to your little bunker and you can do my job."

He smirks at D'Ardo and saunters past all his men, perfectly unafraid of them all. D'Ardo turns on me the second he's in the Mustang. "What the fuck are you doing?"

I turn on him and every last one of his pathetic little poser flunkies take a big fucking step back when they get a look at me. "You wanna try that again? Because I'm not one of your men, you don't get a say in what I do, and when your bitch-ass stopped taking my calls I decided I had to find another avenue to get what I need."

His eyes take on that crazed sheen, the one that says we're about to come to blows.

Good.

Fuck him.

"If you've got a problem then you need to say it now, brother, because I have shit to do."

I step away from him, knowing he's got nothing to say to me, and he waits until I'm back at my car before he calls out to me, "You mean you need to go back to the docks and fuck your little whore? You're pretty fucking dense pick some pussy that's already been broken in."

Brother or not, no one will speak about Odie like that in my presence.

No one.

His men don't see me coming, they're bleeding out on the ground before D'Ardo notices I'm not playing around and my cleavers are out. He smirks, thinking this is like every other one of our fights, but he's fucking wrong.

Nothing about this is like old times.

I will gut him for talking about her like that, for turning into a deranged fucking shit without me noticing, for not answering my fucking calls while she was out there being raped and tortured by the cartel he *pays* for drugs.

He takes a swing at me and I duck, ramming my shoulder into his stomach and taking him to the ground in one move. He grunts at me, kneeing me in the ribs but I've always taken pain well. I'm above that shit, slamming my fist into his face until I know I've snapped his fucking teeth.

"Alright, you grumpy fuck, get off me," he wheezes.

I don't listen. I don't stop hitting him until the sweat is running down my face and the Coyote is yelling out at me from the car.

"You know there's cameras here and the Twelve are obligated to come after you if you kill him, right?"

Fuck.

I'm still fucking tempted but maybe this is enough of a reminder to him. Maybe he'll pull what's left of his head in now I've rearranged his face.

He's coughing blood and bleeding down his shirt when I step away, wiping my hands down my own shirt. I don't look at him again as I step away, swooping down to pick up all of the cleavers I've left in his men. One of the guys is still gurgling on his own blood and I stomp on his throat with my heel to finish the job.

I pause with my hand on the handle of my car door, glancing back to where he's still trying to get himself upright. "Listen to me brother, and listen well. You ever say that shit about her again and it'll be your last words. I'm not your fucking pet. You don't own me, you're not my boss. We roll together, that's it. Either you sort your shit out or we're done."

He glares back at me. Well, I think he's glaring. His eyes are all sorts of fucked up now and he's going to struggle driving back down to the docks like that. I could help him, drive him back like the last time we got into it, but I wasn't lying to him. I'm fucking *done*.

I light a cigarette and wish I had a fucking whiskey as I start the Mustang, ignoring the wide eyes the Coyote is giving me.

"I thought you guys were tight?" he finally says as we hit the road.

I keep my eyes on the road, too much wildlife out here at night. "We are. Sometimes he needs a reminder that even the Jackal can't take the Butcher. Sometimes he forgets where he started."

He started in the same group home as me, learning how to fight and kill and survive from me. I wasn't expecting him to become so fucking power hungry though. I guess because I never wanted that shit I never expected him to want it either. Little did I know he'd want to become the king of all things evil while I just wanted a quiet, blood-soaked life with a bombshell to go home to.

Fuck, I want to go home to her.

"So tell me about this job of yours? I can figure out my price and you can wire it across before I get out of the car." the Coyote says, touching the dash and fiddling with the buttons.

"Keep your fucking hands to yourself. I'm craving blood pretty hard right now and there's no cameras here to stop me from gutting you for getting your greasy fingerprints on everything."

He smirks and holds up his phone. "This thing records

everything around me and sends SOS texts when I'm threatened. The Crow is about to call and check up on me thanks to you."

Sure enough the phone rings. He snakes and bullshits his way through it, calling us friends. I could fucking puke at the sound of that shit.

When he hangs up I ask, "How does the Crow's dick feel up your ass? I always assumed you were sucking him off on the sly, wasn't expecting you to be getting reamed as well."

The Coyote laughs. "Man, he'd have to take his fucking suit off for that shit. He doesn't have it in him."

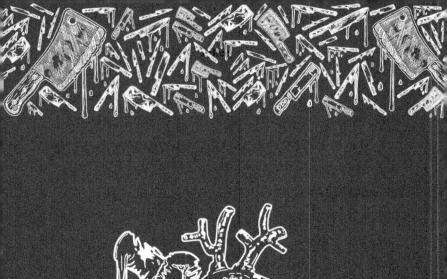

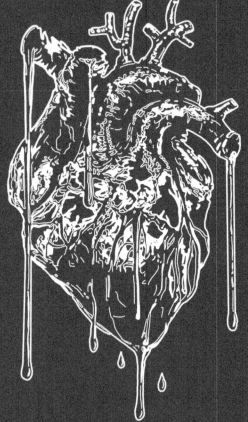

CHAPTER SEVENTEEN

ODIE

I'm bored.

There's only so much wandering around the house and drawing with the same blue pen I can do before my mind craves more.

I try watching the television but nothing holds my attention. I have a cleaning day, scrubbing out the bathroom and then ripping apart the kitchen to clean that as well but the entire apartment is spotless so there isn't any real satisfaction once the job is complete.

I can't take it.

So I watch the food channel for days, soaking in the American ways of cooking and trying to find the perfect recipes for pizzas and burgers. Those are Illi's favorites, whenever we order in he always chooses them. The problem is I hate the bread here so I don't want to use that for my burgers so I make a very rational and not at all impulsive decision.

I learn how to bake my own bread.

The first few days it goes terribly and I worry that Illi will be upset that I'm wasting the supplies in the house. He doesn't, in fact while I'm frowning over the flat mess that my loaf turned into he throws a pen and notepad in front of me and tells me to write a list of whatever I need.

Which is great because I don't want flat bread.

Day four I make the perfect loaf. Illi eats half of it with dinner and I preen like a child.

Day six I make bread rolls and we have burgers. He tells me they're the best he's ever had but I'm sure he's lying. He does eat three of them so… maybe.

Day eight I make sourdough and eat it with cheese and cold meats. It's like being home again and I sit on the living room floor on the rug and cry.

Illi tells me no more bread after that.

I find myself bored again.

I need to find an outlet for all of my energy but asking Illi for anything else seems… wrong. Rude and unappreciative for all he already gives me without asking for anything in return.

So I make pasta.

That lasts two days before Illi declares over dinner, "No more carbs, I'm going to get fat at this rate. Can you learn how to grill meat or make sweet potato fries?"

Bleh. I hate sweet potatoes. He laughs when I scrunch my nose up at him. Though he's right, I'm finally back to my old size now I've been eating all of my attempts at the perfect dinner.

It's on the tip of my tongue to ask him about maybe getting some colored pencils, but I can't. He got home a little after dawn, covered in dirt and blood and grease, and our 'dinner' together is at 8am. I've switched over to his waking hours easily and I find I can't sleep unless he's in the bed with me. Such a strange thing.

"Is there something you need, baby girl?"

Damn him. He can read me so easily and yet I struggle to ever know what's going on in his head. I can't ask him for anything, but maybe I can find another way. "I was wondering if we could go out today, to find me some... ah, *employment*. I know you said it's not safe here, but maybe I could go somewhere it is safe."

He sets his fork down with a frown. "You want a job? What do you want to do?"

I smile at him, nervous and trying to hide it. "I need some money. I found a place in the nicer area of the Bay, over by—"

"What do you need money for?" He cuts me off, drinking his beer. We've discovered beer doesn't have the same effect on my stomach that the harder liquors do so he's switched to one of those with dinner.

I frown and poke at my food. "I would like to buy something. This *employment*, it is temporary. It's in a little cafe and I could make tips until I have enough money for what I need and then I can come home."

His lip twitches upward when I say the word home but he still looks angry.

"Baby girl, whatever you need, I will give you. Anything. No getting a fucking job just to buy something you want. Tell me, I'll have it here in under an hour."

I clear my throat and swirl my fork in the pasta. "I don't want to inconvenience you any further. You have already done so much for me. I can work, I do not want to be a burden to you any further."

He carefully sets his beer down on the table and stalks over to where I sit at the other end, looming over me. My heart skips a beat but I feel no fear. He still looks the same as the first day I met him, a monster made of all muscle and tattoos, but I know now that looks are deceiving and he might be a killer but he's no monster to me.

He takes my hand and tugs me until I stand up, then he catches my cheek in his big palm and cradles my face. I stare up at him and, for the first time since I arrived in America, I feel the flutters of arousal in my stomach. It scares me.

He leans down like he's going to kiss me, but instead he murmurs, "What do you need, baby? I'm your man, I'll get you whatever you need. That's how this is going to go. Money is not an issue for us, baby girl. I'm good at what I do."

I know it's not a real issue. I have seen the obscene amount of money hidden in the panels that slide away on the walls, but I'm still uncomfortable having him buy me things.

He's already done so much for me and all I do for him is... bake.

His eyes narrow into a stern look and I finally tell him, "I would like some paint and canvases and a few brushes. I miss painting, I want to do a portrait of some of your tattoos. They keep dancing in my head while I try to sleep."

I didn't mean to say so much, definitely not the part about his tattoos but once the truth starts to come out all of the details follow it.

His thumb runs over my cheek gently and then he steps away from me. "Grab a coat, baby. We'll go shopping for everything you need. Everything, we'll bring the whole fucking store back home if that's what you want."

A quiet laugh spills out of me. "I don't need much, *mon monstre*."

Mon monstre.

My monster.

A blush takes over my cheeks and I step away from him, whirling towards the coat rack to find something that will work for me to leave the apartment. Butterflies swell in my chest and I feel giddy, it's such a strange sensation.

"Grab the black one, baby girl. We're taking the beamer."

Illi holds my hand the entire way down the stairs and helps me into the car as if I am a delicate lady and not about to leave the house wearing all of his clothes. I look ridiculous but his eyes follow me as if I'm wearing Chanel and dripping in diamonds.

We take out the BMW, the same one he picked me up from the airport in, though he winces as he helps me in. "It's the safest car and has the most trunk space. I'll replace it if you want me to, baby girl."

I shake my head at him. That memory is like an old wound. Something that hurts if I fuss with it but the hurt is about how close I was to being safe. How close we both were at avoiding all of the pain and mess that came because I didn't speak up and he made assumptions.

I quite like the car.

It is a very smooth ride and the windows are tinted so dark no one can see in. Once we're on the road Illi sets his hand on my knee in-between gear changes, squeezing a little each time before he lets go.

The sun starts to shine through the windows, even with the tinting it feels amazing. I smile up at it. "I've never felt so much… peace before. Thank you for that, Illi. Thank you for taking such good care of me."

He smiles a little and then a little frown forms between his

dutifully as he walks around and opens my door. He watches everyone on the streets like they're armed and about to start shooting at me. I don't know enough about this city to know if he's being overprotective, so I tuck myself into his side and let him glare out at everyone.

The warmth of his body soaks through my clothes and into my skin, settling into my bones like a brand. I'm addicted to being with him, having him this close to me and sheltering my body with his. He has become vital to me and my survival, something to anchor myself to in this crazy world I've been dropped in but... I don't think I'd choose anything else. I think he's truly what I want for myself.

It's wonderful and terrifying.

When we walk into the store it's clear Illi isn't here to find the basics because he doesn't just buy me the bare essentials I need to start painting again. He buys me an easel, the finest brushes in an array of sizes, oil paints in every color and that my father would never have dreamt to buy me back home. He buys me everything and doesn't once ask questions or raise a brow. If I glance at something, it goes into the shopping cart.

The shop assistant follows us around with a fine sheen of sweat over his brow, wringing his hands and jumping every time one of us addresses him. Illi holds my hand sweetly, gently as if he's afraid of crushing it in his big hands, and I feel... safe.

I startle a little at the total once everything is rung up but Illi doesn't hesitate in handing his card over.

He leans down to whisper in my ear, "Last chance, baby girl, anything else you need? You sure you don't want some pencils or something? The guy said you might want them for... something."

I smile and stare up at him, squeezing his hand. "I have everything I need right here."

As soon as the words leave my lips I know what I really mean. I don't ever want to leave him. Not now and not ever. He might not be a *good* man but he's the best man I have ever known and I don't think I will ever find someone better.

He stares down at me and I frown back at him, murmuring, "*Mon monstre?*"

He grabs our bags in one hand and tugs me out of the store with the other, ignoring the looks the assistant gives us. I tuck my hair behind my ear, sure that I look like a mess, and he growls as he untucks it.

"You look beautiful, even fucking better because you're wearing my coat. Don't get self-conscious just because that dick can't keep his fucking eyeballs to himself. It's me he's freaking out over anyway."

I nod and tuck myself in closer to his big body. He curves around me like a shield and walks me out to his car, opening the door and helping me in like a true gentleman.

I spend the entire drive back to the apartments grinning and laughing with excitement, listening to all of the little stories Illi has about the city he claims to hate but knows so intimately.

We get back to the apartment and he refuses to let me carry anything, directing me back up the stairs and to grab the door for him while he carries everything up with ease.

There's a bumping noise below our feet and I startle, looking over at Illi. "Is there something under us here? A tunnel or something people can get into the building with?"

He frowns down at the ground and then glances back up to me. "It's okay, baby girl. My workshop is downstairs. Something must have fallen over. I'll get you set up and then I'll go check it out. Grab the door, baby."

I do, trusting him implicitly.

He walks everything into the living room, setting it down on the couch with care. I grin at him, excited about spending the day painting and sketching. "Is there another room I can paint in? It will be very messy to have here."

He shrugs, getting to work setting up the easel and positioning it so I'm looking out over the water. He knows exactly where I like to sit and the exact spot that catches the afternoon sun. I blush when I realize just how much he watches me, the care he takes in giving me space to lay around and deal with my demons. He knows just when I need my quiet, when I need to lay there and process exactly what has happened to me.

I also know that he doesn't want to talk to me until after he's washed his hands. Sometimes not until he's had a shower, on the mornings he comes home covered almost entirely in blood.

He's too good to me.

"Is this everything, baby girl? If the store was missing anything we can order it for you. Anything."

I smile and start to open up the paints, squeezing colors out onto the palettes and mixing them. "This is perfect, *mon monstre*. Thank you."

He leans forward to kiss my forehead, his hand cupping the back of my head gently. Then he steps away, leaving me to my work.

I lose all sense of time but in the best way possible.

When I finally come back to my body, my painting is done. The first sunrise I had seen here at the apartment now shining back at me in an array of wet oils. Tears fill my eyes as I stare at it, my eyelids drooping. I haven't slept for hours and hours, *mon monstre* will be up soon.

I glance back and find him sleeping on the couch, his arm behind his head angling him so I know he fell asleep watching me paint.

I stare at him, burning the image of him sleeping there into my brain to paint later and then… then I'm brave.

I crawl into his arms and fall asleep with him, comfortable even when he pulls me in close.

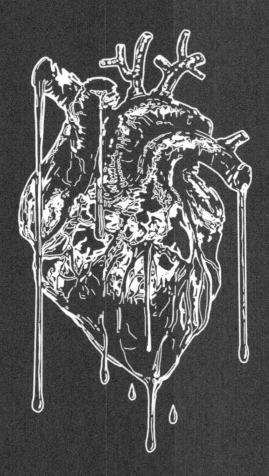

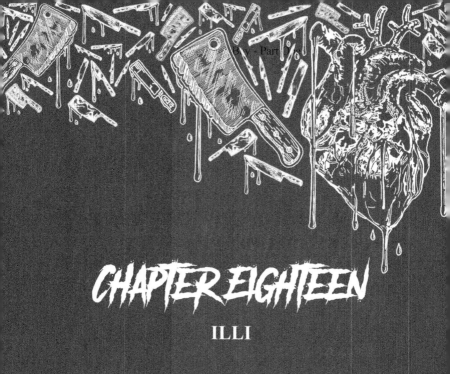

CHAPTER EIGHTEEN

ILLI

I get the call from D'Ardo a week after I'd beat the shit out of him.

My house reeks of paint all the time and I'm fucking gleeful about it. I never knew Odie was an artist. I mean, she was always doodling on scraps of paper and the backs of her hands, but it's not until I see that sunrise that I know she's an artist and a fucking talented one at that.

She paints during her every waking hour and I swear to fucking god, it's like watching the life slowly drain back into her. She laughs and smiles, jokes with me, and dances around in the mornings before she gets to work.

I know we can't stay in the docks forever, this isn't the right place for a girl like her to live, but now I have a plan.

I'm building her some big fucking mansion with an art

237

room, something with a view that she'll love and paint. We'll be fucking happy there. She's going to be happy there and I'll keep the warehouse for my work.

I just have to go deal with this dickhead first.

Just so long as he's got his head out of his ass. I kiss Odie on the cheek as I leave, the giggle she gives me sends blood to my dick, and I practically fucking skip down the stairs to my car. I check the guy in the basement, still breathing, and because I'm in such a fucking great mood I give the fucker some water.

What can I say; I'm a fucking saint, man.

I get into the car, ready to hunt down the lead the Coyote had given me, when D'Ardo's call comes through.

"I have a job for you, if you're interested. Something quick and easy."

I rev the engine as I take off in my Mustang, a cigarette lit between my lips. "So you're not going to be a dick anymore, then? You've decided to remember I'm your oldest and most loyal friend?"

He grunts down the line at me. "You could have reminded me without shattering my cheekbone, asshole. I've cut three of my men apart just this morning for trying to make a joke about it."

Serves him right. "What's the job then, dickhead? I'm on my way to something but I might be able to squeeze you in."

He chuckles under his breath. "A pick up. I've already told the guy you're coming so he's hiding under a fucking rock for you. You like them pissing themselves at the sight of you, don't you Butcher?"

I do but I don't like the way he's saying that. "What's the guy done?"

He laughs and then I hear the grunt as his face hurts. Good. "He's helping me out with a project. Nothing big, he might not even be the guy I need but it's worth a shot. I'll pay you double your last fee, take it as my apology for talking about your... new woman."

The pause feels disrespectful but... double the fee... the mansion I'm going to build Odie is half paid for with that alone. "Sure. Send me the details and I'll stop by with him later."

I hang up and head out to the fishing district, farther up the coast. The streets here are cleaner, less working and the homeless population thins out the further away from the slums you get.

I park my car up and head out to find a good vantage spot.

The Viper needs to know all about the Chaos Demons' business in the Bay. They're originally from Texas, though they have a few chapters dotted around the country, they never get this close to the Bay normally. The shipments that I caught Chance on are a new deal, something they're only been doing the last few months, and they've been flying under the radar mostly. Whatever the Viper thinks they're up to, it's big.

He's paid a lot of money to me to chance up leads.

Three mansions worth of money over the last few weeks, more than I usually make from him in the fights. I haven't even thought about going to one lately, nothing interests me more than the chase for Odie's trust and affection. The drive to get her to want me like I do her.

I'm going to own her in all of the ways you can't buy at the auction and fuck me, it's going to taste so fucking sweet.

I can't think about it while I'm working or I'll find myself face-to-face with a Demon and a rock hard dick. Bad combination.

It's been too fucking long with these blue balls on mine.

Worth it.

I stand in the shadows and wait, looking out at the giant fishing boats as they start to come alive. They usually head out just after midnight and the time is almost here.

I light another cigarette as I wait and I hear the roar of the motorcycles as they descend down into the lot. Fuck, there must be forty bikers here, an impossible number to slip through the city unnoticed.

I hold my breath, stub out the cigarette and wait until they've parked up. Then I see it; there are Unseen amongst the Demons.

Traitors.

Well, well, well, I wonder if the Boar knows about this shit going down in his city with his men? I stand there and keep watch, only picking up bits and pieces of the conversation but enough that I know exactly what the Demons are up to.

The war with the Unseen has been taken to a whole new level.

I stand there for three hours, listening in and taking in as many faces as I can. There's a lot I can tell the Viper about his businesses but there's a helluva lot more I can sell to the Boar.

A lot I can tell Roxas and Harbin to keep them out of the firing line too.

When it's finally safe to leave without being spotted I leave, checking the info D'Ardo sent through and swinging past the office buildings to pick this terrified guy up for him.

He's unconscious and tied up in my trunk in minutes.

He's a nerdy looking guy, all glasses and cheap suits. Fuck knows what D'Ardo could possibly get from him. Probably a chemist, someone to help out with his solvent houses. The cartel have been bringing meth into the country in fuel tanks, easy to hide from border control, then the shipment goes to the solvent houses to be processed and packaged for sale. D'Ardo has eight of them set up around the city, spread out enough that if one of them gets busted by some rookie cop who doesn't know any better, the whole operation doesn't go down at once.

The guy wakes up in my trunk on the way over and starts yelling and thumping around. If he kicks the taillights out I'll fucking gut him. I park up next to D'Ardo's car for an easy transfer over and shrug my leather jacket on now the nights are starting to cool down. I want to be in and out, the beautifull girl waiting back home for me at the front of my mind, but I need to get a read on D'Ardo before I go.

Is he really back in his box or am I going to have to remind him?

The Dive is busy tonight, more gangsters and bikers than I've seen for a while. Makes me twitchy, especially when I see a few of the rats who were just out meeting the Demons. Nothing fucking worse than a rat.

I find D'Ardo in the back at one of the private tables, drinking and watching the fights. The guys in the cage are total amateurs, fucking pathetic.

He smirks at me and waves a full glass of whiskey at me. "Did you find the guy?"

I grab the glass and knock it back in one go, motioning for the bartender to bring me another. "Of course I did, getting him here was fucking nothing. Where's my money?"

He chuckles under his breath, his eyes staying on the fight, and I struggle to keep my cool. The arrogance coming off of him is still a palpable thing and it grates on me.

He'll always be the skinny, desperate kid I met in foster care to me.

"The bags are under the table. Where did you leave him? I'll get him picked up."

I check it's really there first, because I know just how fucking bad *the Jackal* really is at paying his dues, and once I see the loaded duffles I jerk my thumb at the back loading docks. Two of D'Ardo's dumbass flunkies head over to collect the nerd from where he's gagged and bound in the trunk of my car.

I drink the second glass while I watch the last of the fight, one of the guys tapping out way too fucking quickly for my taste. I scoff at the sight, turning on my heel to get the fuck out of here and back to my place.

D'Ardo throws his arm out in my direction, something he does when he's had too much to drink. "Stay. One more drink won't hurt, or have you turned into a pussy now you have one in your house?"

My jaw clenches but I take a seat. How the fuck he knows about her, I have no idea but I'm going to gut whoever it was that told him... unless it was the kid. She would have only done it to stop one of his jealous rages and I wouldn't blame her for it.

I drink one last drink with him, certain it's the last one we'll have as friends. He's not getting that I'm not his to lord over.

I'm the Butcher of the fucking Bay, and I'd rather gut him than be inducted by him.

The Viper insists on having his information in person.

It was bad enough getting stuck at the Dive with D'Ardo, but now being called into his strip club... couldn't get any fucking worse.

I leave Odie happily cooking and singing under her breath, paint still streaking her arms and her hair. She looks fucking edible and as soon as I have this job out of the way I can focus on her, namely getting her comfortable with being under me because I need to worship her skin with my tongue, eat her out until she's screaming my name, and then squeezing my cock with her pussy as she comes all over me.

That's exactly what I fucking need.

The strip joint is called New Blood and it's the only one on the south side. D'Ardo has put the other two out of business earlier. He took out the owners and every time someone thinks about opening a new one he takes them out too.

The moment I step into the darkened building and smell the desperation in the air I want to fucking leave. I'd rather take on the entire Chaos Demons MC than watch these girls shake their asses on stage. A new song starts and the fresh meat saunters out on stage, her body is amazing but the dead look in her eye is fucking telling. I wonder how much coke D'Ardo has her on to get her to swing her hips on stage like that, I wonder just how much it takes to keep the girls pliable and blank at all times.

He's mastered the dosage.

"Johnny-boy, take a seat and join us."

I shouldn't have fucking come.

I'm about to rearrange his face all-the-fuck-over again. The Viper lifts a glass at me from where he's getting a lap dance… no, wait, the stripper is naked and bouncing on his dick. There are private rooms for that shit but I suppose it's a night for pissing me the fuck off. D'Ardo is sitting at the other end of the booth and, fuck me, the kid is tucked in next to him.

I fucking hate him.

I'm going to fucking kill him for bringing her here. For wanting to be the king of the Bay so fucking bad he's willing to sell his soul and our friendship.

I never had those ambitions. I just want to be left alone to drink, fuck, and kill how I want. I want a bank account that's fat enough that I never have to think about money again.

I want the French siren at home tucked up in my bed to belong to me forever because I feel like she's branded my fucking soul without asking for my permission and I need to know I have the same hold over her.

I don't want to be sitting here in some fucking strip club with a posing dickhead who wants to push all my fucking buttons to try to get me to snap.

If I snap I'm going to hack him into pieces.

I can't get the kid mixed up in that shit.

I sit, raise my hand for a glass of whiskey then change my mind and ask for two, sliding one over to the kid with a look. She takes it with a nod, not looking my way. No, couldn't do that with D'Ardo right there. He'd happily break her open right now if he thought I was trying to get in his way.

The Viper grunts and gets the girl off of his lap, zipping his dick away with the kid sitting right the fuck there. Pisses me off more than it probably should but I think this is as close as I'll get to a sister and she's, what, fourteen?

Fucking dickhead, the lot of them.

"I heard you have my information, Butcher. Took you long

enough."

I turn my head, very slowly, until I'm looking at him. "You wanna rephrase that? I'm not in the best mood."

The Viper grins at me, completely unfazed. Maybe when he nutted in that stripper his brain went with it. "I heard you're not getting any action from that whore. Must be rough, going all in for one chick is a bad idea."

My eyes flick over to D'Ardo and he shrugs at me. "If you don't want the Bay knowing about her you probably shouldn't kick down every fucking cartel door. A lot of people are pissed off at you, man."

I clench my jaw, trying to decide just how far I'm willing to go tonight. The kid finishes the drink and pushes the glass away from herself. Her hand goes down to rest in her pocket, she's signaling she's ready for when I kick off.

I'm not doing it with her here.

"If you want the Demons out of the Bay you need to go to the Boar. Half his men are jumping ship. You'll never be clear unless he cleans house. That's it. That's all you're getting from me. Wolf, I'll drive you home. Go get in the Mustang."

D'Ardo's eyes flare at me but the kid follows my lead, grabbing the keys from my outstretched hand without a word. I ignore him completely, my attention on the Viper.

"How are you going to explain it?" I say.

He frowns at me. "Explain what? I'll tell the Boar to sort his MC out. You did good work, the money is in the bag."

"No, I meant how are you going to explain your missing fingers?"

He frowns at me but the cleaver is already out of it's sheath on my thigh and I feel nothing but pure fucking satisfaction as I take off the last two fingers on his hand. He screams and snatches his hand away, leaving behind the ring finger and the pinky I've just removed for him.

I lean over and grab the digits, dropping them into my pocket, and then swoop under the table to grab my payment. "These are mine now. If you ever talk about my woman like that again, I will take on the entire institution of the Twelve just for the satisfaction of gutting you like the cunt you are. Are we clear?"

The Viper is sweating and muttering curses about me under his breath but I ignore it entirely. Like I give a fuck about this piece of shit.

I turn and walk out. He calls out to me, "You'll never fight in my cages again, Butcher. Fucking never."

I raise a finger at him, just so he's really clear on how much I do not give a fuck about his cage fights, and head outside to take the kid home. I get my money into the trunk of my car before I'm hit in the head with a baseball bat.

It's a decent strike and I'm dazed but my height works in my favor and I'm not knocked out, just falling onto the back of my car. I manage to catch myself but I'm going to fucking feel that later.

I push myself up and turn to find D'Ardo grinning at me, though it slides right off when he sees me still standing. Yeah, fucker. Even with a baseball bat you can't fucking take me.

"You spineless little fuck!"

He rushes at me and I let him take the first swing, clearly I'm feeling fucking charitable, but the second one doesn't land. He might have won the Game to become the Jackal but none of the men he faced were anything like me.

I have him flat on the ground in under a minute.

I only stop strangling the little fuck because the kid opens the car door and knocks me out of my rage.

"You know it'll be all sort of hell to pay if you kill him, right? Curfew is in ten minutes."

I land one last punch, feeling his jaw snap under my fist. I stand and think about curb-stomping the cunt but something stops me. Call it nostalgia but I just fucking hesitate, then I turn away and head back to my car.

Matteo hacks up a lung, spitting blood on the sidewalk. "Just remember, if she wasn't born in the Bay, then she doesn't understand this life. How could an outsider ever really get the Butcher?"

I smirk at him, the utter fucking dickhead. He has no idea how sharp my baby girl's teeth really are or how perfect she is for me. Fuck, if I were a man who entertained the idea of religion I'd think she was made just for me.

If there is a god, he isn't welcome in the Bay.

I drop the kid off at the group home, watching as she walks in as if she actually needs me to. My phone starts going off in my pocket, a shrill screeching noise until my ringtone, and my stomach drops.

The alarm.

Someone is in my fucking house with Odie.

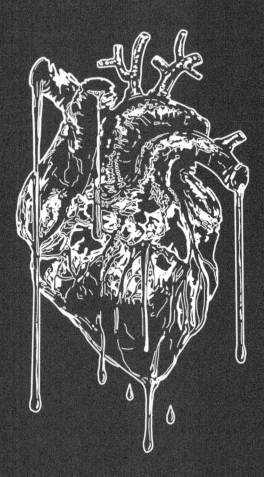

CHAPTER NINETEEN

ODIE

I decide to paint Illi.

Maybe it's curiosity, maybe it's infatuation, but I can't stop thinking about his lips when he grins at me, or his eyes when he watches me so intently while we eat together, or the little tattoo he has under his eye. There's so much of him that I'm curious about, I feel as though I'm standing on the edge of… something. Something important, something that will change who I am as a person. I don't know if I'm ready for that yet, but painting him seems like the best way to work through those feelings. I lose myself in the strokes, mixing colors and working up the layers over and over until he starts to come off of the canvas, a monster that owns the parts of me only I can give away.

I'm so engrossed in what I'm doing that I don't hear a thing until the front door opens and the alarm stops beeping and starts wailing like a siren.

It's not *mon monstre*.

It's not Lips or the doctor.

I stumble away from my canvas, knocking it to the ground as I scramble away. I know nothing about how to protect myself physically. Except then I remember the gun.

The gun.

I bolt into the bedroom, my heart in my throat and my hands a shaking mess, but I get a hold of the gun and whirl around, expecting the man to be chasing me but he isn't there. I creep forward, realizing too late that I've left my phone behind and praying Illi is on his way home to me. I make it to the door, the gun aimed out and my arm only trembling a little. I'm not scared of shooting the intruder. I'm scared I'll miss.

The man is still standing at the front door, swaying a little but a scowl of his face.

I do not recognize him but he's covered in blood and wounds, definitely the result of torture. He looks me over, and my throat closes over as the dread settles over me.

I'll turn the gun on myself before I'll let him take me.

The sway gets worse until he stumbles forward and has to catch himself on the kitchen counter. I raise the gun a little higher, aiming for his chest.

He puts one hand up. "Where's the Butcher? Is this his place?"

I shake my head, words too much for me right now. The

alarm is still loud in our ears and I edge along the wall until I can get to my phone.

His eyes drop down to the phone as I grab it. "Look, I just want to get out of here. Are you... have you been kidnapped? I can get you out of here."

I dial Illi's phone number and he picks up instantly, "Tell me you have your gun, baby girl. Tell me you've got it and the door is locked."

"I have it. There's a man here and he's covered in blood. I can... shoot him?" I don't know why but I need him to tell me to do it.

He swears viciously down the phone. "Keep your gun raised and if he takes a step towards you fill him with lead, baby girl. I'm three minutes away. Stay on the phone, tell Chance I'll gut him if he tries anything."

The man watches me carefully, his eyes shrewd as he searches me. I'm wearing one of Illi's shirts with a bigger neckline than usual, and a pair of his sweatpants, the waistband pulled in tight and the legs rolled up so I don't trip on them.

My arms are bare and the burn marks are visible.

I forget they're there now most of the time. Illi doesn't ever look at them or comment, he treats me like a queen. It's hard to be reminded like this about how visible my damage really is.

"Fuck, what has he done to you? Everyone in this fucking city is a rapist psychopath. I'll get you out of here, find you a shelter or something, in another city that isn't Mounts *fucking*

Bay. What's your name?"

My arm falters a little and the phone slips away from my ear. "You think it's the Butcher? No. He saved me. He is good to me. A good man."

He chokes on his laugh and sweeps a hand down the front of his body. "Would a good man do this, sweetheart? He's paid to make people bleed for information. He takes money to cut people up. He didn't become the Butcher for rescuing women."

But I already know all of this and my life has taught me an important lesson; trust those who treat you well, not those who are supposed to love you.

Illi speaks in my ear and I lift the phone up. "Don't stop him from leaving, baby girl. Just keep your ass in the apartment and that gun in your hand. I'll hunt him down later. Let him go."

Stupidly, I nod. Then I catch myself and say to Chance, "The Butcher is on his way home and he's not happy that you are speaking to me. He knows I do not want to speak to any man other than him ever again."

He nods and keeps his hands up, backing out slowly. Once the door is shut behind him I force myself to stand and watch the security screen until he's off of the property. It's only a matter of seconds between him leaving and Illi arriving back home.

He doesn't chase after his escaping prisoner.

No.

He tears out of his car and takes to the staircase with such speed that I think his feet only touch the ground twice between the ground floor and the landing outside the apartment door. He screams out my name as the door nearly comes off of it's hinges as he bursts into the room.

"Did he touch you? I'm going after him right now, tell me what he did to you?" he says as he bundles me into his arms roughly.

He doesn't usually touch me with such urgency and now he's pressing me into every line of his hard body. I can't breathe but I'm not scared.

"He didn't touch me. He was in a lot of pain and disoriented. I think he was looking for you and when he saw me he thought you were keeping me here against my will. He tried to talk me into leaving with him."

His arms tighten around me. "Fucking piece of shit, I'll gut him."

I wrap my arms around his waist and stop him from moving away. "No, he was trying to help me. He offered to get me out of the Bay, to some other city. He thought you had done... this."

When I motion at the burns on my arms he grunts out a reply that is more displeased sounds than actual words. I rub my face on his chest, taking in the masculine scent of him and happy until I smell the liquor.

I lurch backwards, slapping a hand over my mouth but the bile doesn't stop coming and I have to scramble to the kitchen sink to empty my stomach.

Illi doesn't offer any help, just stands there looking at me like I've punched him. "I'm sorry."

He shakes his head and turns on his heel. "Fuck, don't apologize. You can't help that my touch makes you sick. We'll get past it."

The way he won't show me his face has me questioning if he even believes himself, but I have to fix it. I have to set him straight. "It's not your touch. It's the alcohol. I can't—I can't smell the alcohol on your breath. It was... it was always present when they would... come to me."

He swears viciously under his breath and stalks off into the bedroom. I hear the shower start and then I move to close the apartment door, keying in the alarm code to reset it. The last thing this night needs is that man coming back to try to 'rescue me' or kill Illi and actually catching us off-guard.

I wonder if we'll ever live here without being on alert.

I wonder if Illi would ever move.

I don't want to go back to France though. I can't imagine ever taking this man back there and showing him the hollow pretense that was my life. He lives an honest life. What you see is what you get.

My parents had always played pretend. Pretend they're rich and not rotten to the core. Pretend they were of fine breeding when really they were drug dealers and pretenders. Pretending they loved me.

Pretending they even cared a little.

I move over to where my easel is on the ground and find my

painting ruined... worse, there's paint all over the rug and the pristine, polished floor. My lip trembles and I do my best not to cry but the adrenaline leaves me in a rush and I fall to my knees in the paint and sob.

"Baby girl, you need to stop crying because I'm about to go bleed out half the Bay for you. I'll find that biker piece of shit and carve him up."

I look up and find Illi crouched over me, his sleep shorts on and no shirt covering his impressive chest. "I don't want you to find him. He wasn't bad, he wanted to help me."

He scoffs, grabbing one of my elbows to pick me up out of the mess of paint and tears I'm in. He sits me on the couch, not caring at all that I'm ruining the leather, and moves to the kitchen to grab me a wet cloth. The thought that I'm destroying his house and all of the lovely furniture he's picked out... it makes the tears come all over again.

"You need to stop crying. I can't control myself when you start up and if you don't want me chasing after Chance right the fuck now, you need to stop."

I take the wet cloth and scrub at my face with it, spreading the paint around some more. "I can't help it. I was... I was scared that he might want to take me. Then I saw my painting and it just—it pushed me over the edge of my control. Maybe I was due for a cry. Girls need it sometimes."

He nods and walks over to the mess of my canvas, the image no longer recognizable, and picks it up. He holds it out, moving it a little this way and that, before putting it back on the easel. "Was this me? Were you painting me, baby girl?"

I clear my throat and swipe the cloth over my face one last time. "Yes. I paint things to work through feelings. I'll need to paint you all over again now I have to work through this too."

He turns on his heel. "What about this? The part where I told you to shoot the dickhead if he touched you? The part where I came home smelling like the cartel did? Which part?"

I hold his eyes, no matter how much I'd like to look away. "The part where you locked a man in your basement and tortured him. The part where that's not something a good man would do and yet I don't care. I trust you did it for the right reasons."

His eyes flash, his spine snapping straight as he stalks back over to the couch. I do my best not to cower under his height and the sheer size of him. I roll my shoulders back and meet his eye, the pride there shining through. It makes no sense but nothing about this man ever does.

"I never once said I'm not a bad man, baby girl. I do a lot of bad things but when I said I'll never hurt you, that you never have to fear me, I meant it. I'm a good man to you and you alone. I don't give a fuck about anyone else."

Curse my broken soul but it takes everything in me not to curl into him, to take the intimacy he's clearly offering me. "I understand that, but that man… he offered me sanctuary. I could see the sincerity when he saw the burns on my arms. Could you not let him go, for me? Has he hurt you in some other way?"

He chuckles under his breath, leaning in until I can feel the heat of his body against mine. "Baby girl, no one hurts me. He's a job, nothing more. I got what I needed and we can let him go. He might come back for us someday though, baby girl. His daddy is a big player and if I don't go after him it could burn us later."

I nod and chew on my lip, craving his touch and fearing it at the same time. I hate this. I hate what's been done to me, that I can't even give him what I want to.

He sees this on my face and backs up.

My temper flares out of nowhere, frustration and pent up anger unleashing on the one person who doesn't deserve it.

"I don't want to be treated like fucking glass!" I hiss at him, furious that tears start welling up in my eyes again. I'm so angry that I've been so badly broken that I could *scream*.

He holds his hands up where I can see them but his eyes are fierce as he takes me in. "I'm treating you like you're important to me because you are. I can fucking wait. I can wait for-fucking-ever if I have to because I'm not going to be the next guy to fucking hurt you. I'm going to make sure that I'm it for you for the rest of my fucking life. I'm going to love you and protect you and fucking carve up anyone that tries to get close to you. I'm going to put a baby in your belly and we're going to be so fucking happy together. I'll do anything to make sure you're here and mine, Odie, fucking *anything*."

The trembling in my arms gets worse and the tears start to fall. "You shouldn't want me. How can you want me like that? I can't be the seductive woman you want, that woman is dead."

He walks over to the fridge and grabs a couple of beers, offering me one and shrugging when I wave him off. I want to break something. I want to find my father and scratch his eyes out, spit on him, break his bones for doing this to me. Training me to be a *good girl* who obeys his orders and lays there in silence while she's raped.

That's not who I want to be!

"Do it. I can see the fire, baby, let it out."

My temper is unbelievable and now I want to claw his eyes out too. I stand up, just barely stopping myself from stamping my foot like a petulant child. "Stop fucking calling me *baby*! I am not *yours*. How can I be when I can't stand the thought of being touched? I will not have sex with you or any other man willingly, I know it! And I cannot sit around in this apartment waiting for you to decide what to do with me. You'll get bored of playing house with a broken woman. How can you not?"

His eyes flare and burn into my skin with their intensity. "Oh yeah? What else, Odette? Tell me what else will and won't be happening here."

My lip trembles. His voice is pitched low and dark but he doesn't look angry. He sets the beer down on the coffee table and moves to stand in front of me again. I'm tall for a woman, curvy in the right places, and yet I look tiny compared to him.

"I'm not sitting on a pedestal for you to show off to your friends. I'm not something for you to possess."

He nods at me, one of his shoulders lifting into a half shrug. "Sure. That's all perfectly fine. You wanna hear my list of demands?"

My legs nearly give out on me but by sheer will alone I keep myself upright. I wave my hand dismissively, like this is a reasonable conversation and not a screaming match between a broken woman and the monster that guards her. "Go on."

His lips stretch into a smirk. "You already know what I want. You're not going anywhere without me knowing about it and keeping you safe. This is Mounts Bay, it's not a safe place for anyone, let alone a fucking knock-out like you. You're sleeping in my bed, period. I won't touch you until you beg me to do it and I promise you, Odette, you're going to fucking beg. You're not going to look at any other man. You're going to stay alive and right here in my apartment and you're going to try to find some joy or zen or some shit. You're going to stop crying over shit that doesn't matter, you're going to paint and bake and fucking destroy my apartment for all I care. They're my demands."

I swallow. Everything on his list is exactly what I want, everything he's giving me and now I crave from him. I desperately want it all and for it to never end but I can't accept the part where I am some *treasured* person to him. That's not the woman I am, not anymore.

I have to warn him away, even if that leaves me with *nothing*. "I can't be that person for you. I can't even look at a man without feeling repulsion. Not even… for someone I love like you, *mon monstre*."

He leans forward until his nose nearly touches mine. "I don't see repulsion, baby girl. I see fire and rage and blood and, fuck me, that's my favorite fucking cocktail; the Molotov kind."

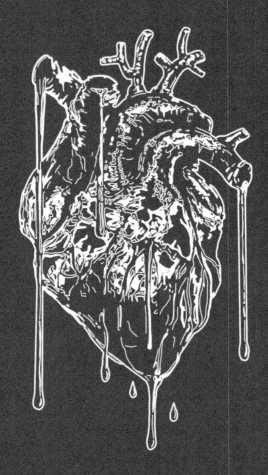

CHAPTER TWENTY

ILLI

I wasn't lying when I told Odie I wasn't going to hunt Chance down and kill the fucker.

But I also didn't tell her I was going to find him and make sure he isn't going to come back here with his MC and set the warehouse on fire while we sleep. I've spent weeks torturing him, I highly doubt he's going to leave here and forget about that.

I'm not letting Odie get hurt by this shit, not ever again.

She's getting closer to me. Her outburst was a great fucking sign, she's getting frustrated over this stalemate we've reached and she's getting ready to move on… I could fucking nut over the thought of it, it's been that fucking long.

Patience is a virtue and I'm fucking paving my way out of

hell with that shit.

I call Harbin on my way out for the night, once I've triple checked the alarms and made sure Odie has her gun at her side. She was fucking lucky Chance was half dead when he came up and she had time to get to the bedroom to grab it. I helped her pick out a holster and fit it before we went to bed. The sight of her standing in front of her canvas with the gun on her thigh... I'm going to enjoy it in the shower later. Those fucking legs of hers... I need them wrapped around my fucking neck while she rides out a brain-splintering orgasm on my face.

Fuck.

I need to find some focus and I need to find it now.

Harbin picks up and grunts down the line at me like a grumpy fuck. "What's wrong with you?"

He snorts. "I can feel the war coming, man. I can feel that shit in the air, I'm just trying to figure out which one will start first, you feel me? Your friend-"

"We're not friends. He's made that fucking clear." I cut him off.

He sighs. "That's the best news I've heard all week. Did you hear Grimm's heading to the Bay to take over? The Boar must be fucking sweating."

I scoff at him. "Yeah, I was the one who gave the Viper the heads up."

Harbin laughs. "I heard that intel cost him some fingers. I hope you made the dickhead swallow them."

Nah, I popped those suckers into a jar. I'm starting a collection for my girl, all the parts of people I take for disrespecting her. I'm going to give her some heads on platters soon.

"Speaking of Grimm, have you seen his kid wandering around the docks? He's run off on me."

Harbin groans at me. "Are you for fucking real? Man, it's bad enough you took him! I can't believe Roxas didn't talk you out of that shit."

I pull the car into the lot at the biker bar, the Choke, on the other side of the docks. It's less popular which makes it a great place to hang out and not bump into D'Ardo. "He didn't even try to talk me out of it. Fuck, he gave me the fucking *map* to find him. I just need to have a chat with Chance, one final talk to make sure he's leaving this place for good. I'm at the Choke, come get a drink with me."

He mumbles something down the line to me, grumpy but I take it as an agreement and hang up.

There's enough guys that drink here on the regular I can hit up about Chance, a few of them owe me and others who just want to stay on my good side. Growing up in this place and becoming a big player on the board means everyone is quick to spill their guts to you. Even if it's just to avoid you spilling them for real instead.

The mood in the place is fucking terrible and I move towards the bar to find some whiskey and some familiar faces.

I spend an hour catching up with some old contacts, no

one knowing anything worth running out for. I work through the room, only skipping Domnhall O'Cronin because he's a mouthy, useless dick who would lie just to fuck me over. The kid he's with looks fucking miserable, all dark hair and moody eyebrows, and I give him a sarcastic salute with my beer bottle.

Finally Roxas and Harbin arrive, motioning me over to the booths in the back.

Not a great sign.

I cut straight to the chase. "Did you find him?"

Harbin gives me a look over the top of his shot glass. "He's the least of our fucking problems, man."

Roxas, serious and ignoring the drink in front of him, does a casual look around the room but I see through it. He's scouting, making sure we're not being watched. Something's up. "You need to get away from the Jackal now, man, before he takes you down with him."

I try not to let the irritation show on my face. I'm so fucking over hearing about how insane D'Ardo really is. He's a fucking poser, someone who was a great friend but lost his head once he made it to the big time.

Harbin nods like he knows exactly what I'm thinking. "I get it, man, but he's doing shady fucking shit and it's only getting worse. Between him and the Boar, the Bay isn't going to be the shining Utopia it once was. It's going to be rubble."

I drain my glass. "I get it. They're both fucked and they're taking us down with them. I have a new plan. I'm taking my girl and the kid, and getting us the fuck out of here. D'Ardo can get the fuck over his little obsession."

They exchange a look and then Harbin tries again. "Nah, man. You need to listen. He has a fucking bomb, it's big enough to take out the state once it's finished. That guy you picked up for him? He just put it all together. The Chaos Demons want it, that's why they're hanging around. The entire city is going to be full of crazies, all of them hard over this impending nuclear war."

He drains his glass and scrubs a hand over his face. "Do you think the Jackal is crazy enough to detonate the thing? Do you know why he wants it in the first place?"

I nod. "He wants to be the biggest player. That's all he's ever wanted, to be the biggest guy in the room. Took a baseball bat to the back of my head when I called him out on his shit."

I hear a throat clear and look up to see the O'Cronin kid standing by the table. Harbin leans back in his seat, his eyes narrowing. "Are you eavesdropping for your old man, Aodhan? We're not the types to let that shit go."

He scoffs at him, completely unrepentant, and I almost laugh at him. Almost, but the conversation at hand doesn't exactly have me in the best fucking mood.

Aodhan steps a little closer and jerks his head at me, "I heard you asking around about the biker you lost. How much are you paying for the details of where he went?"

Well.

He has my attention. "I've got a little green on me. Did Domnhall send you over? I don't take his word on anything."

Aodhan scoff. "Good, he's a fucking thief. I've been working on the boats at the docks. I've been seeing a lot down there lately."

I give him a once over, then turn back to Harbin. He pauses for a second and then shrugs. I pull my wallet out and pull out a wad of green. The kid glances over his shoulder and makes sure Domnhall still isn't watching before he takes it and stashes it away.

Interesting.

"The cut up biker went down to the boats and waited around for the next lot of Demons to show up there. His younger brother was pissed to see him there. Said something about a missing shipment but Colt didn't back down. He didn't say you'd taken him."

Fuck.

Fuck me. "Did you just say Colt? I took Chance Graves."

Aodhan shakes his head. "You definitely took Colt. Chance is a frequent visitor to the Bay, I could pick him out of a line up blindfolded at this point. He's a fucking asshole, too big for his biker britches. Colt never comes down, he's always at Grimm's beck and call back in Texas."

I scrub my hand over my face. This just gets worse and worse. "How do you know this much about the Graves?"

Aodhan shrugs. "You know the score man, if you wanna

eat in the Bay you learn to see everything and fucking *nothing*."

That's a fair point. He turns to leave and I stop him, curious about this fucking kid who came from nowhere. "What are you going to do with the cash, kid?"

He stares me straight in the eye and I know he's not lying. "I'm going to feed my Ma and my little sisters because Domnhall doesn't. You need anything else down at the docks, gimme a call. I see a lot."

I just fucking might.

I check out the boat docks but there's nothing there.

I'm definitely going to pay for taking Colt Graves, no question. Bikers have a fucking twisted way of doing things but oldest sons... yeah, Grimm's coming after me for sure for torturing his future Prez sonny-boy. There's so much bad juju going around at the moment I might just need to skip town for a few weeks, make sure my girl and I don't get caught up in any of this bullshit.

I've never thrown someone under the bus for my work before but I'm tempted to nark on the Viper for once. I won't, I have standards and my pride, but fuck him for this shit.

I get back to the apartment and find Odie scrubbing the floor, on her hands and knees and I swear I have a religious experience over the sight of her. Her hair is shining down her back and her ass… my fucking god, I want to slap it while I pound into her from behind.

Right.

Cold shower time. Icy water is what my dick needs right now.

"Hey, baby girl. How was your day?" I call out, prying my eyes away from her and hanging my leather jacket up.

She makes this happy noise in the back of her throat, the one she always makes for me and I've started dreaming about how she'll sound naked in my bed, all soft and sated. "I think I've gotten all of the paint out! I'm so relieved, I was worried it would ruin the flooring! The rug is ruined though. We'll need to replace it, I'm so sorry, *mon monstre*."

I literally could not give less of a fuck about the rug. "No sweat, baby. Did you paint me again? I want to see it, just let me grab a shower. I don't want you seeing me all bloody."

I'm not bloody but there's whiskey on my breath and I'll never fucking forget the feeling of her lurching away from me to puke. That reminds me, I need to chase up the cartel with Roxas. Everytime I see him something else fucking comes up. I need the Bay to settle the fuck down for five minutes so I can start my hunt. I need to right some wrongs for my girl.

I shower quickly and then head back out to the living room to find Odie. I don't put on a shirt because there's nothing better than the lusty looks she gives my bare chest. Fuck, it goes straight to my cock and I've become a glutton for punishment these days.

She stands there with her back to me, covering the painting from my view with all of those curves of hers. It's a fucking *great* distraction but I forget about the painting altogether for a second there. That fucking ass of hers. Fuck me.

"It's only my second try. It's not... perfect yet." She says, chewing on her lip a little. I can't see her doing it, but I hear it in her voice.

"Baby girl, I don't know good art from shit art, but if you've done it then I'm sure it's perfect. Those hands of yours wouldn't do anything less than that."

She glances over her shoulder at me, her hair falling across her face and I wish I could take a photo of how she looks right then. If I didn't already know she is it for me... this is the moment. The ocean clear in the window behind her, the colorful pots of paint everywhere around her, and my shirt stained from all of her hard work clinging to her body.

Fucking perfect.

She grins a little wider and steps to the side, ducking her head away so she doesn't see my reaction.

She's a fucking savant.

The painting is fucking everything. I barely recognize the man staring back at me. The Butcher I see in the mirror stares back at me but he's different. Fierce but more than that, possessive. Strong and capable. Sexual.

Fuck, this is how she sees me.

"Baby girl, you're too fucking good for me. I'm going to do everything in my power to be this man for you. I'm going to be this man if it fucking kills me."

She grins and her face tips up, wrinkling that nose of hers at me. "You are this man, *mon monstre*. I don't think I've done you justice at all. Come eat with me. I cooked us some food."

I take her hand and lead her over to the dining table, seating her next to me where I can tuck her under my arm. She hums at me, all fucking happy, and I grab the food to lay out for us both. Over my dead fucking body is she serving me. No, she can take a load off of her feet after cooking for me and let me take care of her for a while.

The food is fucking good.

If I'm not careful I'll end up putting on a hundred pounds eating with her. She refuses a beer but I pour her a glass of wine and she sips at it delicately. I can always tell when she likes things, the corners of her mouth twitches happily.

"What are you painting tomorrow for me, baby girl?"

She shrugs a little. "I'm trying to do the sunrise but I can't get it right. The colors… they're not quite right. I need them to make me weep."

That sounds fucking awful but I keep my mouth shut about it, digging into the food instead. She laughs at me, the sound contagious until I'm grinning back at her.

"And how was your day, dear? Kill many men?"

The attitude on her, fuck me. "Nah, quiet night. I'm taking

some time off soon. We need to get out of here for a while, just until things quieten down a bit."

She frowns a little. "I will miss the apartment. I love it here. Where would we go?"

"Wherever you want to go, baby. Is there anywhere else in the States you want to see? Maybe Canada would be better." I think it over and the options get worse and worse. I need to talk to Roxas about where the MCs are a little less active.

Fuck it, the Caribbean must be nice this time of the year.

"Has something happened? Has... that man caused you trouble?"

Yes. "No, baby girl. This place just isn't good for you."

She frowns, her temper flaring to life. "I don't want to be moved around like that. This is your home, I want to stay with you here."

I shake my head, draining my beer and getting up for another one. "It's not safe. I need you safe, I can't think of anything else when you're in danger."

She sets down her fork carefully, her eyes narrowing at me. Fuck, someday I'm going to have her nails scratching down my back and her teeth leaving marks in my shoulder, I can just fucking tell.

"My father hid my mother and I away all of the time. I lived out of a suitcase, moving from cottage to cottage in the night and never really having friends because of it. I'm not doing that again. I'm not... I'm not weak, *mon monstre*."

I don't fucking like that.

Not one bit.

"No." I say, and for a second I think I've been too harsh on her but that backbone of hers... fuck, it's hot to see. She knows exactly what I'm capable of and yet she trusts me to use those talents to keep her safe. I can rip a man apart with my bare hands, slice a man up and butcher him to fucking nothing, but I would never hurt her.

I wait until I have her full attention and then say, "I'm not going to put you in a box and hide you away and stop you from living the life you want to live. I'm gonna teach you how to fight. And then I'll teach you how to gut a man, three times your size, and I'm gonna teach you how to do it without hesitating. And then you know what I'm gonna do? I'm gonna make sure you never have to use that skill. If we leave the Bay, it'll be together and we'll come home as soon as this shit blows over. No hiding, baby girl."

The frown on her face stays put but she nods and finishes her dinner. It takes me until the meal is over, but I get the tension out of her again by the time I usher her off to get ready for bed. I'm ready to call it a night... morning, whatever.

But first, I need to put a call in. I wait until she's moved off into the bathroom and then I make the call. "Hey, kid. I need a favor, you got some time tonight I can take up?"

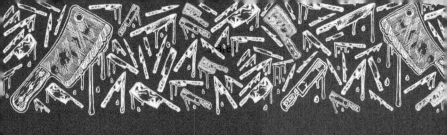

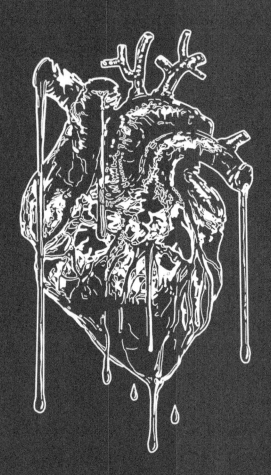

CHAPTER TWENTY ONE

ODIE

Someone in this neighborhood has no respect for those trying to get some rest.

Loud music started around midnight and has played non-stop since. At three am I give up trying to sleep and crawl out of the bed, padding out into the large open-space living area on bare feet. *mon monstre* is nowhere to be seen and the entire warehouse is pitch black, but I know it well enough now to tiptoe around without doing any damage.

I curl up in the big leather armchair that looks out over the water, my legs tucked under myself and a large sweatshirt over my body. It smells like Illi does. It's not a bad smell at all, and when I'm not thinking, I drag the fabric up to my nose to take a deep inhale of his scent.

I need to get a hold of myself.

I stare out at the waves, and the moon hanging in the sky, reflecting on the water so beautifully it's easy to forget that I'm stuck here in this hellish city. So stunningly serene that there couldn't possibly be drug dealers, sex traffickers, pimps, and gangsters on every corner.

I sigh and slump back a little more, rubbing my cheek on the sweatshirt again absently.

I hear footsteps up the staircase and for a second my heart freezes in panic, and then the security alarm beeps as it's shut off and I relax. Illi told me only he knows it and I trust him on that. He's too guarded to let anyone else in his space. He doesn't let me off of the top floor and he made it clear to me no other woman has ever slept in that bed, so I'm not about to be confronted by some girlfriend of his.

That traitorous part of my mind whispers to me again, I would hate to meet his girlfriend.

I shove it to the back of my mind. I have no interest in this man, he can go out and have sex with any woman he wants. It certainly won't be me.

The door opens and I hear his voice and the voice of a woman. My heart drops and my stupid lip drops like some heartsick girl. Stupid, stupid woman!

Then he flicks the light on and I blink against the harshness of it, waiting for my eyes to adjust.

"I brought someone to see you, baby girl."

My jaw clenches at the nickname, how dare he call me that

in front of this other woman, and then I finally blink and see the young girl from the auctions standing with him. She's tiny next to his bulk, all bones and big, blue eyes, but my heart stutters at the sight of her.

She was so kind to me, so genuine.

I'm glad to see her again.

I force my lips into something that could be called a smile and nod at her, relaxing when she does the same. She nudges Illi gently and he chuckles at her, turning on his heel and taking off, jogging back down the stairs. The girl secures the door, checking it twice, before stalking over to the mini bar in the corner, poking around in it.

"Do you drink?" She asks, her voice low and kind of rough. She looks tired, like she's been up all night and her clothes still smell of smoke.

"Only wine."

She nods and walks back over to the fridge, she pours us both glasses. I murmur a quiet thanks and sip it slowly. It's good wine, expensive and smooth on my tongue.

"Illi told me you're having trouble adjusting to being here." She says, and a short laugh tumbles out of me, ending on a sob.

"I am in a foreign country, so different to my own, where I know no one. I have no one. I'm trapped in a house with a man I do not know, after being abused by others, and he says I cannot leave so yes, I am finding it hard to adjust," I speak so quickly I think she'll have trouble keeping up but she nods along with me, sipping slowly and glancing out of the large windows at the water. It's so peaceful, so serene out there as the sun starts to rise.

"Do you have family to go home to? A boyfriend or something?" she asks without looking back at me. I'm thankful for the privacy, it's easier to talk about without her seeing how desolate I really am.

"I have no one. My father sold me off to pay his debts, my mother stood by and let him. I have… nothing."

She nods and sips her drink again. "My mother was a piece of shit too. Illi's wasn't too bad but his dad was a deadbeat. I know you're ashamed but you really shouldn't be. There's no judgment around here about that kind of shit."

I swallow and say, "Did your mother sell you?"

She snorts. "She was too dumb to do that and she never really left the slums to find out. She might've, if she realized how much she could get for me down at the auctions. Would've kept her in drugs for a few years."

I scoff and take a big swallow of wine. "Is that the way of the world here in America? You have children to sell off when you need something? It's so strange."

The girl shrugs. "It's the way of the Bay. This place isn't for the weak-hearted."

I glance down at my hands. "It's not the place for me, then. I saw him, you know. I saw what he did to those men. I couldn't have ever gotten out of there by myself, no matter how much I tried. I just… I laid there and took what they did to me, closing my eyes and praying I'd die. I'll be thrown out the moment Illi realizes I'm no good for him or any other man now."

She leans forward a little in her seat to strip her jacket off, showing off the tiny little outfit underneath. I don't know where she's been all night but there isn't much to the outfit she has on. She sees me staring and smirks at me, lifting one shoulder in a sort of shrug. "I had to blend into the crowd and girls don't wear much to parties at the docks here. You probably heard it from here."

Ah. So that was the noises that have kept me up all night. Such a strange place to live that Illi has chosen. "I wasn't judging. How could I ever judge someone who came to help me?"

She smiles and stretches her legs out, wincing slightly. "You can judge me if you want to. I've done a lot of bad shit to stay alive but living here, you have to decide to survive and then follow through with your decision. This place, here with the Butcher, he's given you something most people don't get. You've got time to decide if you want to survive or give up. He's giving you time to heal and remember who you really are. Lot of girls would kill for the same… especially from him. There isn't a safer place in all of the Bay right now because he's not just protecting his territory."

I frown at her and she smiles back wryly. "He's protecting someone he cares for. Whether you like it or not, he's seen something in you he likes."

I snort, something so unrefined and gross that I would be slapped by my mother for doing so, and say, "He saw the same pretty packaging that resulted in me being sold over and over again. He will grow sick of it, especially if he decides to try me out."

A chill takes over me at the thought, even as a small part of me, buried deep inside my heart, whispers that he's had every opportunity to touch me and has stopped himself. Even when he looks at me with desire, he doesn't touch me.

The girl stares at me for a moment, her eyes taking in every little inch of my face and hair, my neck and the swell of my breasts that's evident even under the sweatshirt. It's hard not to squirm under her eye, even knowing she's not being rude about it.

"I've seen him with women before. I've seen him with some very attractive and confident women, with their asses hanging out, some who the whole damn city knows what they can do. I've never seen him like this. He's playing for keeps. Between you and I, there isn't much better you can find in a man than the Butcher."

Again, I do not like hearing about these other women. Not at all but I refuse to admit that, even to myself. "If he's so great then why don't you want him as well? Shouldn't you be warning him off?"

She laughs. She flat out, tips her head back and roars with

laughter. It's infectious, I want to laugh with her. "Oh, man. My night has been too long for you to be making those jokes. Nah, I'm not into guys. Or girls. I think I might be asexual or something, I have no interest in anyone or anything, except getting out of this shit-hole city. I just know enough guys to know he's a good one. One of the best."

I smile back at her and she reaches over to take my hand. "My name is Lips. What's yours? I mean, I know it from when we rescued you but I think I should hear it from you."

I startle. I hadn't even realized we skipped something as simple as introducing ourselves to one another. "Odette. Odette Archambault. My friends... well, the people who I used to think of as friends call me Odie."

She smiles again, and squeezes my hand a little. "I'm your friend now, Odie. If you really want to go back to France, I'll do what I can to get you there. I can look into your dad, see if it's safe for you to return."

I smile and nod to her, it's a very kind offer, but when she moves to stand I think of something much smarter to ask of her. "The doctor, he called you little Wolf."

She lets out a breath and nods slowly. "That's what I'm known as here. If you ever find yourself in trouble again, you can tell people you mean a lot to me and they'll think twice about hurting you. Same goes with the Butcher, but you probably already know that."

I smile at her, imploringly. "Could I ask a different favor

from you? Would you teach me how to kill? I would like to be able to defend myself if I need to. I think if I'm to survive… this, then I need to know how to."

Her eyes widen a little and I ramble on. "I don't think I'd ever be able to do it, to kill someone like you do, but at least if I know then maybe I have a chance."

She nods emphatically. "Absolutely, I'll show you. I just—I don't want you to ever try to use it against the Butcher unless you need to. If he tries to hurt you then definitely, but I can't have you killing him to leave here. I'll get you out the second you want to leave, okay?"

I hadn't once thought of using this against him.

I could never.

He's twice the size of me and faster than any man I've ever seen move. He gave me a gun that I could use at any moment to kill him, but from the moment I laid eyes on him I've known it's pointless to even try to fight against him. Cruel fate because that's what got me delivered to the cartel in the first place, but I nod as if I'm promising.

She smiles and pulls out an old phone, nothing fancy or even decent really, and taps away at it.

"I've let the Butcher know I'm going to come back in the morning to train with you. I need to get back to the group home before the workers do their next rounds."

Group home? "How old are you? You look young but you don't speak like a child."

She scoffs. "In human years I'm fourteen. In Bay years I'm pushing fucking thirty, everyone ages different here. Listen, I know you're going through hell right now. What we saved you from... I'm not even going to pretend to know what that's like but I know you're going to get through this. I know it because you're giving the Butcher so much hell he called me in for backup. That means something."

A smile dances around my lips.

Called her in for backup.

That the big, hulking man needs such a little girl to help him... and that he would even call her, maybe he's not such a monster.

Maybe.

There are noises coming from the basement.

Illi leads me down to the lower level to use the gym there. It's set up with all sorts of machines I don't know how to use and I instantly regret asking for training. Lips is already there waiting for me, dressed in all black and stretching her arms over her head. Her clothes are tight to her body and I glance down at my own baggy clothes in dismay.

I won't be able to move in these.

She smiles at me and holds up a bag. "I brought you some real clothes, shit that the Butcher hasn't sweated all over in some macho-man claiming bullshit."

I blush but Illi grunts at her, snarking out, "She can train in my shit if she's comfortable in it."

I am comfortable in it but I also want to learn and... maybe I'd like to find a new normal. A normal where I love my body again. What is a better way of learning that then learning how to kill a man with it?

I move into the bathroom to get changed and Lips comes with me to talk about what we have planned for the day. Her voice coming through the bathroom door makes it a little easier to get changed without getting panicked about how revealing the workout outfit is. It molds to my body, clinging to every curve and showing the swells of my breasts in the neckline. The burns there have healed enough that they've started turning white. I no longer hate looking at them but I worry about Lips seeing them. I take a deep breath and when I open the door she's waiting with her back to me. She is wearing the same style of shirt, though she's too small to have the same curves. I startle at the sight of her back though.

She's covered in scars.

Burns, cuts, stitches, punctures, this girl looks as though she's been tortured.

She glances over her shoulder at me with a wry grin. "I thought you'd be more comfortable once you realized I'm way more cut up than you are."

I blink at her. "I didn't know... I didn't realize this had

happened to you too."

She looks at me for a second and then reaches out to link her arm in mine, careful about the touch, and starts to lead me into the gym area. I'm not good at this sort of affection but she's so little and sweet. I'll get better at it.

"I've been trained to become a killer. That's what I do, Odie. I kill people and I sneak into hard to reach places to get information. Part of my training was done by a bad man. He hurt me because he likes it, not because he was teaching me anything."

My eyes fill with tears for her. She has protected me and cared for me from the moment we met, to know she's been through something so awful... my heart breaks. "I hope you killed this man. I hope you tore him apart."

She smiles but it's sad. "Someday, maybe. I have to survive the Bay first."

I nod and we come to a stop on the mats. Illi is in the corner, using one of the punching bags. He's not wearing a shirt and I think I might pass out like some Victorian lady at the sight of him.

Lips giggles at me. "You're drooling. Literally drooling, wipe your mouth."

I roll my eyes but when she turns away from me to stretch I wipe it just to be sure. She walks me through stretches, then stances, then when she's happy with my form she turns to me.

"Hit me."

I stare at her like she's lost her mind. She smirks back at me. "I've dealt with worse than you, I promise. Even if your punch actually lands on me, I promise you it won't hurt me."

She's a child, barely tall enough to reach my shoulder. If I punch her and it lands, I might truly hurt her. She reads this all over my face and cocks a hip at me.

"The Jackal snapped my leg into three pieces with his bare hands. Your punch is nothing to me."

I feel sick thinking about it, but I attempt to punch her. She blocks me easily, critiques me, then instructs me to try again. We do this for hours, over and over again, until I'm sweating and feeling all giddy from the endorphins of exercise.

Illi moves through the exercise equipment slowly and when he's finished he hits the showers, slouching on the bench to watch us when he's finally clean.

I can't concentrate with his eyes on me.

Lips spots my distraction instantly and giggles at me again. "Fine. We're done. You did great, you should work on those stances a few times a week and you'll be a killer in no time."

Illi's eyes flare and he gets up, thanking Lips and talking to her as he walks her out. I hit the shower and when I'm done I stare at my naked body in the mirror for a few minutes.

I think I'm ready to stop hating myself for what was done to me.

I think I'm ready to love myself again.

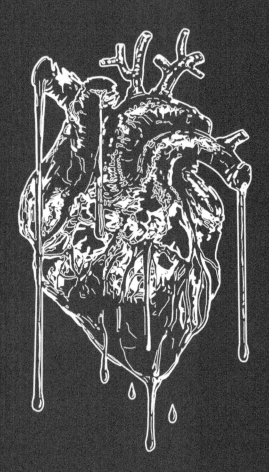

CHAPTER TWENTY TWO

ILLI

It takes the Viper a few weeks to get over himself, but he does call me in for another fight. He probably thinks he'll be able to have me killed there, that his fighter is good enough to take me out, but there's no fucking chance.

The payoff is double the last.

Easy money and good night out for me and the boys. I need to introduce them both to the kid, get another couple of sets of eyes on her. I need a plan to get her away from D'Ardo and I get the feeling I'm going to need the bikers' help.

I leave Odie with a new canvas and the promise of Chinese for dinner. She's never had it, something about her mom hating the smell of it, and I promise to bring her the best the Bay has to offer.

I don't give a fuck if it's sappy, the grin she gives me is

everything and I want to kiss her so fucking bad I see red over it.

Definitely a good night to beat the life out of some dickhead.

I call Harbin and Roxas to meet me at the Dive, then I flick a text to the kid and see if she's game for pissing D'Ardo off. She replies that she's on a job and will meet me down there. She works too much and she needs to fucking eat more.

I'm buying her a fucking burger.

The Dive is the busiest I've seen it in months, overrun with gangsters, too many of them walking around with the Jackal's grinning tramp stamp. I instantly regret telling the kid to come down but fuck it, I'm in the mood for a bar fight.

I head straight over to the Viper, ready to clear the air and make sure he's not about to pull a fucking weapon on me or some shit. He wouldn't do it. He knows that his cage fights are only renown because he doesn't ever allow tampering. As a fighter, you know the moment you step in that you're on your own, your skill against your opponent.

It's fucking perfect.

The Viper sits at his private table, knocking back a shot of tequila with his heavily bandaged hand. He grimaces when he sees me. "You couldn't just fight and fuck off like old times? I only invited you because you're the local attraction. The out-of-towners like to give you a try."

Yeah, they all think they can take me on and make a name for themselves. They're wrong. "I just wanted to make sure you're over your little... moment of stupidity. You keep my girl out of conversation and we can go back to getting along."

He scoffs, pouring another shot awkwardly. "We've never gotten along, Butcher. You don't play well with authority figures."

What a fucking joke that it. "You're a washed up cage fighter who, once upon a time, won a fight in a forest. I'm not impressed, man. But green is green, and I'll take your money with a smile on my face."

He smirks. "Just so long as I don't talk about your girl? Fine. Works for me. Get in the fucking cage, I'm betting on you and hoping I lose."

Whatever, no big loss for me.

The guy I'm fighting is fucking massive but the problem with steroids is they make you slow, sloppy. He doesn't enjoy me pointing that out to him, and he enjoyed having his windpipe crushed under my boot even less. It takes me maybe three minutes, easy work for fucking good money, and I have the entire night left to finish my other jobs.

I find the kid at the bar with a drink.

D'Ardo's driver is with her, his arms crossed as he flirts with some biker bitch. The easy grin he's giving her slides right off of his face when I arrive.

"Boss doesn't want you talking to the Wolf."

I flag the bartender down, order some food, and then turn back to him. "If you tell him, I'll strangle you with your own intestines then I'll sell your body to cannibals. Nothing would make me happier than knowing you're being shit out of those psycho's colons."

The kid pulls a face at me, her eyes widening when the food is put down in front of her. The Dive is exactly that, a fucking dive bar, but the cheese fries are good and the double burger is decent enough.

"Luca, we're friends. The Jackal will... get past his issues eventually," she says with a smile, and the guy backs off.

She is so much fucking nicer than anyone else I know, she just handles people with zero bullshit. To the point, don't fuck with her or she'll stab you.

Effective as hell.

"Eat the burger, kid. I owe you one," I murmur and sit next to her. I know she won't eat with her back exposed like that, she is too alert. Maybe with me watching out for her she'll relax a little.

She frowns at me and I order her another drink. I'll get the little Wolf drunk if I have to to get some fucking food in her. "We're meeting some guys here. I need you guys to meet, get along, swap info. All the good shit."

She shrugs and pokes around at the fries. Once I stop watching her she finally digs in, eating like a starving kid. Well, I guess that's exactly what she is. I remember how little the group home gave us.

I watch two more fights, both of them underwhelming, when Harbin and Roxas finally arrive.

Harbin frowns at the kid but Roxas just steals a couple of fries while he orders a drink. I could fucking stab him for it but he winks at her playfully, clinking his glass with hers and sits beside her at the bar.

"The infamous little Wolf. What do we owe the pleasure of meeting you tonight? Are we killing someone or are we being lured somewhere to die? I've gotta tell you, I usually like my bait older and with more tits."

If looks could kill, Roxas would be a goner. Lips has one hand in her pocket and I set my drink down to punch the asshole. Harbin even manages a real scowl at him.

"She's fucking jailbait, dickhead," he snaps, and Roxas laughs.

"No shit. I can't believe the Jackal wants you so bad, no offense. You look about twelve years old."

The kid turns to raise an eyebrow. "You wanted me to meet this guy? Cool, are we done here?"

I rub a hand over my face. "He's a good guy to know in a fight. Look, I get he can be a dickhead but I've also seen him take on four other bikers, unarmed and wasted, and walk out of it alive with a trail of corpses behind him. You need all the friends you can get. Options that aren't that cockhead D'Ardo."

She snags one last fry and then pushes the half-eaten basket away from herself. She hasn't eaten anywhere near enough and I frown back at her.

Harbin looks her over and then sticks his hand out. "Harbin

Jameson. That idiot is Roxas Kierstone. He likes to piss people off to see how they work, don't be too offended. He was probably hoping you'd try to stab him so he could see your knife. You're kind of a big deal around here, Wolf."

If Harbin had said that to D'Ardo he would've preened, made jokes about how fucking great he is, and milked the moment for everything it was worth.

The kid almost looks embarrassed, uncomfortable with her skill and talent for killing being praised. She's too fucking good for this life.

"Right. Just so we're clear, you three are the only people left that I trust. If the Wolf needs anything from you two, I'll pay the price. Same goes the other way, little Wolf. I need us all across the situation if we're all getting out alive."

The kid looks the bikers over and shrugs. "The Boar has always paid me well. Are you guys loyal to your Prez?"

Fuck. Sore subject. Harbin stares at her for a second and then says, "We're loyal Unseen. We don't always see eye-to-eye with the Boar and his inner circle. Is that going to be a problem?"

She shrugs. "I'm a pretty simple girl; you stay out of my way, don't backstab me or sell me out, we're cool."

Roxas leans back on his stool to keep his eyes on the hot piece of ass that walks past us. "Do we need to shake on this shit or are we best fucking friends now?"

I roll my eyes. "Right. We're looking for the cartel Odie was sold to, the Wolf has been going through her contacts.

Anything?"

She rubs a hand over the back of her neck. "Yeah, a few leads I'm chasing. It's a bit hard around school and the group home curfew but I'm a resourceful kind of girl."

Roxas tips his head back and roars with laughter. "School? Fuck me, I didn't realize the infamous Wolf worried about that sort of shit."

I take another shot of whiskey. I'm going to need the whole bottle at this fucking rate. Harbin looks the same way.

The kid raises an eyebrow. "My brain is how I'm getting out of this shit-hole city and this fucked up life of mine. Pretty sure you can't say the same."

Huh.

So she does have an escape plan. Good to know. "Thanks for looking into it for me."

She shrugs again, her eyes scanning over the bar. They snag on a few guys here and there but she doesn't see anything that alarms her too much. "Odie is worth it. She's worth the work of finding these guys and bleeding them out."

I knock her shoulder with mine, as close to a hug as I think she'll allow anyone.

I turn back to the other two and finally follow up on the question that's been fucking killing me. "Did you find out who the missing guy is?"

Roxas frowns and sucks at his beer. "Yeah. Good guy too, has his problems but solid as fuck. Did your girl say what happened to him."

Fuck. "He's dead. A brutal death at that, one I'd like to hand out to the fuckers who bought her, you feel me?"

The joking mood leaves him entirely. "Yeah man, I'm with you."

I take a few days off and stick around the warehouse.

I spend a lot of time in the gym, working through the stances and positions the kid had shown Odie. She hates doing weights but she enjoys using the punching bags with me. She's hot as fuck when she's angry and smacking the shit out of it, better when she starts kicking it as well. I take her into the shooting range and make sure she's getting some practice time in there too. After a few hours she's fucking glowing with my praise, the feeling of self-sufficiency doing wonders for her broken sense of self.

Then I watch her paint.

She gets nervous if I start off watching her, so I always take my time in the shower or fixing myself something to eat. Then once she's in the swing of things, I sit back with a beer and just watch her. The paintings she's coming out with… fuck, she needs to be in a gallery somewhere, someday.

The painting of the little seaside village she once lived in back in France is idyllic, the airplane out in the desert with two men walking back to it makes my teeth hurt, and the dozens of paintings of the sea outside the living room window, none of them quite right for her, blow me away.

I ask her why she paints the view so often over dinner and she blushes into her soup. Yeah, she's going through a soup phase. I'm not a fan but she's happy so I keep my mouth shut. She's trying to figure out what her life here in the States looks like and I'm not going to mess with that process.

"My first morning here, I hadn't seen the sun in weeks. I sat on the floor, just over there, and I watched the sunrise. I didn't know if you were going to hurt me like those other men had and I didn't know if you wanted to kill me, but those hours sitting there and watching the sunrise... that felt like a gift, *mon monstre*. Something so precious and vital to my survival... I felt like you had recharged me and I could take on whatever came. I had no idea what an amazing life I was going to have here. It makes that morning even more special to me."

She ducks her head away from me as she eats, dipping her spoon so fucking delicately. Not a single fucking slurp from this goddess, she's fucking dainty.

When we're done eating, I pull her away from the dishes and over to the window, right over the spot she just said was so fucking amazing.

"Stay here, baby girl. I'll go grab the mattress."

She frowns at me, looking around like a bed frame is going to magically appear. I chuckle at her, stalking over to the bedroom to grab everything we need to lay out in the living room in comfort to watch the sun rise there together.

The smile she gives me is as if I hung the fucking moon and stars for her.

I get everything together and tuck her in one side, triple checking the alarms and locks before climbing in the other side, leaving the usual amount of space between us.

She rolls over and molds herself to my side instantly.

Holy fuck.

I have a stern conversation with my dick but it's no use. I'm as hard as fucking nails as she strokes my chest, grinning up at the sky as it slowly starts to turn pink. I lay there and plan out our lives, just as soon as I can get a handle on the situation at hand. I have to get the kid away from D'Ardo, kill everyone that's ever wronged my girl, square things with the Chaos Demons, and figure out how to disarm a nuclear fucking bomb D'Ardo has hiding in his basement.

No biggie.

"*Mon monstre?*" Odie murmurs, and I bury my face in her hair.

"Yeah, baby girl?"

"I think I would like you to kiss me. I think I would like to try that, if you would like to."

If I would like to.

As if I'm not laying here thinking about work and blood and bombs so I can distract my dick from how fucking perfect she is in my arms.

"Yeah, baby girl, gimme those lips," I murmur, and she tips her head back to look at me, her eyes clouded with lust for me.

Fuck, I should've dragged this mattress out a little sooner.

I lean down and kiss her softly, trying to be gentle and a gentleman and definitely not suck her bottom lip between my teeth and fucking nibble on her. Except that's exactly what I do because I'm fucking weak and she's everything to me.

Her breath sucks in and I think I've fucked everything up.

Then she moans.

Fuck *yes*.

I tug her until she's a little more settled over my chest, one of my hands in her hair and tilting her head so I can kiss her deeply. The hesitancy in her burns away pretty fucking quick and one of her hands come out to cup my cheek, her thumb stroking over the tattoo under my eye.

The hand that isn't tangled in her hair runs down her back, stoking her spine gently until I get to that ass of hers… fuck me, I force my hand into a gentle squeeze but someday… someday that ass is going to be mine to spread open and squeeze and spank whenever the fuck I want. I'll own every inch of her and she'll own me too.

Fuck, she purrs into my mouth and rubs herself against my chest, her thigh rubbing against my cock in my sweatpants.

I'm going to fucking nut myself like a teenage boy.

I pull away, staring up at her and she blinks those big blue eyes of hers. "Is this okay? Just this?"

I nod, and bring her lips back down to mine, hungry for everything she'll give me now. Fuck, she's everything. *Everything.*

I kiss her until the sky starts to brighten up, and then I lay there with her and watch the sunrise. She murmurs to me all of the colors she'll need to paint this one, all of the mixtures she's going to try and the techniques she'll use. I understand none of it but I listen as if my life depends on it. I don't want the moment to end, so even after she falls asleep on my chest I lay there, holding her against me, watching the waves crash against the beach.

When I wake up that evening, right as the sun sets, I find Odie sitting cross-legged next to the mattress with a paint brush tucked in her hair and another in her hand as she works on the floor.

The sunrise she paints is magnificent and I hang it above our bed. Something only for us.

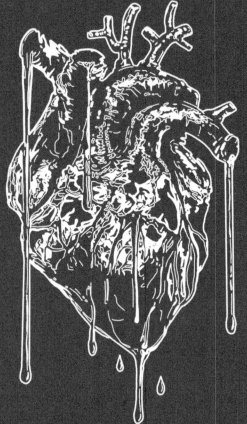

CHAPTER TWENTY THREE

ODIE

I decide to find my father.

I don't know if he is still alive, if my first husband killed him for lying about my virginal state, but I need to find the truth. *Mon monstre* goes back out to work the day after we kissed in front of the living room window.

It was the most perfect moment of my life so far.

And the aftermath of that moment? Now, I sleep curled up safe in his arms every night. He kisses me all the time. When we wake, before we sleep, when he's making us breakfast, and when I'm covered in paint and excited about my latest project. The only time he doesn't kiss me is right after he gets home when there's blood on his clothes and liquor on his breath.

So I ask him about using the computer. He doesn't ask me what for, just hands it over and tells me all of the codes. I stare at the search bar for a few minutes, as if typing my father's name in will summon him like some demon from the depths of hell.

Eventually, I get over my fear and look him up.

He's alive.

He's also in prison.

I don't feel any better. Well… I feel a little better that he's had his liberties taken from him the way he kept me trapped for years. I search up my mother and find nothing. Not surprising, my father always kept us out of his business, that's why he moved us around so much. Then I search for Louis and find nothing, no mention of an arrest or his death. His social media is minimal but there are a few photos of him at parties with his arms around beautiful women. I feel nothing, no betrayal or despair that he's moved on from me.

He probably never felt anything for me anyway.

I was nothing but a pretty face for him.

I search for all of the men who assaulted me, the ones whose names I can remember. Nothing. I wasn't really expecting much but for there to be no trace… It feels a little insulting.

I get up and try to shake my mood off. I can't paint with these sorts of thoughts in my head, the jittering taking over my hands until I'm trembling with something that isn't fear.

So I cook.

And I cook.

And by the time Illi arrives home, covered in blood from head to toe, we have an eleven course meal waiting for us on the table.

His eyebrows shoot to his hairline but he doesn't make a comment, just walks to the shower and gets to work cleaning up. I open him a beer and set it out on the table, pouring myself wine. Illi always makes sure there's something for me to drink even though I prefer to do so sparingly. I don't want to turn into my mother, relying on the alcohol to function and survive my life.

Even on my worst days, I don't let myself drink more than a glass.

Illi comes out as I get the freshly baked bread rolls out of the oven. "Has something happened, baby girl? Let me fix it."

I shake my head and let him take the tray from me. I grab fresh butter because there's no way I would go without real butter for my bread.

I serve us both, taking a little of everything and putting it on Illi's plate. He thanks me with a kiss, his tongue slipping into my mouth and teasing out a moan from me. God, the things he can do with it.

My legs turn to jelly at the thought.

"I'm sorry for going overboard," I murmur and he shrugs.

"Everything looks great, baby girl."

It tastes even better. I'm happy with it all, grinning as I tear into the bread roll. Illi chuckles under his breath at me.

"What?" I smile.

He shakes his head. "You're either laughing or crying over

bread. I don't fucking get it but I love it all the same."

I sigh but the smile stays put on my face. "I had a hard day today. I needed the carbs, as you say."

He finishes off the beer and heads in for another one. "Tell me all about your day, baby girl. Let me take the load from your shoulders and see what I can do about it."

I frown down at my plate.

He comes over to me and pulls me out of my chair until I'm in his arms. I stand there and soak him in, drawing his strength into myself as if I can borrow it. He lets me sift through my thoughts for a few moments and then he pulls back, tipping my chin up with one of his big hands. The scars and tattoos there tell an entire story of who this man is, but the important part is that he is mine.

"Tell me." His voice is more insistent than he usually is, pushing me to give him what he wants.

I shouldn't feel so embarrassed and exposed in revealing this but I'm not used to being encouraged to have an opinion, let alone one that is quite so... horrific.

"C'mon, baby girl, show me that fire," he murmurs, the hand on my chin dropping down to splay out over my chest, his palm over my heart. He's so big compared to me that it feels as though he can cover me entirely, consume me until there's nothing left and we're one. I think I'd like that.

"Coming here, being sold off to those men, it was like having my heart ripped out and spat on. I want their hearts in return. I want something so... vital to their existence to be mine now. I want to collect them and keep them and to know that wherever their souls end up, they will never be complete thanks to me."

His head tips back, his eyes hooded and dark, and says, "What a stroke of luck, baby girl, I'm the perfect man for the job. I will hunt every last one of them down for you and I will bring you their hearts. Nothing but the best for my girl."

Something flutters in my stomach. I like being his girl. I... I love it.

"*Mon monstre*, nothing would make me happier," I murmur back, and a slow smirk stretches over his face.

My monster.

Because he *is* a monster, he can tear grown men apart without feeling an inch of remorse and you do not become the Butcher without really owning it, but he's mine, and I'll love him for it. The more I know him, the more I know that he was born to be mine and to protect me from all of the evils in this world.

He looks out over at the food we have on the table. "Are you finished, baby girl? We need to sit down and go over a few things. It's not going to be a good chat but we'll do it together."

My heart clenches in my chest. "Have I done something wrong?"

His hand drifts back up to my face to stroke my hair back. "No, baby. I have some questions about what happened to you...

I need some details if I'm going to be bringing you some hearts. Whatever you can tell me will help."

The food in my stomach turns sour and I'm suddenly cold. "I can try. Just... I need to put a sweater on."

He lets me go and I move to the bedroom to cover up a bit more. I know it's not actually cold but I need the layers if I'm putting myself out there for him to see. I need to cover up my skin and pray he's not disgusted with what's left of me.

Once I'm covered and I'm sure I'm not going to be sick I join him on the leather couch. I sit at one end, as far away from him as possible. He doesn't push, just reclines back against the pillows like this doesn't bother him but I can see the anger in his eyes, the killer lurking there and waiting for a threat to come out.

It helps me take a breath.

"You said your father sold you to pay a debt? Do you know who that was to? You were listed by an anonymous third party."

I have no idea what that means but I nod. "His men called him Señor Mecedo. I was only with them for a few days."

He nods and doesn't say anymore, a clear indicator for me to continue but... the words are hard to get out. He's given me so much time to work through this quietly though. I need to tell him. "They took me as payment for my father's debts. He runs a small drug dealing business in France. He was never a big player but he liked to think he was the king himself. He did very well, except he started sampling the product. He ended up an addict and taking too much of the shipments for himself. That got him in trouble so he... sold his property. He told one of my uncles that I wasn't a legacy because I'm a woman."

Illi's face hasn't changed at all and that helps. It's like the information isn't upsetting him so maybe it's not so bad.

"When they... checked me and found out I wasn't a virgin, they sold me. There was an older woman who forced me to shower and took the photos. Then I went to the Alcatron house. I only heard that man's name there. No one else. None of the men ever spoke English to me, just him and some of the maids. Oh, and one man who grabbed me when I tried to run. He told me he would slit my throat and rape my corpse so I would stop trying to run. Then I saw... I saw the dogs and I stopped trying to run."

Illi leans forward in the chair, his hand tracing over his thigh in a rhythmic pattern and I realize it's as if he is tracing a knife there. Sometimes , when he comes home late, he still has the thigh holsters on and I've seen the cleavers he keeps there.

"How many?"

I swallow the bile creeping up my throat, my chest tight. "Does it matter?"

His jaw tightens. "Yeah, baby girl. It matters. I'm killing every last person in that house but I need to know how many I'm hurting the most. I need to know which ones die screaming and terrified and in unimaginable ways."

The pressure in my chest eases a little. "Six. There were six men who raped me there."

Illi has to stand up and stare out at the water to not rage out. That's what he calls it when he gets angry and walks out of the apartment, kicking and punching things until his fists are torn to pieces.

I can breathe because it's clear the rage isn't directed at me at all, the bloodlust in him aimed entirely at the men who hurt me. I stare at his tense shoulders and it helps me to get the rest of the story out, what little details I have.

"Alcatron and his brother were the most frequent but there were four others that were allowed in from time to time. They were all higher up, the men he trusted with bigger jobs. The day he called me downstairs to kill that man, they were all sitting together and smoking cigars. My father would never sit with his low-level dealers like that."

He gives a curt nod. "Anything else, baby? Anyone else so much as side-eye you? I want a clean sweep, we're not missing a single fucking person here."

I clear my throat. "No, that's it from the cartel. I just… I wasn't some virginal maiden, this shouldn't be so bad." I sniff, and he turns to meet my eyes.

"I need details about your past boyfriends too but we can come back to that. You can be scared, baby girl, but I know you're not going to let this win."

I glance down at my hands. He thinks I'm so much stronger than I really am but... I want to be that woman for him. For the both of us, because I hate sitting here in five layers of his clothes just so I can talk about some... disgusting pieces of rapist shit.

I try to lighten the mood, to find a way back to the calm we had over dinner. "There was only one boyfriend and you do not have to worry about him, he's a.. terrible person. He's already found another woman to warm his bed, the poor woman."

He quirks an eyebrow at me. "You can do better than that, baby girl. Tell me what he really is."

I giggle. "Fine, he's a gutless piece of shit."

The curse makes him smile and he comes back over to sit with me, the rage clearing just enough to hold me safe again. "Did he cheat on you? The dumb cunt definitely didn't realize what he had."

I huff under my breath at him. He thinks far too highly of me. "Probably but he's a piece of shit because he helped my father bring me to America to be sold off. He didn't even attempt to fight for me. He had the... *audacity* to tell me that I should just have a baby to get freedom. He said a male heir would buy me travel home, like I would hand over my child for the sake of my father's business."

His arms tense around me and his breathing goes shallow. I frown at him but when I see the blank look on his face I ease gently away from him. This entire conversation is a minefield of cutting little details and betrayals that will set us both off.

"I need his name, age, enough detail to find him. I'm going to bleed him out for you, I'm going to kill him so bloody they'll whisper about it in the streets of the Bay for fucking centuries to come, baby girl, I promise you."

I smile at him, taking his hand in mine and trying to deflect away from his rage for a moment. "Are you sure you're killing him for selling me out? I think you're just angry that I once enjoyed another man's touch."

His eyes burn as they touch my skin, what little of it is showing under the protection of his clothes. "Baby girl, he was dead for touching you then but now he's going to die screaming for abandoning you when you needed it. I'm glad you're not still in love with him though, I can be a jealous fucker when other people covet my girl. Tell me you're mine, Odie. This entire conversation is fucking with my control."

I smile and squeeze his hand. "It was a lifetime ago, *mon monstre*. I did not yet know my heart beat elsewhere, in this chest of yours. Now I trust you to keep it safe for me."

He moves faster than he usually does with me, tugging me up and into his lap and covering my mouth with his. He kisses me until I can't think straight, one hand fisted in my hair and the other pulling me in tight against his chest.

I cannot exist without this man and all of his demons, the shadows that play in his eyes when he thinks about the vengeance he's going to wrought for me.

"Listen. Something real fucking shitty happened to you and

I get it, you never want to touch a man again. That's fine. But I know you'll get over that. There's too much fire in your eyes for you to let this beat you. So, someday, you're gonna beg me for my dick, and I promise you, I'll give it to you so good you'll never feel the ghost of that piece of shit's hands on you again. I'm patient. I can wait."

I take a shuddering breath. "I think maybe… that's not so far away. I think I'm close to that."

He murmurs against my lips, "Let me take you out to dinner, baby girl. We should get out of the apartment, let our hair down. I can take you out on the good side of town and show you the better side of the Bay. We need to get away from the bad shit here for a night."

That sounds wonderful but it also sounds like he's hiding this side of town from me.

I understand, I haven't exactly been the strongest person for him so far, but I don't want secrets and the half-life of being protected like that. "Take me somewhere you like going. Take me to something that matters to you. I want something real."

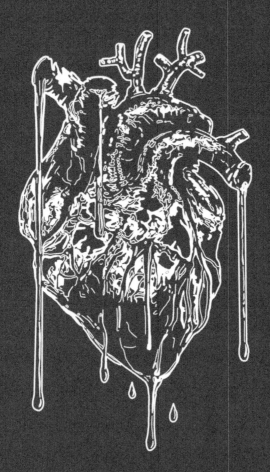

CHAPTER TWENTY FOUR

ILLI

I'm taking my girl to dinner and making her mine tonight.

I feel like some virginal teenage boy just thinking about it but I couldn't give less of a fuck. She's ready for something. The kisses are fucking killing me but she's right there, ready for me to make her mine and move past the fear.

First I have to survive the fucking day with her without busting a fucking nut.

Luckily, I'm on the treadmill when my phone rings.

"Do you want the good news or the bad news?"

I hit the stop button and motion to Odie that I'm heading into the shooting range to take the call. She grins at me and waves from where she's doing yoga on the mats with the kid. They're both doing fucking obscene poses and there's no way

319

I'll be able to concentrate on Harbin's call while I get a front row view of just how far my girl can stretch.

"The bad. We both know the good won't be that good."

He chuckles. "I don't know, it's pretty fucking good. Fine. The bad news is that none of my contacts can find the cartel. I've found where their next shipment is being dropped off to the Jackal so I'll keep an eye out and see if I can follow them back somewhere. If I can find their warehouse, I'll find Alcatron and the house of horror for your girl."

I blow out a breath and lean against the wall, staring at the targets across the room. The deaths I will give these men… carving their hearts out for my girl will be the greatest fucking honor of my life. I'd sent through everything Odie could tell me the moment she'd fallen asleep in my arms after our conversation, ready to get this shit done.

Delivering them to her is now my number one priority.

"So what's the good news then? Did you get sucked off by the barmaid with the tits?"

He chuckles down the line. "Yeah, buts that's old news. Chances are, you're not going to catch any fallout out for your escaped prisoner any time soon."

Fuck, that is good news. I'll have a little more time in getting a new place for Odie. "Tell me the Devil took Grimm out. That would be some great fucking news."

He grunts. "I wish. But the Viper did pass your information onto the Boar and he had to come crawling to me about it. We held a little club meeting and cleaned house. The Mounts Bay charter of the Unseen just lost more than forty members for being filthy rats. The Demons have others hiding in the other charters, we're working on them too but this buys you some time. Grimm just lost his pipeline."

Fucking music to my ears. I hear the girls laughing together and moving to hit the showers. Lips always hangs around and makes sure Odie is comfortable before she leaves because she's honestly a fucking great kid.

I feel the need to adopt her or some shit, how fucking weird is that?

"Tell me you made the Boar grovel. I want the details over drinks later."

He chuckles. "It was decent. It was worth helping him just for the gutted fucking look he gave me when I told him how many you'd seen. He likes to think he has this MC locked down but honestly... he's too lenient on the new blood. He grew shit too fast to keep his head above water with the Twelve. That's not how you run a club."

No truer words spoken. "I'll grab a drink with you tomorrow night. I'm taking my girl out for the night tonight."

I don't know why the fuck I'm telling him this but, fuck it, maybe it's nerves?

He chuckles. "Avoid your usual bars, everyone will enjoy poking and prodding at her too much just to see your reaction. Plus, if she's the beauty they all say... Roxas will definitely try his luck. You know what that dick is like."

Fuck. No. "He'd lose more than his fucking fingers. I'm not letting her near the Dive… or the fucking Choke. Fuck, it's hard to think of somewhere on the south side I would let her go."

Harbin roars with laughter and says, "You might need to move to a better zip code, man. A woman like that, down here? A recipe for disaster."

Nah, it's a recipe for me gutting enough men that the others pull their heads in and stay the fuck away for my goddess of a girl.

I hang up and duck into the gym bathroom to get ready. The girls go upstairs, whispering with each other, and when I give the kid a look she shrugs at me.

"She asked for help, what am I supposed to do?"

Right.

Help from the Wolf of Mounts Bay is not supposed to involve giggling but I let it go, the sound of them both happy is everything to me. I take extra care in making sure nothing I'm wearing has rips or blood stains on it, picking out shit that looks good enough that she knows I'm putting in effort but nothing that makes me look like a fucking dickhead.

I'm not the Crow, for fuck's sake.

I call out to the girls to let them know I'm having a quick cigarette and getting the Mustang warmed up, then I head down to the garage.

The night is warm and calm. It's early enough that the

nightlife hasn't started up yet, only a few cars out and none of the street girls. I get halfway through the cigarette before the roar of a motorbike comes past the boundary line of my property. I shut the alarm off, sure that it's Roxas here to start shit with me like the utter fucking asshole he is but it's not him or Harbin straddling the hog.

I look up to find Colt fucking Graves sitting on his bike, his cut hanging off his shoulders like a badge of pride. He looks much better than the last time I saw him, chained to my chair, wrapped in cable ties and cuffs, and dripping with blood and sweat.

The look he gives me isn't one of vengeance.

Nope, he's looking at me like he's assessing me, taking note of how I look and what I'm packing. Jokes on him, I never step foot outside of the warehouse without two guns, eight knives and at least one cleaver... usually three.

I could shoot the little fuck, take him down and drag him back into the basement to finish the fucker off but the fact he's sitting there has me hesitating. What if Harbin was wrong and half the MC is about to show up?

Well, that and the fact he offered to help Odie out.

That gets him brownie points.

Don't know if he was just saying it to get her to lower the gun but the fact he thought of it... it has me hesitating.

"I ain't helping you, I'm not a fucking snitch." he says, and turns away from me to stare out at the water.

What the fuck does that even mean? I huff at him and unlock my car, the beep loud through the quiet street.

"Are you going to come after my brother again? Take him out to get what you need?"

I glance back to make sure Odie and the kid don't step out of the house while this idiot is around. If he pulls his piece out and aims it at her... well, I don't want her seeing what I'll do to him. "It was a job. I got it done without you squealing so it's over. Don't hold a fucking grudge, boy, because I'll skin you alive if I see you again. And if you bring your daddy down here I'll level the Mounts Bay entirely to the fucking ground if I have to."

Colt nods and looks back out over the water. The fuck is he doing? I grab my phone, ready to call in for backup when he turns back to face me again. "Don't take your old lady to this fight tonight. It ain't the place for her. I come from a world of an eye for an eye, you feel me? She coulda put a hole in me, I wasn't thinking right when I walked up those stairs. Yet she just told me to get out and you didn't come looking."

Well, fuck me. "I put you downstairs, man. Are you expecting me to believe you're going to let that go?"

He adjusts his cut, rolling his shoulders back. "You weren't there for me though, were you? You wanted Chance. Sounds like something happened to me that was meant for him, I don't need to hold a grudge for that, 'specially not when he sent me in his place, knowing you were there to grab him."

Right.

I'll have to double check Roxas's sources but, fuck me, that's a sibling squabble I want no part in.

I nod slowly. "I hear you but this sounds an awful lot like snitching to me."

He grins and shakes his head. "Nah. Snitching means saying something to you that would betray loyalties. There's nothing about what's going down tonight that I want any part in. Not everything in the Demons is about brotherhood. Some of it is about an old man who's fucking crazy and the men that follow him."

I nod again, because that's the fucking stone cold truth right there and something to remember later, in case I ever need to take the Demons out. I can't think of any reason I'd want to haul my ass out to Texas to deal with Grimm but it's good to know his son might be swayed. You should always take note of who might switch teams because the one they're on is rotten to the core.

He nods back at me slowly, kicks his bike to life, and leaves without another word.

The Bay never gets fucking old.

Lips has brought her a dress that almost takes me to my knees in it's perfection. Red and tight, it touches on all of my favorite parts of her and scoops down to show so much cleavage I want to bury my face in it. My mouth waters at the very idea of getting her out of it. The heels she's in means she's almost perfectly at my height, I only have to dip a little to kiss those perfect lips of hers. Lips pretends to gag at us when she sees the face I pull and I ruffle her hair like she really is my annoying kid sister. I get the kid back to the group home safely and then I take Odie out to the suburbs.

Once we're on the road I tell her, "We're making a quick stop off first, baby. I need to show you something."

She watches the entire city go past the window like she's memorizing it all. I find myself thinking about what parts she's picking out to paint later, just to see if I'm right. Sometimes we pick out the same parts of our nights that mean something, sometimes she finds the smallest details that pass me by entirely.

I hope she doesn't paint the house we're going to.

She laid her heart out for me the other night, laid out all the little shadowy parts she was broken over, so it's only fair I give her the same.

It's time she knows how it is that the Butcher came to be.

I pull up, parking across the street and she doesn't make a move to get out. She looks out at the house while I send a quick text out to the only other people I trust in the world right now about my little visitor. I don't need any of them being taken down in whatever is being planned. If they choose to try to save others… that's on them.

Everything I care about is in this car right now.

"That was your house? When you were a child? The photo of your mom was here," she murmurs and I take her hand.

"My father was a bit like yours. Thought too much of himself, too little of the rest of his family. I think he loved us, however he could, but it wasn't enough to put us first. Nah, his gambling always came first. He loved putting money on the fights."

She is looking out of the window still, but her hand comes out and takes mine. It's so fucking small and delicate in mine, all fragile bones and smooth skin. Fuck, I'm so obsessed with this damn girl.

"He got in over his head, like all men do. Lost his business, lost the house... eventually he lost my mom too. The Twelve, they're the main criminal organization down here, the bookie hacked my mom to pieces. Sent her to my father in a box. He knew I was next so he sent me to a group home... like foster care. The place is infamous here. They don't feed the kids properly, they don't force them to go to school, the entire place is corrupt. I waited there for my dad to come back. He never did. I learned there how to fight, I was bigger than the other kids. Eventually I was recruited by a local gang to help out with a big job... only the guy in charge was that same member of the Twelve. The guy who killed my mom."

Her hand squeezes mine so tightly. I can't look at her or the house, it's too fucking raw, even all these years later.

"I remember exactly how my father used to cut apart whole carcasses. He was a real butcher, you know? He would talk me through the entire process, name each cut as he went. I was only a fucking kid but he thought some day he'd be handing the business over to me. All he did was pass on the skills that have made me the biggest threat on the streets here."

Her thumb strokes over the scars on the back of my hands. "You killed the man who killed your mom?" She murmurs, low and sweet.

I scoff. "I killed the entire crew. I had to, or at least I thought I did. The Twelve live by a code, they work together to run the Bay's underworlds. If someone takes one of them out the others are obligated to deal with it. So I got rid of all of the witnesses when I killed the Adder. They figured it out eventually but when the Barracuda came after me I killed him too. The rest of them figured out I wasn't going down easy and cut me a deal. They would leave me alone, give me work, pretend I hadn't taken them down to the Ten, and I'd leave them the fuck alone."

She nods and smiles at me. "Thank you for telling me. Is that why Lips is known as the Wolf? Is she... one of those people?"

I start the car again, getting out of this place would be for the best right now. "Yeah. The kid did what she had to do to survive. I don't blame her at all. She's a good person."

My girl smiles and nods again. "She's lovely. She has helped me so much. Is there... something we can do for her? Isn't she at that awful home now too?"

Yup, she's starving there with the other poor fucking souls. "She's a little jumpy about it. I'll do what I can. I promise, baby. Fuck, let's go get that food and forget about this shit."

She grins at me, her face lighting up. "Are you going to wine and dine me?"

I have the perfect place. "Of course. Let your man take care of you, baby girl."

She grins and stares at her hands, all coy and shit until I'm trying to adjust myself in my seat.

I take her to the nicer side of the city to a tiny, hole-in-the-wall restaurant I called earlier and made the reservation too. Okay, fine, I called them and gave them the lowdown on how important this night is for me and just how bloody I will make their deaths if Odie so much as frowns at her plate.

They pissed themselves, but they agreed, so it should be a great night.

I open my girl's door for her and then tuck her under my arm to walk her in, getting a fucking *great* view of her tits in that dress. Fuck me, the kid was trying to kill me with this thing. I wonder quietly to myself where the fuck she got it.

I owe her.

Big time.

We're seated in the corner booth like I told them too, so I can see exactly what's happening in the room and we don't get jumped by some lowlife fucking gangsters.

Odie blushes beautifully as I help her into her seat and I

call the waiter over to get us drinks straight away. I want Odie comfortable and relaxed, not drunk, so I get her a glass of wine for now so she enjoys the meal.

There's hardly anyone else here, but the few couples that are keep fucking staring.

When my girl squirms in her seat and picks at the neckline of the dress I lean forward and say, "Baby girl, we both know it's me they're staring at. It's human instinct when there's a monster in the room."

She giggles and drops her hand away. "If only they knew, *mon monstre*, what you could really do to them, hm?"

I'm fucking obsessed this woman.

I can't wait to worship her.

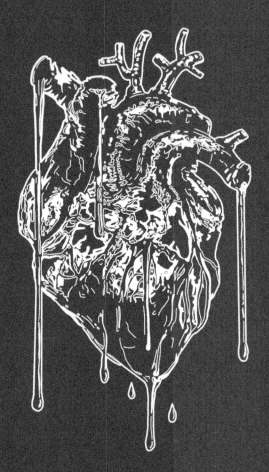

CHAPTER TWENTY FIVE

ODIE

Mon monstre drinks water the entire night.

I don't think I've ever seen him have dinner without at least a beer, and butterflies start in my stomach. I don't know… exactly how far I will be able to go with him if he wants to be intimate but I want to at least try.

I know that sex can be wonderful. Louis wasn't a particularly passionate lover, but he always made sure I enjoyed myself and that I was comfortable so I know it's not all pain and humiliation but there's something holding me back still.

I don't want it to though.

I want to be with him and feel the worship on my body that he gives me with his eyes.

He drives us home, his hand clasped firmly in mine, and murmurs low stories to me the entire way about the pieces of his city that he loves. This may be hell on Earth but it's also his home, the place he has spent his life and carved out his own place in it. I find myself loving it too.

When he parks the car the flutters in my stomach only grow, my heart starting to beat harder and my nipples tightening so they're clearly visible though the thin fabric of the dress. His eyes drop down at the sight and when he bites his bottom lip I groan, my head tipping back and the heavy lust in the air drowning me.

I want him.

Something from him.

"Baby girl, I want you to know you can say no at any time. But I want to take you upstairs and take that fucking incredible dress off of you. I want to see every inch of you and then taste it. I want you to feel owned by me the same way I feel owned by you."

I clear my throat, swallowing around the dryness. "I would like that very much. I think I'm ready to beg now… if that's what you would like."

A rumble lets out of his chest, like he's more beast than man right now. He gets out of the car faster than I ever thought possible and before I have the chance to get more than my seatbelt unbuckled he tears my door open, reaching for me and lifting me out as if I weigh nothing.

I wrap my legs around his waist, my arms around his neck and I bury my face into the crook of his neck for a second, breathing him in and steadying myself with his scent. I feel at home in that smell, safe and cherished.

"Gimme those lips, baby girl, I'm a starving man."

His kiss is like a brand, the only one I'll ever crave, and I wind my fingers into his hair to tug at it. I wasn't expecting to want him this much. It hadn't ever felt like this before, this desperate and frantic. It was always a civilized act, even though I was hiding the relationship from my father, it was never this way.

I want to breathe him in until he's all I'll ever know.

"Fuck, baby, I gotta get you up these stairs and in our bed right the fuck now." He groans into my lips, but when I try to unwind my legs from his waist he grunts and hitches them back up.

"Don't even think about moving, baby. It's my job to get you up there and it's your job to keep kissing me until I'm fucking dying for you."

I can do that.

It takes him three tries to get up the stairs and two tries to get the door open, alarm reset, and the door locked behind us again. He's extra careful with it, even with the distraction and I'm thankful.

I think I'd die if we got interrupted like this.

This moment and this intimacy is for us only, any other people around would poison it. *Mon monstre* and I, we're cut from the same cloth. We bleed the same way, loyalty and fire and blood. It's all we know and no one else can come close.

He finally sets me down in the middle of the bedroom and shrugs out of his jacket, throwing it down on the floor. He never leaves a mess, he's meticulous in his upkeep of the house, and my eyes are glued at the sight of it there for a second.

"You still with me, baby?" he murmurs, and I startle away to meet his eyes again.

"Of course, *mon monstre*. I just… never mind. I'm with you." My voice is like a croak, desperate and parched.

He grins at me, that slow and easy thing, and he runs his hands over the waist of my dress, feeling the fabric and stroking me gently. I don't catch on to what he's doing until he turns me, finding the zipper and dragging it down my back.

My heart leaps into my throat but the panic doesn't set in, just the nervousness of being with someone for the first time. He pushes the dress away from my shoulders, skimming it down my body until I'm left in only the lingerie I'd picked out for the night. Lips was kind enough to bring over what I needed and when Illi sucks in a breath sharply at the sight of me from behind I'm thankful I thought ahead.

The red lace is stark against my pale skin, the sheer fabric leaving nothing to the imagination while also hiding just enough. His hands are gentle enough as he reaches out to stroke my ass but then he gets in a squeeze and groans like a dying man.

It feels amazing.

He slowly turns me back around and groans when he sees

the matching sheer lace of the bra, my nipples dusky and tight and begging for his attention. He doesn't once look at the healed scars, still a little too pink to be completely ignored. He just runs his hands up my curves until he is cupping my breasts, kneading them gently. They fill his hands completely, I've never been small or model thin, and there isn't any disappointment to be found on his face.

"Lay down, baby girl. Let your man take care of you."

A shiver runs up my spine as I back slowly away from him to the bed, sitting down when the backs of my knees hit it. He kicks out of his boots and then reaches up over his head to pull his shirt off, the muscles in his torso flexing invitingly. He parts my legs without me thinking, the lace between them growing wet. I've never been so turned on, and at the mere sight of him I'm turning into a puddle.

"Fuck yes, baby, gimme those eyes of yours," he murmurs, and I look back up to him. He unbuckles his pants, dropping them to the ground and stepping out of them. His boxers do nothing to hide his erection, the thick length of him straining against the fabric. Something close to fear pools in my stomach but I swallow it away.

Fear has no place here.

He plucks at the waistband and says, "I'm gonna leave these on for now, baby girl. We'll see how we go. Now lie back, there's a good girl, just like that."

I move at his every command, nothing ever too much for me

to give him. He covers me with his body to kiss me again, his hand cupping my chin and moving me as he wants me. He sucks his way down my throat to my chest, rasping his teeth over my nipples through the lace until I'm squirming underneath him, my hands digging into his hair and tugging at it.

"There's the fire I know you have, baby, gimme it all."

I struggle to breathe as he tugs the lace cups away from the fleshy mounds, sucking and biting like a man possessed. My hips start to move and gyrate under him, pressing up against the hardness on his stomach. I'm so wet he must be able to feel it through the lace, my arousal for him all-consuming until I'm a shaking mess.

Finally, he kisses his way down my stomach until he's comfortable between my legs, staring at my lace-covered pussy like it holds all of the secrets of the universe. I blush a little but I'm shaking and breathing too hard to care.

He sits up to gently slide my panties down my legs and leave my pussy bare for him. My heart stutters at the molten look in his eyes as he slides his palm back and forth, his fingers fluttering over my clit in a teasing touch as they pass by. I can't think beyond his touch.

"This is mine. I'm not like those men that took from you, I'm not going to hurt you, but that doesn't mean I don't own this. I'm going to treat this pussy so good you'll never fucking regret being mine."

I already know I won't ever regret it.

He gives me one last look, waiting until I croak out a desperate, "Please."

Then he buries his face between my legs, licking and sucking until I feel my entire being break apart and come together again, a new and better woman.

When the feelings finally pass, I expect him to get up, to pull his boxers off and to push himself inside me, but he only grins at me and then pulls my legs until they're wrapped firmly around his neck.

I've never come more than once during sex.

I come four times before he finally climbs back up my body, his mouth wet with my arousal, and a grin so wide on his face you'd think it was him who had just orgasmed his brains out of his head.

He bundles me into his chest, my body still shaking in the aftermath, and runs his hands all over me. He finally unsnaps my bra and takes it off, throwing it across the room. I lay there and wait for him to push for more, to make some sort of move that would start the next act.

He doesn't.

He lays there and holds me to his chest, his erection still as hard as steel and digging into my thigh.

"*Mon monstre*, did I do something wrong?" I whisper, my head still tucked into his chest as his hands stroke over my back.

"Of course not, baby girl. We have all the time in the world and if I go there with you right now... fuck, I'm too fucking pent up. I don't wanna be too rough with you. Not until you're ready to take me like that. I told you, I'm not ever going to hurt you. That means not tonight. I'm not ever losing your trust, baby."

I nod, disappointed and sort of happy that I can feel that way. Maybe I'm more ready than he thinks. I run my hand up his chest, marveling at the colors of his ink and textures of his scars. "I do trust you, *mon monstre*. Even if it's the death of me, I trust you."

I wake up naked in Illi's arms and I want to spend the whole day there. I want to taste every inch of him, the way he did me. I want to offer him everything he could ever want with me.

He groans at the look in my eyes, moving me slowly away from his chest so he can get up and start his night. "I would've killed any man I needed to get you baby, but to see that look in your eyes directed at me? Fuck, I would've never thought I'd get you."

I huff at him, a little grumpy he's getting up and heading out for the day when we could spend all the time in the world wrapped up in each other. He swipes his thumb over my bottom lip, tugging at it before his swoops down and gives me one of those blistering kisses of his, the ones where he gets a fistful of my hair and tugs until I gasp. It's there, the passion he feels for me, and I know that someday he's going to unleash it on me and

I'll beg for more.

"I'm a very lucky woman, to have lured a man like you into my life. I guess I should stop hating this face and body, because even if they cursed me with the pain and horrors they also got me you." I murmur into his lips, still pouting at his leaving.

He doesn't take well to that, his eyes narrowing at me. "Let's be real here, baby, it ain't the sweet curve of your ass or your lush tits that makes me want you so fucking bad, I'd kill any man that gets in my way. It's the fire in your eyes and the curl of your lip when someone disgusts you. It's how fucking angry you are. You're every bit as damaged as I am and I fucking love it. I'll keep you here with me until you're ready to show that fire to everyone else again. We'll ride this out together, nowhere else I'd rather be, baby girl."

How can I stay grumpy at him with such words of love and devotion?

I slump back onto the bed and listen to him shower, biting my lip when he comes out of the shower shirtless, his hair a mess and the grin on his face a lascivious thing.

"Fuck baby, can you stay there for me all damn night? I'll be back before dawn. Fuck, I wouldn't be leaving unless I had to."

There's something about his words and his eyes that makes me brave, but I cup my breasts and squeeze them a little as I arch my back in a long stretch. He watches the entire movement and I laugh.

"*Mon monstre*, you're drooling."

He huffs out a chuckle, throwing his shirt over his head. "You're damned right I am. One taste and I'm fucking addicted. I need more of that sweet pussy baby. I'm having you for dessert."

I get up and walk to the bathroom with a laugh and if I shake my ass a little more than required, well, I do it all for love.

He leaves me with a kiss, triple-checking the locks and the alarms as always, and I move to make a cup of tea. I'm once again dressed in his clothes, most comfortable when I'm surrounded by his scent.

The house is silent as always but it's now soothing to my fractured and healing soul. I hum quietly under my breath as I work in the kitchen, chopping the fruits and sliding the pieces in the pots to stew. It's busy work, something full of labor but not much thought, so instead I dream about something Illi had said to me once, about babies in my belly.

It's not something I'd ever really thought about before.

I always thought I'd be stuck living at the whims of my father and never settle somewhere for long enough to get a husband and a family to call my own. Louis was never strong enough to tell my father he loved me... not that he really did, but he was my only chance at finding love back home.

Home.

It doesn't feel that way anymore. Home is here, between these walls, wearing *mon monstre's* clothes and baking new things in his big, unused kitchen. The lounge area needs a nice rug to replace the one there with the paint stains. I wonder if he'd let me pick one out? Something plush and warm, with a little splash of color. My eyes drift up to my latest painting of the city skyline where it hangs and my heart clenches at the sight of it up there.

Mon monstre hung it in the most prime position in the whole house, over the large fireplace he has. No matter where you sit in the large open-space living room, you can see it. It means something to him. My work means something to him.

I feel adored.

The smile that won't leave me creeps back onto my face and I busy myself in my work again. *Mon monstre* had said he loved the apple pie we ate for dessert last night. I want to make him one from scratch, the way my mother used to do a long time ago. Back before she lost herself at the bottom of a bottle of wine and my father began beating me regularly.

I try not to think of those things anymore.

I try to remember that I'm so far away from them, so safe here, that there is no chance of being taken back to that time of beatings and emotional abuse.

Once it's baked and cooling by the stove I clean up the kitchen and then move back into the living area. I have images of the little house we visited stuck in my head but it's something too… personal and private to Illi for me to paint. No, I need to get it out of my head in a sketchbook where it won't be on display for all to see. I settle back into the chair and open my sketchbook, sighing happily as I look out at the water.

Then the power cuts off and the apartment plunges into darkness.

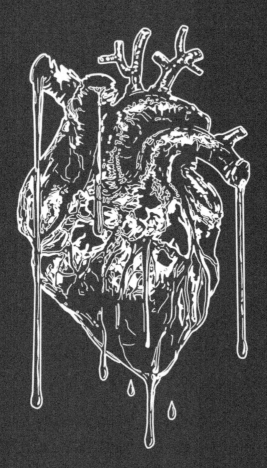

CHAPTER TWENTY SIX

ILLI

I go out on my job with a smile on my face and a pep in my fucking step.

My life is fucking perfect.

Okay, not perfect. There's a whole list of guys I have to kill for what they did to my girl, and I need to find a new place to live that isn't so fucking dangerous for her, and then there's the problems with D'Ardo stalking the kid. But all in all, my life is pretty fucking good.

My girl is back home, healing and laughing and making art. I know absolutely nothing about it but she's fucking happy and I'm going to build her a shrine somewhere nicer than the docks and we'll get messy in her paints and fuck on a canvas for fun.

One taste of that pussy of hers and I'm sold.

But first, I've got work to do. I've gotta see Harbin and catch a drink. I've got to see why the fuck the Viper keeps calling me like some desperate hookup-turned-stalker. I've gotta start checking men off of my fucking list.

I drive to the Dive but quickly find out I can't go there for a drink because there's a gaping hole in the wall. Right. Chaos Demons had their way with the place. Part of me is pissed the Viper survived the attack but, then again, if he's over his tantrum then his money is good and I've got bills coming in I need to pay.

A big fucking mansion.

So the Choke it is, I take off and head further down the docks until I get there, struggling to fucking park now the competition has been taken out.

There isn't a person in the place not talking about what happened at the Dive. The general consensus is that the Demons are fucked and we need to keep them the fuck out of the Bay.

There's also a lot of talk about D'Ardo's bomb.

For fuck's sake.

Apparently seeing the aftermath of a pipe bomb has some guys getting antsy at the idea of a nuclear bomb. Brain-dead fucking half-wits, that's like comparing an arrow with an AK-47. The damage is about a billion times more catastrophic, but I'm glad I'm not the only one who's pissed at the utter fucking dick stain.

Sometimes I wonder at what it is that D'Ardo has as his end game.

A nuclear engineer, all the shit he could possibly need for a bomb, maybe he wants to wipe us all from the face of the damn Earth.

Wouldn't be the worst thing.

Except thinking about what could happen to the country if the Bay is wiped out... I'm not sure how I feel about that. Where would be the hot spot for crime lords and corruption? Where would the skin trade start up again? Everyone knows this is where you come to buy all the best guns, girls, and good times.

Kinda sad to think about it.

"What the fuck is wrong with you now, Butcher? Every time I see you lately you're looking like a puckered asshole."

I drain the beer in my hand and slap a wry smile onto my lips. "Tank. What brings you back to the Bay? I thought we beat the asshole right out of you, guess I was wrong."

The Serpent chuckles and slaps my back. "On a job. Moving something big for a mutual friend of ours."

I quirk an eyebrow. Tank has never been one to put up with D'Ardo's egotistical ways. I choose not to tell him I fucking loathe the guy now, it'll only start a whole new conversation I'm not fucking interested in. "Since when are you D'Ardo's errand boy?"

I ignore the warning look he gives me. I could take out every last one of the Serpents in this place without working up a sweat and the fact that he doesn't call me out on my shit tells me he knows it too.

"A lot of people are interested in what he's cooking up, ya get me? I've learned it's best to keep an eye of that sort of thing, before it blows up in my face."

Blows up.

So maybe everyone really is a little twitchy about the bomb.

I need to get the kid away from him as fast as fucking possible.

I nod and grab another beer. "I'm not too worried about it. There's a lot he still needs, a lot that will be too fucking hard to get."

Tank scoffs and turns in his seat to check out the room, to eye up all of the guys around us just to be sure there's no one here that could go running. Gio is far too careful with this place, I doubt D'Ardo has ever stepped foot in here before. Even being the Jackal has limits to where you can go.

"He already has all of the hard shit. After the dickhead Coyote got him the nuclear materials, the rest has been too fucking easy. If we're not careful, this whole fucking town is going to be gone. Now, I have a home to go back to but this place being wiped off the map... that kind of changes things. Changes a lot of things."

I sigh and nod. Looking around for Harbin or Roxas but finding neither of them. They hadn't texted me back either. Fuck it, I have a job to do tonight, I'll have to catch up for drinks later instead.

"I'm out of here. I'll see you the next time you're in the

Bay."

Tank shoots me a wry grin of his own. "I heard you have a woman now. Never fucking thought I'd see the day."

A lovesick stupid fucking smile tugs at the corners of my lips. "Never met a chick worth settling down with before."

He chuckles. "What, and this one is?"

I roll my shoulders back in my jacket. "This one is worth it all, dickhead."

The job is so easy I don't know why the Viper is paying me the big bucks to do the drop off but green is green.

I drive out to the drop-off point, chain smoking my cigarettes as I plot out the rest of my week. I need some fucking leads on the cartel. I'm itching to bleed them out.

I make it to the truck stop, drop the bag off, and turn to leave when I spot it.

There are legs sticking out of the bushes.

It's the Bay, finding a dead body isn't that strange, but the shoes on the chick's feet stops me. I don't claim to be a fashion expert but no Mounty girl wears those sorts of heels. Red soles and an emblem on the strap that looks like diamonds and believe me, I do know diamonds.

They're designer so the corpse is some rich bitch.

I step carefully over to the body, pushing the bushes aside to get a better look at her, just to make sure she's actually dead. Something about it being a woman... it just doesn't sit right with me anymore. I don't think it ever did, I just ignored the sick feeling because it wasn't my business.

As soon as I get a good look at her warning bells start screaming in my head.

She's naked. Her eyes open so her cloudy eyes are staring sightlessly up at the stars and her limbs are splayed out all over the place without a care. I don't recognize her at all, definitely some rich bitch senator's wife or something, but I know for sure that this isn't a hit or some cover up for an accident.

This was premeditated murder by a serial killer.

Okay, I get that technically I'm a serial killer but that's my job. I take out other people who live in the murky underworld of Mounts Bay. There's a very clear difference with what I do and the work that's laid out getting colder by the minute at my feet.

The guy who did this is compelled to kill for his own sick pleasure. Sexual pleasure for sure because you don't carve a woman's chest open, break open her rib cage and plant a fucking lily in her chest, dirt and all, without it being some kind of sexual thing.

I'm about to turn away, make sure I didn't leave any of my own evidence behind, and then leave her to be found by someone who'll call it in when I spot the card.

Right.

This guy leaves calling cards.

That's not fucking weird at all.

I crouch down so I can get a good look at it without touching the thing. It's a scripture verse, this guy thinks himself moved by a higher purpose.

"The seed is the word of God. - Luke 8:11"

Oh, great. Just what the Bay needs, fucking zealots. I don't know much about this kind of thing, but I'm fairly certain if there were a god, he doesn't want women murdered and plants growing out of their corpses.

This time when I turn to leave I actually go, getting into my mustang and hitting the highway and gunning it towards home. I try to forget about the woman entirely, I have my own girl warm and welcoming at home waiting for me, but sometimes you know when you find something that will change your life.

The kid was one.

Odie was another.

And now this.

I don't like it. Not one fucking bit.

I know it the second I drive the Mustang into the garage. Something is wrong.

There's tire tracks leading into the garage and both of the doors are open. I check my phone, my stomach full of lead but there's no missed calls from my girl. There's no way she wouldn't call if someone showed up here... no fucking way.

I tear my way out of the car and up the stairs but I'm too trained, too well honed not to see the evidence around me. Dirt, rocks, grease, there's been people in here. Men in fucking boots.

My cold, dead, worthless heart begins to race in my chest.

The front door is fucked. The lock snapped off as if someone used a battery ram to get in and the power is out in the entire building, the alarm never having a fucking chance to go off.

There's two dead men in my kitchen, bled out from bullet wounds in their chests. For a second, one useless fucking second, I think she's killed them and is now hiding and waiting for me to get back here.

She's nowhere to be found.

And, fuck, do I try to find her. Every room, screaming out for her to hear me, but nothing. She's fucking *gone*.

A roar of pure, filthy rage claws its way out of my throat as my chest begins to heave. Where is she? Where *the fuck is* she?

The red letters scrawled across the window catch my eye.

My eyes trace over the words written out in blood, over and over and over again. No. I can't have misjudged him this much. He can't fucking do this, not to me. This can't be fucking happening.

The Jackal sends his regards.

ACKNOWLEDGMENTS

To Laura, my ride or die. I swear I could write a whole new novel about how much your friendship, support, encouragement and dick pics mean to me. You're the real MVP of the entire Mounts Bay family and I'm so freaking grateful to have you as my bestie <3

To Katy, thank you for being such an amazing, loyal, and kind supporter and friend. Your friendship means the world to me and your staunch loyalty when shit goes down is everything to me. Also, the dick gifs and MM recs are a total bonus lol. Thank you for being you <3

To Kenia and Flora, thank you for all of your help with translations and for not judging me for butchering your languages terribly. Your help and support mean so much to me!

To everyone in my Facebook group, you all give me life and make this whole journey so much fun. Thank you from the bottom of my blood stained heart.

AUTHOR BIO

J Bree is a dreamer, writer, mother, farmer, and cat-wrangler. The order of priorities changes daily. She lives on a small farm in a tiny rural town in Australia that no one has ever heard of.

She spends her days dreaming about all of her book boyfriends, listening to her partner moan about how the wine grapes are growing, and being a snack bitch to her two kids.

If you want to know when J's next book will come out, please visit her website at http://www.jbreeauthor.com, and sign up for the newsletter or find her on Facebook at J Bree Author.

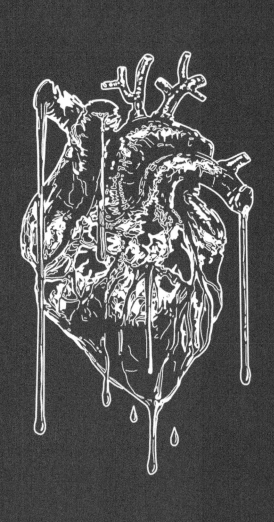